Through the mist he saw her

Modestly his hand felt for his towel, checking the overlay of material for closure.

Her eyes traveled down to the small towel, then up again to his face.

"Don't get any ideas," Chance said in a high voice. "I've got the most dreadful headache."

"My bad luck," Maggie returned.

"Well, maybe next time," he said. "Want to schedule something?"

"Calendars don't go that far." She nodded to the steamy bathroom. "I thought I'd take a quick one," she said.

She moved regally, head up, through the room. He could feel her, actually feel her without touching, as she passed beside him. Static electricity. Two storm clouds on a collision course. Thunder and lightning. That sort of earth-shaking, soul-shattering, body-satisfying potential. It was going to be a long, long night.

Dear Reader,

Spellbinders! That's what we're striving for. The editors at Silhouette are determined to capture your imagination and win your heart with every single book we publish. Each month, six Special Editions are chosen with *you* in mind.

Our authors are our inspiration. Writers such as Nora Roberts, Tracy Sinclair, Kathleen Eagle, Carole Halston and Linda Howard—to name but a few—are masters at creating endearing characters and heartrending love stories. Their characters are everyday people—just like you and me—whose lives have been touched by love, whose dream and desire suddenly comes true!

So find a cozy, quiet place to read, and create your own special moment with a Silhouette Special Edition.

Sincerely,

Rosalind Noonan
Senior Editor
SILHOUETTE BOOKS

JENNIFER WEST
Moments of Glory

Silhouette Special Edition

Published by Silhouette Books New York

America's Publisher of Contemporary Romance

To Robert Greenberg, with appreciation
for being at Taiko at the right time!

SILHOUETTE BOOKS
300 East 42nd St., New York, N.Y. 10017

ISBN: 0-373-09339-X

First Silhouette Books printing October 1986

America's Publisher of Contemporary Romance

Printed in the U.S.A.

JENNIFER WEST'S

current hobby is tracing her roots to see if she has claim to any European throne. In the meantime, she writes novels, television scripts and short stories. Jennifer's husband, son, two Akita dogs and an indeterminate number of goldfish put up with her at their residence in Irvine, California.

OREGON

IDAHO

CALIFORNIA

NEVADA

San Francisco

Death Valley

Las Vegas

PACIFIC
OCEAN

ARIZONA

Los Angeles

Rancho Costa Lomas

Del Mar

San Diego

MEXICO

CALIFORNIA

Underlined places are fictitious.

Chapter One

Chance Harris looked, then took a second, longer look through the insect-spattered windshield. He was forty miles from nowhere out in the middle of the upper Mohave desert and what he was seeing just couldn't be true. Two days before, the late September weather had turned freakishly hot, so hot that even Cadillacs and Mercedes were pulling off to the side of the road with vapor lock or steaming radiators about ready to blow. So what he was seeing could not in reality be there.

He blinked away the road fatigue and shifted forward in his seat, slowing somewhat as he continued down the highway.

At first glance he had thought it was one of those wavy heat images that made an ordinary cactus look like a man being ambushed, arms held up high at right angles. Only this was a walking cactus, and from what he could make out, of the female species.

He cut his speed down further as he came up on her. The woman kept to the shoulder of the road and was walking head up, in the direction of the mountains, as if she were out on a Sunday stroll through some nice cool country lane. The topper was, she had a pack on her back with a bedroll scrunched up. How much weight could she be carrying? Chance asked himself in wonderment. He just couldn't believe it.

Besides the fact that it was the decent thing to do, he thought he would stop just to see what kind of woman could take that sort of brutal punishment.

The truck's wheels crunched to a halt at the road's edge, some feet ahead of her. All he could hear for a time was the vehicle's radiator sizzling and gurgling while he waited for her to come up alongside. He had already rolled down the window, and a blast of hot air filled the truck's air-conditioned cab.

She passed him by.

He couldn't believe that either. She simply walked on past the truck as if he wasn't there. Maybe the heat had gotten to her, he thought. Then he had a flash and understood.

"Hey!" he yelled, leaning out the window. "Hey you, young lady out in the hot sun! I may not look like much, but I'm not a mugger. I am not a masher. Just for the record, this is the voice of a Good Samaritan. So, you want a ride?" No response, just more walking. He noted, incidentally, that her legs were very long and tanned. Stretching his head out the window again, he yelled louder. "No? Okay, then, go ahead and die out there. Have a nice day."

She kept walking. He hadn't had the chance to see her face. Expecting her to stop, he had looked straight ahead, waiting for the time when she would come up alongside and tell him how wonderful it was he had come to her rescue. There might have even been the requisite tear shed in gratitude. Instead, her passing had been a brief dark blur out of his side vision.

Arms relaxed over his steering wheel, he began to wonder now if she wasn't even there. Maybe she was some sort of a desert ghost, a legend come to life. Hadn't he seen such things on those Rod Serling shows? Who's to say such weirdness didn't happen in dead heat like this?

He tipped his lucky hat—a battered fedora—worn at a slant, farther down on his forehead, then started the truck's engine and followed after her at a slow crawl. The horse van he pulled creaked after him. Even in the comparative cool of the truck, the climate punished. How could she stand it?

"Listen, babe," he called out, "there's nothing out there for more miles than you can walk today. So if I were you, I'd take your chances with me. Otherwise," he yelled, "you can consider yourself a barbecued treat to some big birds."

She kept on, and now he was becoming annoyed. Why was she doing this to him? He was feeling responsible and he didn't even know her. This was crazy. She was crazy! She was making *him* crazy!

He slowed to a stop and again leaned his head completely out the window. "Look, no disrespect intended, but are you stupid, or nuts, or what? What I'm doing, here, is trying to save your life." Nothing. Just some more walking. Walk, walk, walk. Nice swing to the hips. He watched her, shook his head. To hell with her, he thought; it wasn't like he could grab her off the road against her will. Wouldn't that be sweet? Lately, he'd had all the trouble he could use for the rest of his entire life. He didn't need jail, too.

It was then that she stopped. Turning slowly, she eyed him from a distance of about twenty paces.

Well, well, he thought. *Well, well, well.*

He tipped back his Indiana Jones fedora to get a better look.

What a woman! She had a face that was something else entirely. Beautiful, strong, totally alive. Like him, she had on a hat, some kind of a felt contraption with a medium brim drooping at different angles. Long wisps of jet-colored hair trailed out at the edges. Her darkly tanned skin made the white of her eyes all the more bright, and the dark of her eyes became, consequently, all the more dark. Her form shimmered in the heat. She wore short safari pants and a black tank top, over which she had on a beige, man's shirt, knotted around the waist. A canteen and a brutal looking hunting knife in a leather sheath hung from a low hip-slung belt. Judging by her muscle tone—not to mention her expression—he figured she would know how to use the weapon.

She began a slow, fearless walk back to where he waited, unexpectedly mesmerized by this dark apparition of feminine power.

Coming to a stop by his open window, she gave him a long hard look and said, "Okay."

"Okay," he said back. Just that.

"Maybe okay," she qualified, still eyeing him with eyes like hard coal. "Let's get one thing straight. I get in this truck with you, you lay one hand on me, you even look like you're going to lay one hand on me, I'll skin you so quick you won't have time to get your fly zipped.''

Chance winced. "You ever considered the diplomatic corps?" Amusement did not exactly ignite her expression, so he said with as much seriousness as he could muster, "Sound's pretty fair to me."

She gave him a final smoldering look and walked around to the passenger side. He unlocked the door and she climbed in, throwing her pack on the floor with a thud. It must have weighed a ton.

"Headed for Vegas?" he asked amiably.

She said nothing. Her legs were up high, feet resting on her things lumped on the floor. They were long, slender legs, but muscular. He felt himself stir automatically. It had been a while since he'd been with a woman, which was partly a good thing. The last woman had caused his present downfall.

"Me, too," he went on cheerily, determined to break down her resistance to civilized communication skills. "Lot of lights in that city. Draws them in. Moths to a flame, wouldn't you say?" From the corner of his eye he saw her pointedly turn her head away. That was okay. He'd risen to a challenge or two in his life. "Name's Chance Harris," he said again brightly. He took his hand from the steering wheel and held it out to the side.

She made no effort to respond to the physical gesture of friendship. "Maggie Rand," she said in a flat voice. She spoke to the side window, not even to him. "Look, it was a nice thing, you stopping. I appreciate it, okay? But I'm not much for conversation."

"Ever?" Chance asked, looking at her. "Or just now?"

She gave no answer.

An hour later, he began to slow. "I'm going to pull off and get something to eat at that truck stop. There's nothing else between here and Vegas. You can come, if you'd like. Or, if you'd rather, you can sit outside and fry. Nothing personal, but I just can't see my way to leaving you alone here with the keys, sweetheart. That horse back there is all that stands between me and starvation. Up to you."

There had to be twenty trucks parked out in front, big rigs, not small jobbers like his. His taciturn passenger climbed out and he checked the horse van. After making sure everything was all right, he walked ahead to the diner. She remained outside, finding some shade by one of the semi trucks. A couple of men whistled, but—surprise—she ignored them.

From inside, Chance watched her through the glass window. It was cool in the diner, almost frigid. He ordered a hamburger and fries, along with an iced tea. Then he stood up, and on the way to the door told the waitress to double the order.

He found her crouched on her haunches, staring down at the blacktop when he came up to her. He didn't care what she thought, he just grabbed her up by the elbow and said, "There's a hamburger and fries waiting in there. Iced tea to wash it down. Come on."

She walked with him for a moment, which, based upon their recent history, he took as a major triumph, equivalent to scaling Everest. The taste of victory came too soon. She jerked herself back and said, "I don't think so."

"What?" He shook his head. "A hamburger's not good enough—you only eat steak?" He was finally losing patience. Both the woman and the heat were getting to him. Then, he said, "Oh" with a flash of insight. "You're one of those, a veg? Relax. They've got lettuce in there. And it's all on the house, okay? Hey, what the hell, your company's been grand. A burger's the least I can do to repay you for all the cheer you've brought into what might have been a long, lonely trip."

She stood where she was, stonily eyeing him. Then she shrugged and started walking ahead to the diner.

"Tell me, point of curiosity...you often go out on afternoon treks in one hundred and twelve degree weather?" he asked when they were seated opposite each other in the booth.

She stuffed a fry into her mouth. Abandoning her remarkable reserve, she had already begun to attack the burger.

With a half-full mouth, she answered, "I had this old jalopy. It decided to die in the desert alongside some of its relatives. So I hitched a bad ride." She reached for another fry. "Guess my judgment of human nature wasn't what I thought it was." For proof, she moved the shirt material a little off her shoulder.

Chance saw discoloration, a round blood mark already formed close to the skin.

"Animal," she said, fury resonating in the single word. "He had a nice car, nice clothes, nice smile, probably a nice wife and nice kids." Maggie Rand shrugged.

Chance gave a nod. "Bad heart though."

"Bad day, when I got through with him. He'll have an interesting time explaining the scratches on the side of his face." She almost smiled.

"You didn't use the—" Chance's eyes moved down to where he could see the top of the knife's handle over the table.

"Only for rabbits. And desperate emergencies. Which this wasn't."

"Ever used it before?" he asked, finding her fierce independence admirable and somehow, although he couldn't say why, sexually intoxicating. To imagine a woman with that kind of fire in bed...

"I've caught a few rabbits in my day," she answered.

"It's the desperate emergencies I was kinda wondering about."

"One," she said, and left it at that.

Chance was finding it hard to concentrate on his food. The woman fascinated him. She was like an exotic cat, something you didn't come upon very often and wanted to study, to see how it moved differently from other cats. She looked so smooth and beautiful. He wanted to reach out and stroke the skin to hear her motor purr. Or maybe, he thought, she would scratch him, too.

An instant scene flashed before him. Moonlight. Naked bodies—his and hers—she fighting him, giving in, taking him with as much force as she used in defending herself. Typical male fantasy. Brutish. Ugly. But, God—all that morality business aside—he wouldn't mind making love to that body opposite him, the body with the arm connected to the hand that was reaching for yet another fry.

He took his eyes off her long enough to signal the waitress and silently pointed that he wanted another order of potatoes.

"You're into horses?" she asked, but more in the way of a statement.

It was the first personal interest she had really showed in him. Ridiculously, he felt almost flattered. "Until last week, I was."

"I love horses," she volunteered.

"Ever ride?" Incredible. They were having a real conversation. Back and forth. Questions with responses.

The shield dropped from the black eyes, and he found himself being appraised with something akin to warmth.

"A long time ago," she said. A row of splendid white teeth showed themselves in her quick half smile.

He fought down the urge to reach out and run his finger along her lips, to insert his finger along the rim of the dazzling pearlescent whiteness and feel the furry softness of her tongue against his flesh, to intrude himself into her magnificent body, to blast through her controlled exterior, to . . .

"When I was very small," he heard Maggie Rand saying, and told himself to shut off his libido, which was on overdrive. "I used to ride bareback in the desert." Suddenly her eyes clouded, and a dark shadow felled the light that had momentarily occupied her expression.

The darkening reminded him of his own recent miseries, and for a while they both sank back into their former state of isolation.

He supposed he had no one else to blame for what had happened to him. But nevertheless, it was a tragic business all the way around. If he thought about the horses he'd go mad. Truly. At first when he'd heard about it, and then when he had gone down to the stables and seen . . . well, it was too much. He'd gone a little crazy. Those four-legged animals were like family to him. He couldn't have loved them any more if they had been his children.

Dead. Twenty-four horses, some of the finest blood-stock in California, burned in the fire set by someone who hated him—and they, just poor dumb beasts, had paid the price.

God, he thought, shivering, *the mentality of some-one who could do a thing like that.*

He knew the man responsible for the order, if not the deed itself. There was nothing he could do about it, either. All that would come of his finger pointing was that he would end up looking like a fool. A fool he might be, but not so much of one that he didn't know when he was in a no-win situation. He knew the face of reality, having stared into its jowls once or twice too often to forget.

He'd known Denelia Hill was trouble from the first moment he had seen her. Blond and tall, with a figure to make Hefner take pause, she had come onto him for three years. She was not divorced, but separated, with every indication that the situation was going to be made legally permanent. Of course he had known better, but what was a guy to do? Finally he gave in. Only, Dene-lia Hill's estranged husband found out. From what Chance heard later, Denelia got a new yacht out of the situation, a second chance at connubial bliss, and he'd gotten his life smashed to bits.

He had saved for ten years, saved every penny he had made as a trainer for some of the finest horses on the Southern California circuit. He'd paid cash for every-thing, for the horse farm, the horses, equipment—right down the line. Which was why he hadn't gotten around to buying insurance. The insurance was going to be next.

Only somehow, in between Denelia and the fire, it hadn't happened.

One horse. He had one horse left; this one only because the filly had been at the vet's with a bad fetlock. And soon the filly would be gone—if he had any luck left. In Vegas he'd offer her up for private sale to one of the shieks and Sangsters—all-inclusive shorthand for the top money men in the international Thoroughbred scene—who were coming to bid at the invitation only shindig. When it was over and he had some cash in his pocket, well, then he'd have to decide what to do with the rest of his life.

The waitress slapped the bill on the table and Maggie Rand's hand went instantly for it before Chance had the opportunity to respond. She scrutinized the numbers, then dug into a large satchel she carried.

From where he sat Chance could see pieces of clothing and then something bright and glittery and metal. Her rummaging stopped momentarily as her hand touched what he could now clearly make out as an Indian necklace, maybe Squash Blossom; he couldn't keep the tribal jewelry straight, but, it was definitely American Indian. As if she felt him eyeing her—and it, the necklace—her attention lifted to him, and she froze him again with one of her dangerous black stares before going back to the business of hunting down her wallet.

There was a telling lag as she surreptitiously surveyed the wallet's contents and Chance, having himself gone through the same ceremony a time or two during his life, knew instinctively there was little cash being held between its thin leather walls. After a time, she placed a few bills on the table and dug into her pocket for some loose change.

"What's this?" he asked, making light of her gesture.

"I ate, I pay."

"I told you, it's a gift, a present. As in from one human being to another, dig?"

She was silent, looking at the meaning behind the moment, it seemed, rather than at him.

"Okay," he said, "so I made a mistake. You're not human." He covered the rest of the bill with his own cash, and swung out of the booth.

Behind him, he sensed Maggie Rand's hesitation to follow. A sinking, slipping-away feeling invaded him with unexpected poignancy. The feeling weighted him with its layers of sadness.

Then, suddenly, there was a rustle of movement and he heard the sack of belongings clink against the table's top. She was coming. The weight lifted.

The heat blasted him in the face as he left the diner. His eyes went first to the van, where he saw the filly watching him. She was a beautiful beast, he thought for the one millionth time; his lone, beautiful little survivor.

The restaurant door swished closed on its hinges and the woman joined him, off to the side. There was no need to look at her. Chance could feel her presence in his gut. He tried to define the vibes, but couldn't. All signals came in garbled. The frequency she operated on was too high, too female for him to receive.

He took off in the direction of his truck. Undulating waves of heat rose up from the vehicle's metal hood. A smell of parched earth mingled with diesel oil and horse manure. To the left, a door of one of the big rig's cabs opened suddenly and a cowboy song wailed out into the stillness. *Gonna love you till there's no more road to travel. Gotta feeling I'm on a road with no endin', babe.*

Going around to the trailer of his own truck, Chance checked out the filly then paused, his eyes following the interstate. Straight, it stretched into an infinity of barren landscape. Then he looked across the truck to where Maggie Rand waited for him to unlock the door. The black eyes watched him. They were as dark and as deep and as forbidding as a night alone on the desert.

Chance hitched his hat down, blocking out the sight of her. "Travelin' time," he said.

Maggie Rand sat as close to the truck's door as she could, an unconscious attempt to separate herself from the man who continually threatened to move into her psychic space. She needed room, lots of it. She felt wild inside, felt ferociously unhappy and discontent. The whole of the desert wasn't big enough to contain all her rage.

Her hand felt inside the top pocket of the oversized shirt she wore over her tank top. The folded envelope was still there where she had put it the day before when she had left the bland little rental house in the San Fernando Valley. How strange the twists of life that had brought her grandfather to that spot.

He had changed his name to Charlie Rand but, unlike her, he had never truly been able to pass for anything other than what he was. Indian Man, the kids used to call him when as a little girl she would walk by his side in the modern air-conditioned malls. He had worn civilized clothes, but his hair was long still and banded by a headband. People thought he was strange, but she thought he was beautiful. He was her grandfather, White Cloud, and she had walked beside him and held his hand proudly and loved him more than anyone, ever, in her life.

Three days earlier she had flown into Los Angeles from Oregon. The trip had been on a whim; or at least so it had seemed at the time. In hindsight, she recognized the decision to visit her grandfather as an intuitive link between their spirits. He seemed almost to have expected her when she showed up at his door.

It came as a shock to see him as he appeared. She guessed he was in his late seventies; no one took down numbers when he was born, dates not being an issue in his native surroundings on the reservation. The once sharp profile had become a brittle parody of his former self; the glittery dark eyes had become opaque and dull. Only his carriage remained light and noble as he glided soundlessly into the main portion of the house with her following behind.

He did not speak of illness, instead asking her about her own life.

There was not much pleasant to say about that, so she made up some extra stories to keep the truth from him. She had been working in Oregon on a ranch, mostly helping with the domestic chores, but once in a while was allowed to ride into the hills and up farther to the mountains to check on the cattle and sheep if the owners found themselves short of male hands. It had been for those moments she had lived.

Her grandfather's face had always grown happily wistful when she related the details of this part of her existence, and so it was on this she elaborated.

That first afternoon of her visit, he had brought out the necklace and handed it to her. She took it as he gave it, silently, with proper reverence. She had been aware then—in the same way as she had known, inexplicably, that it was important for her to make the trip to Los Angeles—that a moment in life was being celebrated, a rite of passage was being commemorated through the transference of this piece of her grandfather's heritage into her keeping. The necklace, Maggie knew, was all he had left of a way of life that had long since vanished.

That evening they had sat long into the night, her grandfather's voice soothing her just as it had when she was a child and he had told her stories of their people's customs and their bravery. But on that recent night, he spoke of her parents, who had died years before in a car accident, and he had spoken of how in their world no one ever truly leaves, but stays on forever in another form with their loved ones. He told her that she would have a good life. At that Maggie had smiled, but bitterly, glad that the night hid the truth of her feelings from the old man she loved.

The next afternoon she returned from the market. She put the bag down on the kitchen counter and called out that he should come to see what she had brought for their feast. It was then that she saw the envelope with her name.

A sliver of fear raced through her spine as she lifted the paper. Opening it, a handful of pale seeds tumbled onto the floor. She let them lie and quickly scanned the note's contents. His writing was atrocious, but she made out the shakey, ill-formed letters and arranged the grammar to form meaningful thoughts.

The seeds in the envelope were from his people's land. They were of a desert flower, having no true botanical name that she knew of, but by her grandfather called the Ancestor Plant. When planted correctly, that is, with the proper degree of love—and with reverence for the plant's inherent power—the seeds contained the spirit of life. These seeds were his essence, and the essence of his grandfather before him, and so on. When he was gone, she was to take them and scatter them in the desert where, if she did so with the proper mind and heart, they would take root and flower, petals reaching for the clouds and the stars and the sun; roots reaching deep into the earth. And through the wind, the voices of the flowers would be carried forever, connecting them always. Heaven and earth were one.

Maggie's fingers trembled as she gathered up the fallen seeds and placed them in the envelope. Then she searched for her grandfather, who was nowhere to be found.

The call came in the early evening. The police had found him at the top of Griffith Park, beside the observatory building. There were no signs of violence. It appeared he had died peacefully, of natural causes. They asked his age, and Maggie said she didn't know.

The following day she made the arrangements for the funeral and told the landlady who owned the rented house to do what she would with his few belongings.

But before she left, she took a city bus up to the top of the mountain where her grandfather had been found. It was a magnificent day in spite of the late-September heat. Huge clouds had formed, white towers building to the sun. The backdrop of blue was vibrant and pure. Below, the vast metropolis of the City of Angels spread out before her, and somewhere, hidden in the distant mists, stretched the Pacific. The wind was from the desert. It was hot and howled about her like a devil, pricking at her skin, pricking at her nerves. Early Spanish settlers had named it appropriately: the Santana Wind, the devil wind.

Maggie turned her head into its force, facing the blast as if having been called. Beyond were the high mountains that cradled Los Angeles. A bit of snow had already fallen on their highest peaks. Her hand went to the packet of seeds folded in her shirt's pocket. On the far side of the range would lie the desert; there her grandfather's spirit would again rise.

The droning of the truck's engine had lulled her to sleep. Maggie awoke with a lurch, surprised to see the outposts of civilization on the horizon. A scattering of tall buildings loomed into view. Closer, road signs touted the pleasures to come in Las Vegas casinos. The daylight had taken on the hue of late afternoon, but nightfall did not worry her. She would easily curl up in her sleeping bag beneath the stars, a cactus for her bedpost. It wouldn't be the first time. The factor disturbing her, as she scrunched her eyes to examine the potential threat, was the gathering of large clouds dropped low over the top peaks of the desert mountain range. A sudden downpour in the desert could create a wall of water that could, within minutes, sweep cars and cattle and people into oblivion.

Still groggy, she felt for her bag of belongings. "This is good," she said, "right here, anywhere."

Chance kept driving, as if he hadn't heard.

"You can let me off here." Maggie said it louder now, irritated that she had to make the effort to repeat herself. She wanted to be alone, wanted to sever contact with the world.

"What's it with you? A death wish?" Chance returned. "There's a storm coming."

She sighed. "Look, mister, all I want—"

"The name's Chance, Chance Harris, and I know what you want," he barked back, overriding her. "You want out." He came to a sudden, jolting stop in the middle of the road, which was empty in both directions. His jaw was fixed tight, his attention on the distance stretching before him. He leaned to the side and reached across her, his arm lightly grazing her body, and opened the door. "Enjoy your evening."

For a long moment Maggie was silent, immobile. The windows were rolled down and the desert air carried the scent of the oncoming rain. A light wind drove a bundle of dry brush scurrying across the road before them.

"Thanks for the ride," she said, and climbed out. With a quick motion, she hoisted her bundle down to the road's edge.

Chance felt her eyes on him. He couldn't trust himself to look into her face. "Close the door," he said flatly.

Slowly, too gently, she closed it, gave it an extra shove so that the catch engaged. "Thanks, again," Maggie said.

"Yeah," Chance replied, "maybe I'll get a badge for my Scout uniform. It'll have a picture of a Looney Bird on it." He fired up the ignition.

Maggie backed off a few inches as he shifted the truck into gear. The truck started to roll, the trailer lumbering after it.

She watched for a moment, then started across the highway with her gear slung over one shoulder. Midway to the other side she stopped and looked down the stretch of road.

The country around her was silent again. Even the red glow of taillights had become an indistinct blur dissolving into the dusk. Within her a silent cry arose, bringing with it a moment's vertigo. She fought, as she always did, against the throb of loneliness. The regret of what might have been open to her—to her and this man she hardly really knew—had she continued down the road with him, lasted only seconds, before she was able to again cloak herself in the resolve of remaining singular. Over the years she had cleared her inner territory of emotional obstacles so that now there were vast, empty spaces in which she might roam without the worry of bumping into sorrow and pain. Anyway, she had things to do.

On the other side of the pavement, the sandy shoulder of the road sloped downward a few feet, then leveled off to the flat expanse of the desert flooring. She angled herself down the sandy incline and looked about her.

The world had turned eerie. There was a pink cast to the sky, against which the clouds stood out in bold relief, their bulbous shapes shot through with shades of pastels deepening into colors of purple-black and magenta, providing the night with a costume appropriate for a violent drama.

She would have to be quick about her mission.

At that moment, a sizzle of light arced across the sky. The hairs on her neck rose up and her arms turned goose-bumpy.

Never in her life had she felt so entirely bereft. All she had were the seeds held tightly clenched in her hand. She clung to them for warmth, almost as if her grandfather's spirit did, in fact, reside within the few dry kernels of plant life. A romantic thought only.

She did not believe in the Indian legends; but she did not entirely disbelieve, either. Her feelings fell into the realm of respect. The truth made no difference one way or the other; she was carrying out her grandfather's last wishes because she loved him.

Maggie began to walk into the landscape. It was dotted with clumps of dried vegetation, looking to her at the moment like the shells of dried souls. Here and there were the plumper forms of cacti, who through some secret knowledge had survived and flourished. Little creatures scurried away with business to tend to, regardless of her intrusion.

It had to be the right place, the seeds needing the perfect spot that her grandfather claimed could only be selected by the feeling one had when standing on it.

At last she reached a place that she felt was suitable for the mission entrusted to her. She tramped around for a bit, continuing to test the ground for the proper feeling of power, and when satisfied, put down her gear.

The spot was a slight mound, the only mound in the otherwise flat landscape for as far as she could see, and on it was a black rock, porous by way of its volcanic origin.

She sat down and studied the ground, thinking of the best way to distribute the seeds so that they would grow. A weariness took hold of her and she felt herself bone tired, her eyes ready to drop closed. All she wanted to do was to sleep forever and ever. An owl cried as it passed by, its wings casting a brief shadow over the mound. She took her knife and scraped at the earth, which was nothing but packed sand. How anything could bloom in the punishing extremes of the desert, she did not know.

Her thoughts were concentrated on her grandfather as she pressed each seed into the parched earth. She imagined him as a young man, and then later, saw him as she knew him, in his maturity. When the last seed was placed into its bed, she said the prayer to Nature, taught to her when she was a girl by her grandfather.

So intently had she dwelled on her private ceremony that the first drops took her by surprise. They were hard and large and spaced far apart. Another came, then another. Maggie rose, enveloped by the silence and the purple dusk.

She turned abruptly, hearing a noise behind her. Her right hand went for the knife at her belt and she whirled around, ready to defend herself.

"I don't know what the hell you're doing, woman, but now's about the right time to knock it off."

Chance Harris stood below the mound, his legs spread apart and his fists hanging loose at his sides like some kind of Oriental martial-arts warrior. He wore his hat tipped low, but she could still make out his face, which was kind of rugged-handsome, and looked like it belonged to the kind of man who had done some serious traveling through life's byways.

Her grip on the knife's handle relaxed.

His blue eyes had been on her all day, every glance holding a question in it. At first the question had been sexual, one that she might have handled easily if anything got out of control; but later, what she read behind the side looks he threw her way when he thought she wasn't aware, was more personally oriented. She didn't like his interest. She felt invaded, as if someone was trying to get into the only territory she had left in which to survive. Maybe it was the Indian in her and nothing even personal; maybe that inner necessity for freedom never left you once it was in the blood.

The rain had begun in earnest. Large, fast drops followed one after the other. Still, Chance Harris waited. His shirt, a blue cotton work shirt, with the sleeves rolled high on his arms, was already becoming attached to his skin.

"Stubborn cuss," he growled, when she didn't move.

Then, with the quickness of a lizard he was with her, grabbing her up from the mound and throwing her at an angle over his hip. She screamed and kicked and thought of using her knife, but her position didn't allow for it and his grip was like a vise. The humiliation of being caught off-guard far exceeded any physical discomfort.

In a moment, he had thrown her into the truck's cab. He slammed the door after her, then came around and got into his side.

They glared at each other in silence for a moment. "Shut your mouth," he said, reading her mind. "Don't even start. I don't want to hear it." He started up the engine and they began rolling toward Vegas as though nothing had happened.

"How much money do you have?" he asked her a mile or so down the road. The rain was beating against the window.

Startled, she shot him a frightened look. Robbery had not occurred to her.

"I'm not after your money, sweetheart."

She turned away, staring straight ahead.

"If you haven't noticed, that's a real storm out there." He speeded up the wipers.

"Not enough for a hotel room, if that's what you're getting at."

"That's what I was getting at."

They passed slowly down the main strip, caught in a mesh of rush-hour traffic. Both sides of the street were a blaze of blurry colored lights through the wet windshield. A little farther down the way, Chance turned into a side avenue and kept going until he was on the outskirts of the town. In time he came to a horse ranch, where he deposited the horse with a groom who un-hitched the van from the truck.

Five minutes later he pulled into the parking lot of a seedy-looking, third-rate motel. "Here's the deal," he said. "Of late I am not Midas, so I can't stake you to a room of your own. Nor am I some kind of a cretin who's going to pounce on your bones. Unless," he added, with a more hopeful note, "you specifically request the service."

Maggie gave him one of her familiar dead-fish stares.

"Didn't think so," he said. "What I suggest—no, insist upon—is that you share my humble, but dry, abode for the duration of the storm, which is—" he took time to pause and listen to the rain pound the roof "—a doozy. To put it scientifically. And, if I'm any judge of storms, this one should last the night. Thing is, the way I see it, you don't have much of a choice, sweetheart."

"Why?" she said stridently. "What's it to you, any-way? What's it to you what happens to me?"

"Honestly?" Chance said, and pulled his hat down lower, as he prepared to get out. "I don't have the slightest idea why I should bother with you. Maybe it has something to do with your sweet disposition." He climbed out and slammed the door so hard Maggie's teeth vibrated.

The rain sluiced down the truck's windshield in thick sheets that all but obscured the image of Chance Harris dashing for the motel's office. In the red neon glow of the overhead sign, he looked to Maggie like a melting devil, his shoulders hunched in, back curved against the downpour.

Yeah, Maggie considered, it was going to be one hell of a night.

Chapter Two

They stood side by side beneath the eaves, mere inches out of the downpour. He felt suddenly embarrassed to be bringing her there. It was a seedy joint, a harsh reflection of the times he had so recently fallen upon.

If you could have seen me then, he felt like saying to his hitchhiking companion. He felt the urge, the need, to puff himself up a bit. *Thing is, I was once a prince. These webbed feet? Don't let them throw you. Only temporary, folks. Soon enough she'll be along—the beautiful maiden; the one with a heart of gold and the special X-ray eyes that can see through this green frog coloring. I'm just hanging out now, waiting for the kiss that will turn me back into—*

Even the numbers on the motel door were disturbing.

He noticed that one of the metal numbers had slipped. Chance glared at the four. It dangled upside down from a thin nail. It gave the row of three digits the look of a complex mathematical equation; something to the something power, a sign to those who passed through the portals that the true use of this shoddy dwelling, this garrish, neoned hostelry for transient princes turned into frogs—and others of similar misfortune—was the summing up of spent lives. At that present moment, his life would tally up in the minus column, more losses than wins. Well, at least there had been the excitement, the drama of it all, he thought. Even losing had it's thrill when you came so close to the golden ring.

"Don't tell me. You're going to stare it open."

Maggie Rand's voice intruded upon his inner sigh. He had drifted off again. It happened a lot lately. Nothing much was going on in his present life anymore, so why not time trip?

Coming back into the real world, he saw Maggie Rand's justifiably impatient expression, thought of apologizing, reconsidered and, instead, flamboyantly flipped the key into the air, caught it with an equal display of flourish, and said, "I was trying to remember the magic word, but since you can't wait for my powers..."

The old-fashioned key was enormous and wouldn't fit easily into the lock. Chance had to struggle for longer than was masculinely chic, and when the door finally gave way, it was to a yawning blackness that smelled faintly of mold and antiseptic cleaner.

He felt inside for the wall switch. A flick, and the focal point of the room was illuminated: a bed. *A* bed, as in singular. A framed print of a clown with a prurient leer hung crookedly over the two thin pillows.

Neither of them moved to enter.

Chance cocked his head toward the interior. "Pretty romantic setting, huh?"

"Is this a joke?" Maggie said, and simultaneously turned away.

But for his quick reflexes, she would have been gone from his side. But he was experienced. Grabbing her wrist, he stopped her flight.

But not her fight. She struggled against his hold.

"Recall," he said, "I am a man who makes his living...*made* his living...working with creatures who are fleet of foot."

She was glaring at him with what he recognized as that now all-too-familiar glint of savage refusal to be hoodwinked into—maybe just possibly—relaxing into any emotion approximating, God forbid, friendliness, warmth, spontaneous humor.

"Tell me something..." he went on conversationally as she continued to make vain attempts to jerk her wrist out of his grasp. Pointedly he ignored her as if she were no more than a fly. Actually she was quite strong, and it was difficult to maintain his stance of composed supremacy while saying, "Is it the picture on the wall you object to? Because there we just happen to agree. I hate a clown snickering over my head when I sleep. Or," he went on brightly, "could it be your disappointment stems from the various exotic scents wafting our way? But wait, wait..." he said, and paused reflectively. "Might it be the bed which displeases you? The one—and only—bed?"

"You must read minds."

"Just another of my little talents."

Her eyes narrowed into slits. "Look, I don't care if I drown out there, I am not going to—"

And then, suddenly, unexpectedly *he* had had enough.

"Look, baby," he said, and dropped her arm, "this may come as a bit of a surprise to you. Thing of it is, I've been driving an entire long day. I'm hot, you dig? I'm tired. And, I may even have my own set of worldly miseries to nurse. Enough of them, dammit, so that I don't need to add a bitchy woman to the list of everything else that's not working in my life. Fact is, sweetheart, I asked for a double room. Turns out this is their idea of a room for two bodies. And, it's their last room." He gave her back one of her stone cold looks. "Maybe, baby, it just so happens *I'm* not in the mood to have my bones ravished, either."

With that, he pushed forward into the room, honestly not caring if she followed him or not. It was a true speech, honestly felt, clearly spoken. So maybe it sounded a little wimpy for a once macho stud. The hell with it. He was too tired to trot out his male repertoire.

He dropped his suitcase on the floor by the side of the bed and went into the bathroom, shutting the door after him.

Maggie thought of a hysterical bride. She almost laughed, but not quite. That would be giving in.

Alone, she stared into the room. An overhead globe in the center of the ceiling filled the place with a weak, yellow glow. Dark outlines of moths lay collected in the fixture's bottom. Her eyes traveled to the print on the wall. She had to admit he was right about the clown. Then her gaze landed on the bed and her eyes clouded with an apprehension that was due less to physical fear than a distrust of her own feelings.

Her mind raced, making her dizzy with the "what ifs" circling her. She had not been with a man for so long, and then she had believed in him and had been wrong. What if this man, this Chance Harris, with his easy smile and easy words and easy ways, were to know that she hadn't let anyone touch her, outside or inside, for so long that sometimes she ached from the pain of loneliness? What if he knew that and he reached out for her and she let him? What if she were to risk herself and end up even more alone in the morning?

God, she thought, clearing her mind, *but I'm tired. And it is a dry place,* she conceded.

After all, inches behind her, beyond the narrow overhang, the rain was coming down in torrents. A low glance to the left and she took in a thin river of water flowing past. It was a fast-moving tributary of cigarette butts, pieces of chewing gum wrappers, torn soft-drink cups and other miscellaneous debris. Let pride rule over reason and she would stand every chance of joining the motley flotilla sailing past.

She had a bedroll.

And, she thought with satisfaction, she had her knife.

Behind her, the rain increased.

Most of all, she had her resolve not to let anyone close in on her heart via her body. Especially this man, for whom such a deed was probably another of his "little talents."

She took a step forward into the room.

Chance had put her out of his mind while he showered. Instead, he had thought of the auction coming up, in which his little filly would be shown alongside some of the most spectacular animals in the horse world. Whatever he was offered, he'd take. It wouldn't be much, that was for sure. But what other choice did he have? He couldn't feed himself, much less the animal, without any money.

The thing of it was, it hurt like bloody hell, the thought of letting her go. Ordinarily he wasn't too sentimental about his horses. After all, it was his business. You bought, you sold; you lived, you died. It was black and white, that simple. It had to be that way.

But this horse, this one horse, with her it was different. Certainly it was not the same. She was the survivor, she alone. She was his tangible hold on the dream he had conjured and made real. For a while anyway. And then, all because of a woman...phfft, up in smoke. Literally.

He dropped the thin white terry-cloth towel to the floor and wrapped a dry one around his waist. The steam was thick in the room, and when he opened the door it flooded out into the bedroom. Surrounded in a damp cloud, he moved forward. Through the dissolving mist he saw her.

She was standing in the corner of the room with her bedroll unfurled at her feet and she was holding a shirt of some sort over one arm.

Modestly his hand felt for his towel, checking the overlay of material for closure. He really had forgotten about her, although now, seeing her there, he wondered how that could have been possible. She was more than just beautiful; she was compelling in a physical sense that could easily keep him up all night.

Her eyes traveled down to the small towel, then up again to his face. "Don't get any ideas," Chance said in a high voice. "I've got the most dreadful headache."

"My bad luck," Maggie returned.

"Well, maybe next time," he said. "Want to schedule something?"

"Calendars don't go that far." She nodded to the steamy bathroom. "I thought I'd take a quick one," she said.

"Great! Ah! Beware of the soap. It left holes in the tile." A knot had formed in his throat as he took in the woman's lean form with its gently molded curves promising...a lot. "Great," he repeated, "a quick dip," and turned away to fiddle with his watch on the nightstand.

She moved regally, head up, through the room, as if she were passing through a crowd of onlookers and didn't want to give them the benefit of her attention.

She certainly had his attention.

He could feel her, actually feel her without touching, as she passed beside him. Static electricity. Two storm clouds on a collision course. Thunder and lightning. That sort of earthshaking, soul-shattering, body-satisfying potential. It was going to be a long, long night.

She closed the door.

He lay back on the bed, his hands folded behind his head, and exhaled a deep sigh.

There was a rattle, a kind of nervous commotion, and he turned to see the bathroom's doorknob moving about as she fiddled with the lock that didn't work.

Chuckling to himself he got up and quickly, slyly, made his way across the room, found what he was looking for by the side of her bedroll and hurried back to the bathroom.

He knocked politely.

"What?"

What. Suspicious. Challenging. So endearing. Chance smiled with evil intent.

"Hey! I know your type of woman, I know what you want," he said in a voice that suggested an X rating. "And I'm ready, and able, to give it to you. Exactly the way you want it."

There was a space of outraged silence, then, "Look, you—" and the door swung open.

Chance dangled her knife before her. "Insurance."

She didn't say anything, just looked. "You're right," she said finally, and reached for the leather sheath protecting the murderous steel blade he was holding up. "For once you know exactly what I want." She shut the door.

"For once," he mimicked happily, and slipped once again onto the bed.

Perhaps he *could* be seriously interested in pursuing his libidinous fantasies. Maybe he wasn't quite as tired as he had originally stated. There was the slightest possibility that he might squander his high moral standards for a brief one-night fling with a stranger he had just met and would never see again. *Hmm,* he wondered, *what were the possibilities of him being given the opportunity to have to live with such moral decadence?*

His eyes slanted toward the bedroll in the room's corner, looking for clues of possible acquiescence to the plan he was hatching. If she had placed it any tighter up against the wall she'd be outside. There was definitely no room for imagining an invitation in her geographical positioning of her bed.

Yet . . . and yet . . . on more than one occasion he had been told "no" one minute, only to discover that with a little patience and a bit of male craftiness, the female negative evolved into a tentative affirmative, which evolved into, say, some very worthwhile moments.

He was lost in a brief reverie of some of those moments when Maggie stepped into his real world again.

She had on a long T-shirt from Oregon State University. Still, the shirt was not long enough to obscure her even longer legs.

Chance groaned. It was going to be a rough night.

He tried to concentrate on the tattoo of the rain outside. Inside was harder to take, the room filled with the kind of deafening ring that silence takes on between two people who have things to say and don't. Or maybe can't.

He could hear her stirring around in the sleeping bag. He lay still, his mind churning. Vague thoughts floated in and out of focus.

The slatted blinds were partially ajar and a red glow, fallout from the neon sign over the office, seeped through the cracks. From where he lay, he could make out Maggie Rand's dim outline on the floor. She was turned on her side, the curve of her hip catching the soft, crimson light. Her face, too, was turned to him, high-angled cheekbones defined and glossy in the rose-tinged light. A river of long, black hair flowed against the bent arm cradling her head.

The desire in him was at its peak. He longed to take her against him, could taste her flesh against his mouth, knew with absolute conviction the explosive heat their bodies would generate together. The hunger created by his mind gnawed continuously at his resolve to be a good guy in the face of real temptation.

She turned away, settling closer to the wall so that her figure was now no more than a dark outline, the color of the neon fire falling on the unoccupied space.

The rain had momentarily let up somewhat, and he imagined he could hear her breathing across the room. Agitated, he sat up in bed. He ran his fingers through his hair and watched her, the unspent male passion giving way to curiosity as she again restlessly tossed her body into another position. He wondered if she could be thinking thoughts similar to his; he wondered if his thoughts might in some way be making her restless.

This time she came to rest on her back. The large dark eyes that had so fascinated him during the day now gleamed in the artificial light. Periodically, their direction would shift and he could read in their movement thoughts being followed. He read trouble in their rhythmic search, and felt a sadness steal into the silence.

He had to do something to break that silence before the sorrow overwhelmed him, too.

"What was that all about tonight?" he asked cautiously, the words cutting in and out as they fell counterpoint to the rain's cadence. "That thing you were doing out there in the desert?"

She didn't answer for a moment, and then, as if she had brought up the subject herself, slowly said, "I had a promise to keep."

He was surprised that she answered, surprised and encouraged. He decided to continue on what could be a roll. There was something of comfort to this back and forth interchange.

"A promise," he echoed, inviting her to proceed.

And then a thought dawned. He was conscious of the slightest prick of jealousy. Something of the primal male had arisen in him at the notion of someone being close to her, the automatic assumption being, of course, that it had to be a man someone. Foolish. He didn't know how the emotion had formed. She was no one to him; a woman with a good body, was all, an intriguing arrangement of female flesh.

"Promise to who?" he asked, with more insistence.

"My grandfather."

"Hmm," he commented noncommittally, and relaxed.

She waited a beat longer, and then, as if she had made a weighty decision to trust him with a few additional words, went on tentatively.

"He died a couple of days ago. My grandfather was an Indian. He had some beliefs. Odd beliefs, maybe, but you know..." She sighed then, abandoning the train of conversation.

"You felt obliged," he finished for her, his hope being to pick up their dialogue.

She turned her head and the dark eyes blasted into him with outrage. "No, not obliged. I loved him. I loved him," she said, her voice breaking even as she continued to hold her gaze steady.

He felt her stare as a brand on his bare chest, as if he had been seared through his skin. He felt himself condemned of presumptuousness. He was guilty of not understanding something that she had apparently thought he would. He should have been silent, should have waited, or maybe not said anything at all. Nothing would have been better than the something that was so clearly wrong.

One thing at least was plain: he had trespassed on the foreign soil of her inner feelings. Women, in general, were difficult at best, but an Indian woman? Did she, he wondered, have a different psyche even from the others of her sex? What the hell could he possibly know? And what could he possibly know of a woman like this one?

"Sorry," he said, and relaxed back into his pillow to think.

An Indian. So. That confirmed his suspicions of her heritage. It shed light upon the wildness in the woman's nature. He had felt it from the first moment he'd laid eyes on her; it fairly radiated from her pores. There was a free-spirited, uncontained quality to her, whether silent or active. Even now, from where she lay, he could feel her power radiate all the way to him.

It explained the black eyes and hair the color of obsidian, straight and luxuriously thick. In the day, it was worn in a braid; not a simple braid, either, but wrapped in a coil like a snake sleeping at the base of her neck. In symbol: slumbering danger. He liked the slumber part, not the danger.

God, she was a beautiful-looking woman, though. He put both hands behind his head and once again thought of the way it would be if they weren't so far apart in the room.

The rain, which had picked up during his ruminations, had again slackened. In the intervals of relative quiet, he imagined he heard a faint snuffling sound. He listened again, and then, amazed, recognized the source.

He leaned up on his elbows. "Hey!"

His eyes had become accustomed to the lack of light, and with the neon from the motel's sign filtering through the blinds, he saw her lying on her back, a bent arm covering her eyes. Her lips moved slightly as she fought back an obvious impulse to cry.

"Hey," he said again, "hey...want to talk about it?"

There was no response.

He remained as he was, not moving or talking, either. He'd learned his lesson.

And then the sobs really came. Deep, soul-wrenching cries rose up from her gut, shattering the silence.

"Baby...oh baby..." Chance said, up off the bed and halfway to her before remembering he had nothing on but his undershorts.

Kneeling, he bent over and took her hand in his. This made her cry all the harder, and suddenly it was she who had risen up and clutched him around his neck with both arms.

"Hey there, easy now," Chance said as if gentling a spooked filly.

"All alone..." she said, her shoulders racked by the emotion. "No one else..."

It was the desperate hold of a drowning child and Chance found himself tightening his arms around her. Something stronger than physical lust arose from the pit of his stomach and swept through his entire being. He was experiencing her pain.

"Oh...God..." Maggie sobbed, her entire body trembling against him. "Oh...God...I feel so alone. There's no one left. No one but me, and I'm afraid," she whispered.

She burrowed into him and he let her, welcoming her need. "Okay, there. S'okay, now. Things'll work out..." he crooned. Her sorrow cut through his flesh, and then, recognizing the sadness as his own, he silently gave in to the grief he had pushed from his mind because it was so large, and ran so deep, and was so terrible.

In his own way, he was clinging to her, too; the sounds of his horses screaming through his mind, the black cinders of his life swirling around him, particles of what had once been all drifting into the void of the future.

She didn't object when he carried her back to the double bed; nor did she complain when they lay twined together in each other's arms. It wasn't sexual now, only the warmth of two cold bodies, finding temporary comfort in the other's presence. For a long while they stayed like that; then he heard her breathing settle, and eventually he joined her in a troubled sleep.

If later, accountability came to be an issue for what transpired, he knew he could not be held to blame. For this one time, at least, he was an innocent man.

He felt her body moving against his—small, spiraling movements with the pelvis, probably first against his leg. Perhaps she was not even aware. But he was aroused. Unable to help himself, he kissed her lightly, tenderly on the side of the neck. It was the kind of gesture that could have meant nothing, there was a sweetness to it; without encouragement, he would have let the matter go and would have probably drifted back to sleep.

But she didn't let it go.

No. Maggie Rand returned his kiss with a deepening ardor that sent a blade of hot excitement tearing through his stomach.

It happened so quickly there was no time for either of them to reconsider. It was as if lightning had struck, and they were two pieces of parched kindling, instantly ignited.

He lifted the nightgown from her body and felt her breasts, which were high and small and full. Her skin was like liquid velvet, and his tongue was instantly upon the hollow of her stomach, moving down, systematically exploring her length.

He could lose himself in this woman, he thought. He could never come up again from this delight, he thought, and tightened his body to control what was happening too fast.

Maggie did not know how it began, and now she could not stop it from continuing. She had been asleep, and then pleasurable sensations—the most deeply satisfying and tender, yet erotic feelings she had ever experienced—came flooding over her, through her. It was as if she were dreaming while being awake. So for a moment she floated in the dream, experiencing the sexual abandonment of her body without, for once, the conflicting voice of her mind to lend interference.

When the inner voice finally surfaced with its familiar rebuke, it was too late.

He was touching her, and in such a way that waves of delight, of absolute bliss drenched her. She felt she was drowning in a liquid ecstasy.

Her own hands and mouth sought him, tasted the clean soaped flesh of the man she had ridden beside that day. His body was incredible, hard and muscular, yet the hands tender and knowledgeable. They knew how and where to press against the mound, and when to release and press again. His tongue wound into her, driving her into a frenzy of need she had never known before. His breath was ragged, the certainty of his movements controlled but forceful...and suddenly she was swept away, demanding, finding herself leading him.

He entered with her guidance. The sensation was intense; they gasped, holding still for a moment, feeling the pulses of their bodies merging. Then he moved slowly, and she moaned beneath him, meeting his movements with a fluid counter rotation.

"Maggie..." he called softly. "Maggie Rand...Maggie Rand..." he said, repeating her name for no reason at all but for the fact that she was filling him completely, body and soul, so that he could not separate himself from the woman whose body had taken control over him.

She gasped and, rigid, bowed herself into him as he drove deeper and cried out in a voice he didn't recognize.

The aftermath was slow, diminishing in gradual spasms of pleasure until they lay side by side, silent once more.

He waited for a time, then turned his head to the side. "Maggie...?" he said, but she had fallen into sleep again.

For a while he watched the woman's face, seeing the wildness now as a natural innocence in her state of repose. The light caught the sharp edges of her high cheekbones, cheekbones that he had so recently kissed. And the mouth. Partially open, he longed to kiss the lips that were neither full nor thin, instead being perfectly proportioned to his own mouth. She had made an attempt to cover herself with the sheet. It had dislodged, and one breast lay exposed to his view, the nipple still peaked.

The most erotic woman he had ever known; would ever know.

Chance sighed and closed his eyes. What the hell had he gotten into? He could love this woman—maybe he even loved her now. Only after this night it was all going to be over. That much of his life was a certainty anyway. He knew wild horses, worked with them; knew the ones that could and couldn't be tamed. She was one of those who couldn't.

Chapter Three

She crept out of the bed, barely daring to breathe. Without a sound she reclaimed the Oregon State shirt lying crumpled on the floor and slipped it over her head.

The morning dampness on the thin commercial carpeting was nothing compared to the chill of Maggie's mood as she crossed the room and bent to rewind her bedroll. A sense of betrayal ripped through her, rousing that familiar, just-below-the-surface anger always in her company. Only in this case the betrayal was inner, directed at herself for having succumbed—as she had been afraid she might—to needs, both of the flesh and of the spirit, weaknesses that made her vulnerable to the possibility of pain. The act of betrayal was her own mutiny against her own self.

As if directed by an unseen hand, she found herself staring back to the place where she had lain that night.

Chance Harris, sleeping soundly, was sprawled on his back. Loose and nude, he rested upon the tangled sheets with one leg bent, an arm down, the other crooked at angle to his face. Her eyes swept down the length of his form, which she had known only in the dark. But for the expanse of paler flesh where he had worn shorts, his muscular body was tanned. Only a slight feathering of hair on his chest interrupted the satiny gleam of skin.

It was a body she had reveled in only hours before, and as she observed his sleeping form, a rush of heat coursed through her like a taunt, reminding her of the pleasures they had shared together.

Familiar flurries of old resentment assembled like an unruly crowd in her mind. With satisfaction, Maggie recognized their faces as old companions. A practiced group of followers, they had gone through their protests time and time again, had waged on her behalf countless internal revolutions. The old slogans began resounding in her head and the banners of distrust and futility and disappointment fluttered on their standards.

On the bed, Chance Harris stirred.

She watched with apprehension as his hand reached out beside him on the sheet. Slowly as if confused not to find her there, his eyes came open. Still groggy, he looked to where she had lain, the understanding that he had been abandoned finally becoming clear.

Maggie saw a fleeting look of pain wash over his face. Rising to his elbows, he looked down the length of the bed and, seeing her, another expression filled his face with a tender, almost desperate urgency.

"What's going on?" he asked quietly, not moving. "What's happening?" His gaze shifted to the rolled canvas beside where she knelt on one knee.

Her answer was to grab her shorts and shirt from her bag. She rose and headed for the bathroom to change.

Only she didn't make it.

Chance slipped to the side of the bed and was on his feet, blocking her way before she could pass.

"Wait a minute," he said, "just hold it. Look, I don't get what's going on here. You're acting like some goddamned tornado. Last night we—"

"I want to get dressed. If you don't mind," Maggie said, and made another attempt to escape the situation.

Taking her by the shoulders, he repositioned her directly in front of him. "Yeah? Well I do mind." His voice was lower than usual, still weighted by sleep. It carried the timbre of passion from the night before.

Maggie shivered. It was happening again, her control dissolving. So close they were. She could smell his musky scent, imagined her own still clinging to him. Memories of their lovemaking flooded her senses. Beneath her shirt her nipples tightened and she made a move to cover the telltale sign of arousal with the garments she held.

"Maggie," he said, forestalling her attempt at modesty with a kiss that left her weak. "Maggie, last night...it was...I've never felt..."

He broke off with a look that left her heart melting. She closed her eyes, desperate to sever their bond. He had said what she already knew. But his words made everything all the more frightening; it was documentation that their experience of each other had been real.

"Baby, I want you again. And again..." His palm found her breast, and he rubbed lightly in circular motions against its peak.

"Chance, no," she said, unable to move as ribbons of involuntary tremors rippled through her.

Hardened, he pressed against her pelvis. She moaned, unable to fortify herself against the onslaught of her own desire.

With his free hand, he lifted her shift and followed the swell of her other breast with his mouth.

"Oh, God...no..." Maggie whispered. "I don't want—"

He angled her against the doorjamb and, lifting her slightly, entered her with a single fluid motion. His lips were on her neck, then on her mouth, seeking with an almost violent male hunger to possess her entirely.

At first she felt the hardness of the wood cut into her back. But that discomfort, along with every other sensation, was reduced to nothing. Her entire being seemed controlled by the urgent need to meld her body with his.

What protests she offered were soon abandoned to the rhythmic flow of their joining. With each thrust the heat took them simultaneously higher. Her body resonated with echoes of his pleasure as he called her name in short bursts of warm breath.

Slick with passion, she held herself against him. He pressed and withdrew, hands expert on her body, all male natural instinct. It began as a rolling tension and blossomed into each cell of her body. With a cry that sent her head back, she arched involuntarily, tightening as a flood of fiery emotion consumed them both.

They came into the world gradually, both spent and trembling. Tears trickled down her cheeks and he brushed them away, searching her face with his blue eyes. "From sadness or pleasure?" he asked, and waited for her answer.

She turned her head away, not wanting to confront the question, but he did and turned her chin back to him.

"From disappointment in myself," she said bitterly.

It was as if she had slapped him. He blanched. His hand dropped and a second later he backed off, creating a space to set her free.

But she didn't move. For a moment she felt directionless, as if she had somehow lost her way. She stooped to retrieve the fallen clothes and brought them up against her. They felt limp and useless, and she thought of the wasted, dead dreams of her youth.

"Sorry," she said, and brushed past him into the bathroom. Turning back to him, she said, "It was a mistake, that happening last night. And now, too. Things just got . . ." Maggie tried to find the word. Her eyes circled the room, searching for an answer. "Out of control." She averted her eyes as she backed into the bathroom.

Leaning against the closed door, she let the tears fall freely down her face. As often as she wiped them away, they replaced themselves with new recruits.

She was out of control, off balance. It frightened her.

The act of sexual abandonment was a fall from her moral ethics; casual sex with a man she did not know and would never see again. But there was something equally disturbing to the tryst. For in those few moments in his arms she had once again felt that elation. Her emotions had soared high and free in some other region of herself, a place that she had long forgotten existed, having filed the map away in the darkest, most inaccessible regions of her heart. It frightened her, that joy, for it meant that she might spin out of control again, lost in some phantom happiness that would dissolve, leaving her with all the emotions of that disastrous time earlier in her life.

Unlike all the pretty blond girls with whom she had attended high school, with their blue eyes and milk-and-honey skin and glittering prom-queen smiles, her skin was a tawny, gold color. Her eyes had glittered with black anger when she was called "squaw," and her straight black hair, worn in a long tail down her back, was lifted and held like the reins of a horse. Perhaps if she had been able to laugh about it, perhaps if she had not cared so much, they would have forgotten about her differences; but she couldn't forgive them, and they, in turn, wouldn't forget to tease her.

She was defenseless. How could she change what she was? Then, being young, she could not accept the differences between what she was not, and what everyone else in her new world was. She did not see the strengths of being unique, only the shame of being unlike the others.

When she was a girl she had nothing to do but to run home to her grandparents' house. She never told them of the taunts; things were hard enough for them, too, trying as they did to make the best out of life in a world in which they could never truly belong. There was no happiness for any of them. The worst of it was, it was for her sake they had moved into the city. They had left the reservation knowing that their ways could not last forever in the modern world's encroaching evolution, and that someday Maggie would need the skills to make her way in this alien world.

When she was eleven, she finally discovered something positive and distinctive about herself. She could run.

She ran faster than any of the girls, even faster than all of the boys, except for one or two of them. By the time she was in high school, she was competing in track meets, and soon enough she was taking medals right and left. Those were the moments she lived for, when, surrounded by glory, she would accept the medals, the flowers, the ribbons, knowing that she did not fit into the cold society of blue-eyed blondes simply because she was more special. Nature had not entirely abandoned her. Instead, she had been blessed with the amazing physical grace and power of her family's people.

It was during the summer after her senior year that the accident occurred. She was in a pre-Olympic work camp for runners. There was no doubt in her mind, nor in anyone else's that she was going to compete and that she had a good chance of winning the medal for the United States. Now, everyone was very high on her being an Indian: it was so totally American. There was in everyone's minds, including her own, the legendary romance of the lone Indian, racing over hot desert sands, enduring, achieving.

But that summer, there had been another girl, one of the blond, pretty ones, who was very fast, too. She came from Texas, and she was everything that Maggie resented. The feeling was mutual. The princess from the South did not like to share her accolades with a "minority," as she phrased it.

The accident happened during the final trials, when the decision was to be made as to who would compete for the United States in the Olympics. Maggie was racing in the lane next to Ms. Scarlett—as even the others called her. They were rounding a bend when Scarlet, beside her, bolted up ahead, then suddenly seemed to falter, almost to fall, except that she didn't. Instead,

Maggie went plumeting to the ground, shattering her knee and making it impossible to compete in any track event ever again, so long as she may live. It was an accident, or so they said. Ms. Scarlet had lost her balance. Her right foot had turned out, tripping Maggie, who was zipping around at a clip at precisely the wrong moment.

Maggie had tried to tell them that there had been no accident. Her grandfather had come to speak up for her, his awkward speech patterns humorously endured by the officials; his nobility and dignity ridiculed in patronizing looks, because he did not have the facility of tongue and the false coverings of their fine clothes. No one heard them; no one seemed to want to listen, and in the end, whatever they said was discounted. In a way it made it even worse, speaking up against the injustice, for they were illuminated as the powerless entities that they had always been and always would be in the eyes of the rich white majority.

On that terrible day, Maggie's future had tumbled around her, shattering into pieces just as surely as her knee had crumbled into shards of white bone.

And that had marked the last of the highs for Maggie. Since then, she had kept a careful guard over her pleasure gauge. What went up, came down...way down. She hated down. So sticking to the middle, lukewarm and safe, cruising the valleys of life and avoiding the peaks, would do her well enough.

As for men—and love—both fell dangerously into the same territory. Whenever she found herself falling in love, the inner siren would blare; there was too much similarity in that thrill, in that floating high of love, to the excitement and exhilaration of her individual triumphs.

She showered and changed into her clothes. When she emerged from the bathroom, Chance was dressed and standing by the window, looking out. He turned his head to the side, but made no move to face her. It was clear by his expression that he had been visiting his own past.

Maggie's energy was somewhat restored, a portion, at least, of her guards posted again. She moved across the room with a purposeful stride that said "places to go, people to meet, no time to tarry over spilled milk."

"I can't pay you for the room now, but I'll have the cash soon. Maybe tomorrow, if that's okay," she said.

He turned to the window again. "Forget it."

She couldn't. "So, if you have an address—"

"Lady," he broke in quietly, "the only address I have is the front seat of my truck. Or wherever these two feet happen to be standing. Let it go. I certainly will."

There was a cold weariness to his speech. It took her off guard. She had planned on some sort of fight, needed the tension to feed her resolve to walk away from him without carrying any emotional debris. This made things harder. She grabbed up her bedroll and the bag with her belongings.

Opening the door, she stepped outside, then reconsidered and crossed back over the threshold. Chance had not moved from his place at the window. His face was immobile, a granite mask.

"So," Maggie said, "how long do you think you'll be here in Vegas?"

"Maybe a day. Just as short or as long a time that it takes me to handle my horse business."

She nodded. "Okay. Well, I'll have the money. Consider that a promise."

He turned finally, drenching her with an ironic blue gaze. "What's all this about? Some Indian code of honor?"

"No," Maggie replied coldly. "My own. Nobody owes me, and I don't owe anybody either."

"No kidding? How nice and neat. Nice and cold."

"That's the way things work in the world."

"Whose world? What world is that, baby?"

"Your world," she said.

"Oh," he said, nodding, "I get it. Lines left over from an old movie script. We're talking about the white man's world and the red man's world. That's what this is all about, huh? They aren't making movies like that anymore, baby. Out of style."

"Hypocrisy and prejudice are always in."

"Tell you something else that never goes out of style, baby. Being a human being is here to stay, too. And people love. An inalienable right. They have instincts for laughter. And sex. And they don't necessarily have to take something good that's working and turn it into a heap of garbage. You want to talk about hypocrisy? Fine. Let's call a spade a spade. You were the hottest, most goddamned passionate female I've ever been with. Fact, baby. Fact. And I've known my share of women, so figure I'm a pretty good judge in that department."

She started to leave, but he came like a streak across the room and grabbed her wrist, dragging her back in to face him.

"You've got fire. You've got so much fire in you, you're going to burn yourself out if you don't open a vent." Suddenly he became softer, his voice almost a whisper. "We had something good, Maggie Rand. We had something better than good. It was great."

"It was okay," she said, her eyes misted with feelings she would have rather denied. She looked down to where his hand still held her wrist, not tightly, but just so there was the contact of their flesh. It was hard for her not to cry. It would be so easy for her to believe him, so easy to give in to what she wanted, but was afraid of losing.

"I've gotta go," she said, not trusting herself to look up. There was an instant's hesitation, then Chance slipped his hand away.

Outside, she closed the door quietly, their future severed.

It was already after ten o'clock when Maggie stood by the bus bench reviewing her options. All she had left was a few dollars. That was no real problem; her fortunes had trickled to levels just as low more times than she could count in her life. Maybe true financial solvency would always be out of her range, but taking care of life's basic needs merely required a bit of mental organization to decide where to direct the physical effort.

It had been her intention to find a job and earn enough money to take her off to wherever she had decided upon. She had thought about going back to the reservation, just packing the "real world" in, but she doubted she would fit in there anymore, either. Civilization had tainted her just enough to make her an outcast. The idea of an office job made her blood run cold; she'd die inside concrete walls. Anyway, her main immediate concern was to even the financial slate with Chance Harris before he took off.

The quickest way she knew of making money fast was to waitress. Cocktail waitressing was the most lucrative in terms of tips, and she needed instant cash. It was a plan.

The bus pulled up to the curb. Maggie stepped in behind an elderly lame woman who struggled up the steps carrying a cane and a large fabric shopping bag. Maggie had only just formed a sympathetic picture of the woman going out to shop, hobbling through stores to purchase her meager supplies, when the bus driver called out with a laugh, "Hey there, Mamie! You gonna milk them one-arm bandits dry again today?"

"Bet your sweet buns I am." She slammed the token into the meter with the gusto of a shot-putter.

"What you made yesterday?"

"Made me enough t'take something better'n this old heap," she cracked back.

Some of the other people laughed and some looked disapprovingly at the woman as she plopped herself down in a middle seat. She did not live up to her image. People didn't like that. People wanted you to stay where they felt you belonged and do what they expected you to do; you were not, under any circumstances, to venture beyond their preordained limits for you. Maggie knew that only too well.

She found a seat toward the back where she didn't have to sit near anyone. Silently, she rode along, looking out the window as the bus braked and wheezed through the traffic. The night's wonderland of blinking, flashing marquees had turned into a faded parody of itself in daylight. Her mind traveled to the hours before, those passed in the arms of Chance Harris. More than anything else perhaps, she had been afraid of waking up in the morning to find the exquisite pleasures of the night without substance in the morning. Glowing, magical, seductive, the experience of passion always turned into a false front, every bit as shoddy and illusory as the Vegas street scene.

She examined each casino as they passed, trying to get a feel for where her best bet might be to find employment. Caesar's and the Hilton attracted, but the Azteca Palace Casino gave off the best vibrations. It was there she disembarked.

The woman in Personnel ran her eyes down the application form, then shifted her attention to Maggie. "A speckled history. Done lots of things." It was a statement, not a judgment.

"I've covered my share of territory," Maggie said simply and without her usual defensiveness. The woman opposite her was in appearance much like her attitude, crisp and unemotional. Maggie could relate to that.

"Would you mind standing up?" the interviewer said. "What we're after...there's a certain look..."

Maggie hesitated, the request striking her wrong. If it had come from a man she would have already been out the door.

"I know," the woman said with a slight smile. "Look, this is Vegas. You and I know there's more to us than long legs and a pretty face. But in this case they aren't looking for a scientist to fill the slot."

Maggie nodded; a bow to Reality. In this case it wasn't her mind that was going to put food in her stomach or pay back Chance Harris.

She stood where the woman could see her clearly and, wearing a twisted smile, did a mocking pivot to display the requisite physical attributes.

"That's it," the woman replied. "The right look. It's only minimum wage. The tips will more than pay the rent, though. Also there's the required uniform. That's minimum fabric." She gave Maggie an ironic smile, its crookedness breaking the perfect mask. Underneath, Maggie recognized the face of a fellow human being with her own scabs and scars.

"So. Who am I going to be? Bo-Peep or Daisy Mae?"

"A bird."

"Tweety-Bird, huh?"

"Well, let's just say the kind Audubon didn't paint. The species has high cheekbones, preferably dusky skin coloring, a great body with no natural padding some places and a good deal in others, legs that don't quit and a right hook that'll lay flat any nature lover who isn't content to just watch the wildlife."

Maggie received her copy of *Azteca Palace Casino Employee Manual*, along with a health-insurance form to complete at her leisure. She was to go straight to wardrobe and be fitted for her waitress costume so that alterations could be completed by the time she arrived for her shift.

It was noon when she left the Azteca amid a crowd of Japanese businessmen in dark suits with cameras slung around their necks. They moved down the steps in a quiet, organized way, following their female tour guide to the waiting bus in the circular drive below.

For a moment Maggie remained standing on the landing of the monstrously huge building made to resemble an Aztec temple. The neon sign in the front of the hotel was turned off, the announcement, "Digger Bellamy's Azteca Palace Casino Welcomes IBM" a muted version of its raucus midnight self. Maggie had gotten little enough sleep herself and would have welcomed the opportunity to curl up and "turn off" for the rest of the afternoon. But she couldn't. There were more pressing matters at hand, such as getting her hands on some immediate money. The job was, of course, necessary, under any conditions, exclusive of her determination to pay off Chance Harris and even the score between them. She was not going to let anyone think she had traded her body for a place to stay; especially not herself. The problem she now faced was no longer employment, but simply that she needed money now, not tomorrow, when Chance Harris was likely to have left Las Vegas.

The bag with her personal belongings weighed heavily on her right shoulder and, absently, she shifted it to the other side. A soft clink-chink of metal invaded her thoughts. Maggie looked down to where she had heard the sound. A glint of silver amid a softer bundle of fabric possessions caught her eye. The thought formed; then, horrified, Maggie dissolved the idea. But no sooner had she chastised herself than the plan returned, even more logical on its second pass across her mind. Her conscience waged a war against that part of her mind which was rational. *How could she do it? How could she even think of doing such a thing?* Because it was sensible, and short of selling her body on a street corner, it was about the only option open at the present time.

Grandfather would understand, she told herself.

But as she took the Azteca's wide marble steps down to the street level, Maggie felt that she was descending into a new, lower level of inner hell. Was it ever possible, once having visited the depths, to climb back out? Or did a part of you always remain there? Did you lose a piece of yourself in such compromises of the spirit? Could you ever truly be whole again once you bartered your ideals?

It wasn't hard to figure out where to go. Every downtown district had them. This city, Maggie knew even before the bus let her out, would have more than enough of its share. In a gambling town, more than one unlucky bettor found it necessary to separate himself from his watch or ring, guitar or radio, to keep the game of life going.

The streets in downtown Las Vegas were more narrow than the wide boulevards where the enormous resort casinos were located. Here the buildings were high and packed close together. Maggie walked along the busy sidewalk. The downtown area was where the people came to gamble seriously. It was not the same crowd who, in between sessions at the baccarat table, ate leisurely dinners in pricey restaurants where tables floated in lakes and harpists on golden gondolas sailed past.

The people passing Maggie as she made her way down the crowded noon-time sidewalks, had the hollow eyes of humans hypnotized by the ring of slot machines and the chant of the croupier's call. She could understand the allure. The energy in the air was palpable, manic in its intensity.

Maggie felt her insides constrict against the artificial world. Not that many years ago there had been open spaces with blue sky and the smell of sage where she now stood on the corner amid a cloud of diesel fuel waiting for the street light to change.

The place she selected was only one among scores to be found off the main track—hidden where their existence would not offend or detract from the spectacular illusion created for the public just blocks away.

The word on the sign above the shop was Pawn, displayed in black paint on a white background. Here there were no flashing lights. The message was take it or leave it, sell it or buy it; life advertised just the way it was. But even here off the main drag there was a billing: in small print—Bernie Fleishman, Proprietor.

Maggie pushed open the glass door and entered.

There were several customers being waited on by as many different employees, none of whom were currently free. She walked around the shop for a while, waiting for her turn. Beneath and behind glass counters and shelves were watches and binoculars and guitars and rings. There were televisions and radios and pots and tape recorders. A fur coat was hung behind a glass case. She saw eyeglasses and a pair of crutches. It would not have surprised her to see hands and heads checked in for cash on the line. The air smelled stale, the rancid odor of desperation and soiled dreams weighting each molecule she breathed.

A feeling of wrongness washed over her, and she turned suddenly, bolting for the door.

"Hey, honey! Help ya?"

A man stepped into her path. He did not have the kind of face she liked, not that it was important, but just his look warned her off.

"Buying or selling?" His eyes traveled over her body suggestively, making no pretense of what kinds of terms he might name to make a deal. "What can I do for you?"

"Absolutely nothing," Maggie said, wanting to put him down, but wanting more to escape the environment. She quickly stepped around him, and then, realizing that she was behaving like an overly emotional child, took in a deep breath and turned back to complete her mission.

The man was still staring at her: partial contempt, partial lust, Maggie gauged. It wasn't the first time, nor would it be the last that she was so evaluated. His thoughts were obvious. After all, in his business, he'd know a bit about people, all kinds of people. He would know instantly that she was either Mexican or Indian, not Italian or Greek, someone of Mediterranean heritage. He would see the sleeping roll on her back and take in the bag slung over her shoulder. She was a traveling woman, and he'd know it; a minority down on her luck, as most minorities always were at some time or other—if not all of the time. God, she despised those generalizations. God, she hated never, never being able to be only herself for what she was and who she was.

"I've got something I'd like to pawn," she said.

"Gimme a lookee," the man said.

Maggie followed him to the counter. She removed the necklace her grandfather had given her only a few days before and, with fingers that had suddenly gone numb, laid it on the glass for his scrutiny.

"Hey, honey," he said, "you gotta be joking."

Maggie looked up, not understanding.

"This stuff is junk on the market now. Better you should try to swap me a hoola-hoop."

"This is a very valuable—"

The man's personality turned. His weak gray eyes hardened into sharp little balls and he spoke in a rushed voice that told her in tone, if not in words, that she could clear out of the place because there wasn't going to be any deal made. "This Indian stuff saw it's heyday like eight years ago. It was big, big, big then. Now it's nothing. Market was glutted. Man who owns this place issued a total moratorium on Indian stuff. We don't want it, 'cause no one else wants it."

Maggie felt anger, panic, and humiliation arise all at once. She felt dizzy from all the emotion, and trying to stabilize herself before she went entirely crazy, she made the supreme effort to be calm in what she now said. As she spoke, she heard herself as if in delay.

"Okay, so the market's glutted, or whatever. I only want to pawn this necklace for one day. I want it back tomorrow. I'll have the money then so there's really no risk for you. This particular necklace," she said, casting her eyes down to the glass where it still lay, "is worth a great deal of money. There is nothing like it available today. It's been handed down from generation to generation of my family. The amount of work, the level of craftsmanship in this—" she swallowed down the emotion welling up "—this necklace is beyond compare. It's worth a small fortune. You have to know it."

The man was quiet for a moment. Maggie watched thoughts shift back and forth behind his eyes.

"Sorry, honey. Can't do. Got my orders."

Maggie returned a look that was every bit as telling as the one he had originally laid on her when she'd walked into the shop. Only the bottom line of her silent commentary read "worm." She'd like to stick that on a marquee.

She scooped up the necklace and dropped it into her bag. A moment later she was through the door and in the streets again. At the stop light she paused to get her bearings. There were other shops. But she felt sick, like she was selling her own child, her own adorable, beloved child, and that no one even wanted it. Double heartbreak.

The light changed and she had taken only one step when by her side she heard, "Hey, Indian necklace woman."

Maggie turned. The man from the pawn shop was a foot away.

"Gotta deal for you. Maybe," he said, and hitched his head back for her to follow him.

Reluctantly, Maggie retraced her footsteps to where he waited. He said nothing more, but led her around the corner and stopped beneath a tattered awning of a small coffee shop.

"Look," he said, "this's just between the two of us, right? I can't buy that necklace for the store. No way. But maybe if you and I can work a deal on our own... You pay me interest direct, see. I'll advance you the cash."

"How much?"

"I can go five hundred."

"Five hundred?" Maggie stared at him incredulously. "It's worth—"

"It ain't worth nothing 'less you got someone to buy it. Which you don't."

"There are other shops."

"They aren't gonna take it, either. Trust me. I know what I'm talking about. You think we're in business to give good stuff away to the competition?"

"And you're just being a nice guy, huh?"

"I've got me some extra money and I can make some interest on it. Why the hell not?" He waited for Maggie to consider.

"What else?" she said.

"What do you mean, else?"

Maggie just waited, staring him down.

"Okay," the man said. "Only other thing—I got no way of knowing for sure you're going to turn up with the money. I'm going out on a limb for you."

"Thanks, you're a prince. But don't worry. I'll be back. You can lay your life on that."

"Look, I retain the option of protecting my investment. Say, if anyone shows up between now and then who's got a serious yen for your jewelry...it's a sale."

"No," Maggie said. "No deal. I can't risk it."

The man shrugged. "Suit yourself, honey." He started to back away, one hand in his pocket. It didn't take X-ray vision to know the money she needed was in there, available. "If you change your mind..." He swiveled on one heel and faded into the flow of pedestrians.

Two hours later, she had visited every pawnbroker in the area, all with the same story the first man had given her. Discouraged, she wondered if perhaps she had been too suspicious of him. He *was* a worm, but maybe she let her personal dislike cloud her judgment as to his business acumen. What he'd said made perfect sense from a commercial standpoint. He had no way of knowing she wasn't just some desperate woman needing a stake to put her through another night at the gambling tables. He had a right to protect himself. So he had some extra cash; like he said, why not do a few deals on the side?

He saw her the moment she arrived. Their eyes brushed lightly and he made a motion for her to go outside. Moments later he joined her and they walked down the sidewalk until they were out of view of the shop.

"All right," Maggie said. "The necklace for five hundred. And I'll be back tomorrow. I swear I'll be back."

They completed the action in the street. There were no goodbyes. The man tipped his finger to his forehead and took off with a jaunty stride.

Maggie watched him for a second. A piece of herself was missing.

The heavy silver necklace weighted the pocket of his sports jacket, dragging the material down. He didn't care about his jacket now. Going straight to the telephone in the back of the shop, he dialed the private number he knew by heart.

She answered on the third ring. The day was turning out lucky all the way around.

"Hi. It's me. Got ya something real nice."

"What's that?"

"Real unique piece. Just like you always ask for. Indian. It's gotta go fast, though, so..."

"Don't try to squeeze me, you little termite—"

"Hey, no way. I'd never." It was in his best interests to overlook the insult. "Truth. The girl I got it from's coming back for it tomorrow."

"Oh, sure. Now you tell the future."

"No, really. This is for sure. I haven't been around in this business this long not to judge human nature."

"Okay, okay. Bring it by."

"See ya," he said, and was already counting his profit before the telephone hit the hook.

Chapter Four

Maggie had until late afternoon before she was to be trussed up in glitter and feathers to wait tables at the Azteca. With the money she had from the necklace, she rented a cheap hotel room, then she showered, changed into clean clothes and went in search of Chance Harris.

He was not at the motel.

Taking a taxi, she asked the driver to drop her at the horse farm she had visited with Chance the previous night. There she was told he was at Digger Bellamy's ranch, having taken the horse to the big sale.

Digger Bellamy was Las Vegas's premiere songster. Everyone knew about him. He was reputedly one of the richest entertainment figures of all time. A legend, he was treated as a monarch in the city. He owned part interest in several hotel casinos and was the principal owner of the Azteca, where she had hired on. Digger's wife, Pru—Prucilla, for long—a former chorine who had hit the proverbial jackpot by marrying Digger, was horse crazy.

The taxi stopped at the entrance of the Bellamy ranch. The driver waited while Maggie considered her options. There was a chain link fence and a gate with two armed guards checking printed invitations. Better she should try to rush Fort Knox.

In the distance, she saw the flags of what was a full circus tent erected on the grounds. Closer in was the Bellamy estate, an immense modern structure fashioned of glass and wood and concrete.

Maggie watched as trucks with horse vans and trailers took a separate entrance to the ranch. She told the driver to let her off a bit farther down the road.

Making herself inconspicuous by a lone, scraggly tree, she let four vehicles pass by until the right one appeared. A decrepit pickup, driven by a trio of Hispanics in the front cab, crept by, the men talking and laughing among themselves. She took off behind them, swallowing dust as she gained on them, then threw her things into the truck bed. A second later she scrambled up the back end to take her place among sacks of feed.

The guards at the work gate thought nothing of her presence. They waved the truck through, barely giving her a second glance after checking the invoices the driver presented to prove they had a legitimate order from the Bellamy estate. To anyone who bothered looking, she would appear as part of the crew, a darkish woman in jeans and T-shirt and boots, bored and crouching amid a tumble of feed sacks.

No one saw her leave the truck and, once in, she was free to roam as she pleased. She deposited her things in an open tack room by the stable area and took off on her search for Chance.

She had to admit, in all her travels she had never experienced anything like the scene around her. The stable area was as vast and modern as the main house appeared from the road. But for some of the minor work hands, the back was all but deserted. The action was now centered in the main tent.

A groom walked by and Maggie stopped him.

"Hey, friend," she said, "what's all that?" She cast her eyes toward the tent.

He answered in English heavily accented with Spanish. "Big sale. Best horses in the whole world. Richest men in whole world."

"No kidding?" Maggie commented, this time using her Spanish, which was fairly fluent. "Tell me more."

In his own tongue, the groom was a fluent gossip, happy to share his opinion along with the facts. What she learned was that the action centered in the main tent where one of the richest, by-invitation-only sales in the history of horse racing was underway.

"If you want to see, just go up, stay near one of the tent flaps. You can see it all from there."

Maggie thanked him and they parted.

Just as she had been advised, she found a place to watch near an entrance, where horses were being led out. For all anyone might guess she might have been a hot walker or one of the stable hands, not chosen to wear a special uniform for the grand occasion, but ordered to remain in the background.

The interior of the tent had been furnished with plush theater seats on graduated stands. There was an elaborate bar with a running fountain of champagne, and an enormously long buffet table piled high with gastronomic delicacies ranging from crab legs to prime rib, to the more exotic fare of steak tartare and sushi.

But the feast was secondary. Everyone's attention was focused on the center arena, where horses with numbered white cards affixed to their flanks were being slowly led before a rapt audience. Maggie was not impressed by wealth; but even she had to acknowledge the display of finery spread before her. There was no one there not dressed impeccably, men and women, alike. The women seemed to be of one cut in their hats and gloves and tailored suits; cold-eyed, they seemed to appraise one another in the same manner they judged the horses—gauging bloodlines and speculating on what financial benefits might be derived from direct association. The men were more animated, but appeared wary, watching each other less and the horses more.

Maggie picked up a discarded program from the floor. It was white leatherette, a handsome piece of work, professionally bound and printed with the sale's schedule and rules, along with information on the horses being offered. Running her eyes down the columns, she at last found the name of Chance Harris as presenter of a long list of entrants. However, there was a sticker, added after the initial printing, with information eliminating all his entries, but for one horse: a one-year-old filly named Darkstar.

Maggie scanned the perimeter of the tent, searching for Chance. When she didn't find him, she left the spectacle to search for him one more time in the stable area.

She found him a moment later by an open horse stall.

He was leaning with his back against the white frame wall. For a moment, she hardly recognized him. Like the others, he had dressed to kill. His suit was black and appeared expensive. He wore a dark tie with a subtle background print of gray and red in the silk material. His shirt was a dazzling bright white, probably new, purchased for the occasion at hand.

No matter what else she felt about him, Maggie had to admit, he was a handsome man. One knee was bent, the sole of his shoe flat against the wood siding. In his hand he held a bottle of beer. A black horse leaned through the upper opening of the stable, nudging his shoulder.

He appeared not to notice his surroundings, not the horse, nor Maggie, who waited before him with the money she owed, outstretched in her hand.

His eyes focused slowly, and she read surprise in his eyes as he acknowledged her presence.

She was going to say something short and smart, punch the money down into his palm and take off, business concluded, relationship terminated. That had been her intention. She would have carried it out to the letter, except that she was not in the company of the man she had left earlier.

A terrible change had altered him since that morning when she had walked out of the motel. And now, well, it didn't seem like she would be giving her speech to the same man. The phrase she had been prepared to deliver died in her mind as her thoughts were taken over by a sense of shock. The usual flip irony had deserted his face, which was now marked by a drawn fatigue that looked to be beyond mere physical exhaustion.

He made no move to take the money from her, and she let her hand drop, forgetting her own problems for a time—even abandoning her pride and ever-fertile anger—to wonder about his situation.

"What do you want?" he said, barely moving his lips. His eyes were steady as he asked the question.

"I—I came to give you back the money." Her fingers were curled around the cash, but suddenly the gesture of repaying him for his kindness to her the previous night seemed the shallow, superficial and selfish gesture that it was.

"I told you, forget it," he said, this time with a coldness she had not thought him capable of.

But she realized the coldness was not actually directed at her; it was more universal. That she could understand, that kind of disaffection for the world in general. She let her hand drop, closing her fingers over the money.

She might not have even been there. The suspended foot lowered to the ground and he turned and started off, tossing the empty beer bottle into a trash barrel.

Maggie watched him go, then went along, remaining a few paces behind.

"Look," she said, "you want to talk about any of this?"

"No." He kept on.

Maggie stopped. Why she didn't just beat it out of there she didn't know. It was just too confusing to come up with any motives for what she was about to do.

"Listen," she called. "Hey you, hard case! I want to talk about it, even if you don't."

This time, he did turn. His eyes, in the past so filled with good-natured amusement, were now flat and unemotional. "Get off my case, woman."

"Uh-uh." When in front of him, she said, "Look, I've known some troubles in my time, too."

"So what?" he said. His eyes were ice crystals stabbing into her.

God, she realized, *she had done that to him, hadn't she?* She had looked at *him* that same way. Well, it was coming back to her in spades now. Begging him, she was damn near begging him to talk to her about his troubles, and the weird thing of it was, she didn't care about her pride. She just felt this incredible sense of...of what? Identification, maybe.

"Maybe there's something I could say, or do. Maybe just to listen might help?"

"Help?" he said, as if she had uttered a new word. Memories moved through his eyes like distant clouds. "There's no help short of a miracle—like turning back the clock—that can do anything for me now."

"It's about the sale today?" she prompted.

He gave her a sharp glance. "Yeah, it's about the sale today. And it's about maybe a whole wasted lifetime, too, if you really want to get down to it."

"I do," she said. "I do want to get down to it."

Chance looked off in the direction of a uniformed groom who was leading a magnificent chestnut Thoroughbred gelding back to its stable quarters.

"Lord," Chance muttered, shaking his head. "I must have been crazy. I must have been quite a sight out there today with my little black pony. Well, at least I provided the entertainment. They had a tent, why not a clown, too? Appropriate. Yup, I must have been out of my mind to think that anyone was going to buy my hamburger meat when steak was being served."

"The hamburger being Darkstar," Maggie said. He gave her a surprised look, to which she responded, "I saw one of the programs."

"Enterprising little wench, aren't you?" Chance commented. There was a glimmer of his old self in the tone of voice.

Maggie took heart. But prematurely, for he started off again, leaving her without a word or so much as a backward glance. She, like the rest of his life, was apparently finished business as far as he was concerned.

"I'm more stubborn than enterprising," she said, and came up beside him. "So," she went on, as if the conversation had never been interrupted, "Darkstar did not get bought."

"She didn't even get a bid out there. She was the original invisible horse."

"How come?"

"Why?" He was walking more slowly. "For a damn good reason. She doesn't have the bloodlines. She's a good little girl, though. But she doesn't have the five-star rating you need in this kind of league."

"Since you know that why did you put yourself through the disappointment?"

"Add humiliation," he said, and this time laughed, some of his humor remaining intact. "Originally when I registered, I had a full house of top-sired horses. She was coming along just to even out the numbers, so to speak. Ten's always been lucky for me. Horse fanatics are superstitious—I'm no different, I guess, though I wouldn't admit it to anyone who wasn't a crazy Indian."

Maggie surprised herself and laughed. Ordinarily she would have been offended. The time didn't seem right to be offended. She felt lighter in his company; maybe it was because with him there was no sham, no pretense at good manners or social charity. It felt good to let down her fences.

"Horses were being sold out there today for eight million bucks. I didn't even have an offer of eight hundred for Darkstar." He paused, then quietly, with affection, said, "She's a hell of a little lady, but it's who your daddy and mommy are who count in these parts."

Maggie didn't say anything, but the uncustomary lightness in her vanished. A pool of resentments, stagnating over her entire life had been stirred by his last words.

"I'm going to talk to a guy I know," Chance said, both hands in the pockets of his slacks. "So, I'll see you around someday, okay? If I see a thumb out on the road, and the woman belonging to it's got a mean look about the eyes, I'll know it's you."

"You going to stop?"

"Hell, no!"

He turned and they both laughed. Then the smiles faded, and there was a kind of sadness emanating from them both.

"You touched me, lady," Chance said. "I won't forget you." He reached out and ran his finger lightly along the side of her face, then beneath her chin.

On impulse she wanted to grab that hand, wanted to hold it in hers. But she didn't; instead, she merely stood there, and in the next second he was going from her. That feeling arose again, the one she'd had when she was standing at the side of the road in the desert and saw his truck fading into the horizon. It was the sense of losing something: a chance, an opportunity, maybe a part of herself. It was a desperate kind of feeling which made no sense at all, and overwhelmed, she yelled, "Chance!"

He looked over his shoulder.

"Is she fast, your horse? Darkstar?"

"She's fast," he said, his expression wondering at the question.

"Fast, like how fast?"

"Like what do you want? Times?"

"Like the wind, is she fast?" Maggie asked, speaking quickly, the words coming in a rush.

"You could put it that way. Kind of poetic, but yeah, I'd say she's fast like the wind."

"Then why not race her?" Maggie said.

She felt crazy, she felt as if she didn't know whose case she was pleading, her own or a horse that nobody wanted. But the words were coming out on their own, from a place that had been closed up for a long, long time.

Chance hadn't moved since she had called his name and while they spoke she'd come slowly up to him, aware that it wasn't what he wanted.

"Look," she said, "if Darkstar's that fast, if she's got that kind of potential, then why sell her? Why not give her a chance to do what she can do best?"

For an instant she thought a spark had ignited behind the tired eyes watching her with something akin to an ancient sage's forebearance. But when he spoke, she knew it had only been her imagination.

"Well, it's like this. The heart's just not in it anymore. Sometimes you try for something, see, and when you lose it...well, you lose pure and simple. But sometimes it doesn't work quite like that. You lose more than you ever thought you'd gain. I guess in this case I lost something more fundamental, something I didn't exactly know I had. But it's gone now. I doubt I can get it back."

"The taste for living," Maggie mumbled.

"Yeah, something like that," Chance said. He gave her a long look. "And judging by your general demeanor, I'd say you tried for something once or twice and it didn't come out too great, either."

Maggie didn't acknowledge the insight; he was carving too close to the bone.

"What'd you try for Maggie Rand? What'd you lose that made you turn so damn sour on life?"

"Nothing," she said, and out of long habit when people came too close to her, whether to her insides or the outside, she backed away. "Nothing much."

Chance nodded. His look penetrated her exterior, and he seemed to read that she had shut him out, and in turn, she read in his face that he didn't much care anymore.

"I'm going to take Darkstar back to the farm over here in Vegas. See if I can unload her on someone less snooty than these folks, someone who just wants an easy trot now and then and not much else from life." He looked Maggie's way with a sad, crooked half smile.

The defeat in his eyes cut into her, shredding the solid wall of her emotions. She liked him better the other way, sassy and cool. That guy she could deal with; this one was hard to hate.

"Yeah, better not to want too much. Hurts less that way when you don't get it. Huh, Maggie Rand? Take care, baby..."

There was no going after him this time. She'd used up her chances and blown each one. It was her speciality, blowing things.

Her eyes stung as she started off in the opposite direction, not knowing exactly where she was going, but having to move. Dimly, she was aware of the sounds of animals and people moving about her. Dimly, she was aware of the world.

The way out took her back near the stall where Darkstar was stabled. She didn't have to make the extra turn, but found herself doing it.

The filly was waiting, alone and quiet, when Maggie came up to the gate. Darkstar stuck her head out and tossed her mane, a polite nod of recognition.

"Hello, girl," Maggie said. She put her hand out flat against the horse's mouth and Darkstar raised her lips to nibble at the natural salt flavor of her hand. "Too bad," Maggie said to the horse, who looked at her with intelligent brown eyes. "Too bad you didn't have the chance to run. Maybe you would have shown them all a thing or two. In spite of what side of the tracks you were born on," Maggie ended quietly. "Hell," she said, and turned away from the pain. Just like she always had, just because pain seemed always to be there.

Chapter Five

It wasn't the first time Maggie had worked as a cock-tail waitress, but this was the first time she had worked in an atmosphere of such opulence and in a costume of such extravagance.

The cocktail lounge itself was raised several feet up from the main casino floor, so that it was both a part of and separate from the gambling activity. The interior of the casino was plush and subdued, with stylized inti-mations of the Aztec theme subtly worked into the de-cor. No one could give points off for garishness here.

The carpeting was a thick pile, done in a clean, geo-metric pattern, which incorporated tones of wine, blue, and an off-shade crimson. Surprisingly, the diverse combination of colors worked together in perfect har-mony. All the hardware fixtures, from railing to lights, were of gleaming polished brass and no price had been spared on the crystal chandeliers over every gaming ta-

ble and also placed as luxurious accents at strategic lo-
cations throughout the building.

Considered one of the class casinos, on a par with the
MGM Grand, the Hilton, or Caesar's Palace, the Azteca attracted the same up-scale clientele. Although the
ubiquitous polyester and Hawaiian shirt contingent
could be found dotting the surroundings, here they were
not the predominant sartorial force. From the corner of
her eye, while ferrying trays of drinks to her own customers in the Azteca Lounge, Maggie was treated to a
continuous parade of gowns and gems, even some furs,
although it was still early in the season. Men wore
everything from formal black and white attire to leather
pants and velvet jackets.

It was a packed house at the Azteca. The atmosphere held a celebratory mood. Digger Bellamy was
mainlining in the Azteca Celebrity Room and his appearance on stage had brought in droves of admiring
fans. Only Sinatra or Wayne Newton attracted the
magnitude of response Digger's show brought forth
from the public. Accordingly, there was barely room on
the casino floor for people to move, and in the lounge
every table and bar stool was occupied.

That was more than okay with Maggie. At a little past
one a.m., she had already taken in close to two hundred
dollars in tips and her shift wasn't going to be over for
another hour. She had discovered a scientific law, ap-
plicable, perhaps, only in Las Vegas: that as the hours
progress, the tips increase, liquor and the surealistic atmosphere of unlimited wealth taking a subliminal toll
on the judgment of usually conservative Kansas cattle
barons and Japanese industrialists.

She was feeling good, actually; something she hadn't
felt in a long while. Although she balanced a tray

heavily laden with drinks over her head, and even
though she had already been standing for six hours, her
spirit was buoyant with emotional relief. It was while in
this elevated mood, with the comforting knowledge that
she had at least short-term financial solvency to which
she might look forward, that she saw him.

Chance Harris had found a place at a small round
table in a section not part of her station, near the railing overlooking the casino. The room was densely populated; he didn't see her. In fact, he seemed oblivious to
everything. His attention was fully on the drink he was
nursing. Just by the tilt of his head and the position of
his shoulders, Maggie could tell the drink wasn't the
first he had put away that night.

She mentally shrugged off his presence and, with
what she chose to see as being symbolically significant,
unloaded her drink tray, as well. Outstretched hands
flashing with diamonds curled forward to accept the
glasses she delivered. The table she waited on contained a thirsty and rowdy group of pudgy, flushed-
faced men and heavily made up women, two of whom
had dye jobs of harshest black, and one who sported a
pinkish, cotton candy mane reaching to below her
shoulders. But they were also a generous table, and
Maggie, already forming another truism from her current night's experiences, was coming to believe there
might be a direct correlation between bad taste and big
tips.

There was something else she could not ignore as long
as she was being so insightful: a moment ago such a
haul would have filled her with a mild sense of satisfaction. Only now the material substance of money seemed
oddly lacking its previous power to delight and soothe.
What now overwhelmed her was an intense spiraling

rush of heat, a primal, Pavlovian response to anticipated pleasures, which wound through her as she stole another surreptitious glance Chance's way. This initial reaction brought forth a secondary one of acute embarrassment. That she should be so physically susceptible to base animal instinct!

Whatever her reaction, internal or external, it went undetected by Chance, who was partially veiled by the constant state of animation around him. Bodies sat and rose and squirmed and twisted and jostled through a sea of other human forms equally dedicated to the goal of perpetuating the interlude of euphoria manufactured by the casino.

Maggie added to all the movement, making her way to a table of patrons who signaled for another round of drinks. Amid all the frantic goings on, only Chance remained immobile, the fingers of both hands webbed around the glass, as if it were a possession he dared not lose. He made for a lone solitary image. Regardless of the churning, milling flow of humanity all about him, he seemed isolated. He might have been sitting on a desert butte with only the wind's howl for company.

The pull she felt from him was compelling, magnetic in its power, and she had to will her eyes away. She was, however, less successful in shepherding the direction of her thoughts to safe terrain. Confusing images overlapped one after the other in her mind. Pictures of Chance nude sprang forth as brief flashes, perhaps remembered, maybe only imagined, composites of reality and emotion: Chance lying on the bed, a man in natural relationship to his body and feelings, a man who had shared himself in all his male, human wholeness—with her. A man whom she had rejected because . . .

Because . . .

Maggie forced herself to go on with the train of self analysis, dared herself to face what she previously could not: that she was not his equal, not in honesty, nor in actual courage. That is why she had run away from him, and why she would continue to run away from everyone and everything. She did not feel equal. She lived in constant fear of her deficiencies being discovered. Once, had she been able to actually make that long run, if she had been able to surpass everyone else on that track, perhaps then she might have lived in peace. But that moment of glory had eluded her. And now she was here, serving watered-down drinks to strangers in a palace of floating dreams.

A man grabbed her rump as she passed by. Maggie whirled on him, more surprised than angry. She saw his face as a blur of drunken, leering features. She thought she should do something, but merely stood there with the empty tray.

"Hey, honey," he said, the words bubbling out from lips thickened by too much liquor, "how much?"

"You already paid your tab, mister," Maggie said, now aware of other eyes on her. She felt naked in her abbreviated costume of burnt orange and hot pink sequins, with the black tail-feathers positioned to call attention to the curve of her buttocks. Tiny goose bumps had risen to the generous swell of bosom appearing over the push-up bra, which was part of the seductive outfit. She was feeling cheapened and used, one more spectacle provided by the management for the entertainment of people who would not see her as a human being, but only as an ambulatory sexual joke. That morning, when she had been so desperate, the trade of self-respect for cash had seemed more realistic than inequitable. Now she did not know.

"I mean, how much for later?" the man warbled wetly. His two male friends waited for the outcome, their eyes soft, slushed with liquor.

"Mister, there isn't any later," Maggie said sharply. "Not for you or anyone else," she added loud enough for those around them to hear.

The man's blubbery lips curled upward into a mean snarl. "Slut," he said. "All you broads are sluts. Showin' everything you got." His eyes cruised the length of her body hungrily and with contempt. "You tellin' me you aren't selling? How much?" he said loudly. "How much's it gonna take for a little bit of fun?" He made a grab for his wallet and slapped a hundred-dollar bill on the table, then another one and one more. "Name your price!" he yelled.

Maggie saw it all in slow motion. She saw her hand reach down for the table, heard the man's shocked intake of breath as her fingers skirted the bills but moved on to clasp a cold glass, its outside sweating with moisture. In one motion, she brought the glass up, saluted him with a mock toast, and soundlessly, effectively dashed ice cubes and gin and tonic into the man's dazed face.

There was a sort of universal gasp of excitement from the spectators. The man rose, fury creasing his face, and Maggie would have been decked by his drawn fist except that the head waitress appeared with a big security guard at that moment.

"No problem, okay?" Maggie's would-be assailant assured the guard. Grumbling, his vengeance spoiled, he slumped into his seat and immediately commenced into a rambling monologue of male bravado downgrading women "like that."

Just as quickly, the senior waitress in charge spirited Maggie away.

"Forget it," she said to Maggie. "That sort of action comes with the territory. Only management doesn't dig scenes where there's the hint of anything unseemly going on. Bad gossip makes for bad business in their books, seeing as how the Gaming Commission has a real thing against vice." She gestured to the far side of the lounge. "Take that section for now. And see if you can keep it friendly. Son of a bitch," she ended, with a glare in the direction of the three drunken men wobbling down the steps, off to find more fun.

Maggie nodded and set off with her tray to where a man was signaling for service. The table was one over from where Chance sat.

As she took the order from the couple, she heard the light, mocking sound of two hands clapping. Sighing, she looked to Chance. He wore his familiar crooked grin.

"Nice going," he said. "Guy's lucky he didn't get the rabbit-skinning utensil right between his eyes."

"I would have aimed for some other part of his anatomy," Maggie said as she passed by. "A place more geographically appropriate."

Chance reached for her wrist and pulled her up beside his table. Maggie sighed again. Standing in a hipshot pose with the tray balanced against it, she said, "I've had my fill of grabby drunks for one night, you know?"

"You think I'm drunk?" he asked, the blue eyes wide.

"I know you're drunk. Now let me go. I've got a job to do and I like eating occasionally so I don't want to lose it."

"Okay, okay, freedom's yours. I'll take a beer."

Maggie nodded and walked off. His eyes were on her tail feathers as surely as if they were hands running over her body. Spinning around suddenly, she confirmed her suspicion and, half in jest and just as much in earnest, delivered a quick, meaningful, universally rude hand gesture that only seemed to delight him more.

A moment later she delivered his beer.

"I think I love you," he said. "In spite of your mean nature."

"You've had too much to drink."

"Come home with me," Chance said. "I'll show you if I had too much to drink or not."

"Thanks, but I'll take your word for it. That's three bucks."

"And I'll take another. Really," he said, smiling.

"Oh, give me a break, man." she gave him a long-suffering look, and set off to service her other customers.

She hated it when he said things like that. Of course she knew when he said, "I love you," he didn't actually mean it. Well, of course not. For one thing, he simply just *didn't*. And besides that, if he *did*, it was not the time or place for a man to make such declarations. The thing that bothered her the most was that it bothered her when he said it. It made something in her heart—that wondrously impenetrable citadel—twinge with terror... and longing—if she were, for once, to be absolutely honest with herself.

An hour later Maggie made yet another pass by Chance's table. There were already six unfinished beers there. The circle of bottles was taking on the look of a mystical arrangement.

"It seems I'm running out of money," he said, when he paid for his seventh bottle.

"Good. I'm running out of energy." Her feet were aching from the high heels that were a part of her costume. "Not to mention patience."

"Your head thing looks good," Chance said. "Makes you look like an Indian." It was an orange sequined cap with a thick band of black feathers that had been liberally doused with gold glitter.

"I'm a bird," she said tartly.

"You don't like being an Indian, do you?"

"I am what I am."

"That's an answer?"

"All right, would you like it?" she asked. "Would you like to be someone who never fits in anywhere?"

"I'd make a place for myself, then."

"There aren't any places for us. Unless we want to be herded like cattle into portions of land where whites get to drive through in campers with their kids to see if we've gone extinct yet."

Someone was calling to her at another table. "See you around." And that was when she saw her, saw *it*.

Maggie froze. Her entire being turned cold and quiet, and the rest of the world was no longer in existence. Her total awareness was trained upon the couple that had stopped near the brass railing.

"No..." Maggie murmured. "No, no, no..."

Chance turned his head to where she was looking. "Well, well..."

Expressions of recognition also appeared on the faces of casino patrons as the man and woman passed through the room. The couple's attention was on what Maggie knew to be one of the white leatherette programs offered at that day's sale. Two burly security guards trailed the famous pair.

The man coming toward them was Digger Bellamy; everyone knew his face. But it was the woman who held Maggie's attention. The female at Digger's side was Pru Bellamy, his wife. Yes, it was the notorious Pru, whose picture was often featured in magazines devoted to celebrity gossip. She was tall and blond, with intense blue eyes and a body that made even the amply endowed appear boyish by comparison.

Digger and Pru had reached the railing. Seeing Chance, they stopped.

"Hey fella, bad luck today," Digger said to Chance.

"Yeah, the breaks," Chance replied.

"Sorry to hear about the horses," Digger Bellamy added. "You'll be back up again," the singer said, with his noted infectious laugh added at the end.

"They can't, though."

Digger's smile faded somewhat, as if Chance had affronted him by realism.

"Well, win some, lose some. That's what they say."

"They lost big."

Maggie had been holding still, faint with despair during the interchange between the men. She had forgotten everything but what she was looking at—the thing Pru Bellamy was wearing. She had even forgotten that she was holding a tray filled with empty glasses. As she pointed to Pru, there was a downward slide of filled ashtrays and glasses. Tray, drinks, bottles, everything ended with a splintering, clinking crash at Maggie's feet.

The space around them became suddenly quiet as the eyes of others were drawn into the drama. In the background, the steady clink-slap-purr of one-eyed bandits taking in coins continued, along with the bells of pay-offs from lucky slot winners.

Maggie's feet were sopping from the spilled beverages; what there was of her costume showed dark stains. None of that even registered, though, as she said, still pointing to Pru Bellamy, "That's my necklace!"

Chance and Digger and Pru all turned their eyes to Maggie, no one saying a thing.

"That's my necklace you have on," Maggie repeated.

The scene turned ugly then.

"You just shut your mouth," Pru said, her words slamming against Maggie like hard flat stones. "This is my necklace and I've got the sales slip to prove it." She looked around with a haughty sense of triumph, as if she expected applause.

"It isn't yours," Maggie replied coldly. "It could never be yours. That necklace is generations old. It's been in my family for the many lifetimes of many noble men and women. It can't belong to anyone without the heart to wear it. That has to be earned, not bought. You can't own some things, no matter how much money you have. I want my necklace back."

Pru Bellamy had listened raptly to what sounded, even to Maggie once she was done, like a ridiculously maudlin speech, the sentiments true, but still... In a casino with the voices of croupiers calling the plays over green felt, the higher principles of life somehow suffered instant devaluation.

"That's wonderful!" Pru said excitedly. "Well, did you hear that? Isn't that just fabulously wonderful?" she gushed to Digger, who seemed not to follow what was happening between his wife and Maggie. His eyes kept straying, as if he thought that by moving his vi-

sion elsewhere, he might similarly transport himself
from the vicinity. "I just love all that old Indian stuff.
It's so real. Hardly anything is real these days, darling."

"Look, all I want is to have my necklace back. I'm
not trying to prove anything. I don't care about making any points or making this some kind of a contest
between us. You're rich, you're powerful, you've got
the world by a string, okay? And all I've got is that
necklace."

"Wrong," Pru said. "I've got the necklace."

"Okay, okay. It's in your possession." That sounded
less permanent, somehow more temporary and hopeful to Maggie than to have said, "It's yours now."
Maggie dug feverishly into the change pouch attached
to her costume and took out her wallet with the money
from the pawnbroker, along with all the tips she had
received so far that night.

She glanced up briefly and saw that Pru Bellamy's
eyes had narrowed and she was doing a rapid, instinc-
tive figuring of how much money Maggie was pulling
out.

Maggie held the handful of bills out to Pru. She knew
she looked desperate and foolish, a pathetic case all the
way around.

Pru refused the money, stepping back haughtily as if
to avoid the touch of a leper.

"Look," Maggie said, trying to be reasonable,
"there's over seven hundred dollars in my hand. The
guy at the pawnshop only gave me five hundred. So
you're making a profit."

"Profit?" Pru responded with affront. "I happen to
love this. It's a genuine heirloom. Just like you said it

was. And as *I* said," Pru concluded sagely, "there's hardly anything genuine left in this world."

"It belonged to my grandfather. My grandfather. Look, please, *please* ..." Tears were burning Maggie's eyes. she was actually pleading, she was crying in public, something she had never done before in her life. "Please," she said, fighting hard to maintain her dignity, "the necklace is the only thing I've got left of my family."

For the first time, Pru seemed to weaken. She exchanged a glance with Digger, who, by his expression, seemed to be feeling some compassion toward Maggie.

"Why not sell it back to her?" Digger suggested. "Ask twice what you paid," he added in a way that Maggie sensed was deliberate pandering to the blonde's innate greed as a psychological ploy that could work to Maggie's favor.

Only it backfired. Pru took the suggestion in the worst way, as if she were being sided against for the benefit of a younger and very pretty woman.

"The hell with you," she said to Digger. "And you, too, honey," she added, sending Maggie a hard look. "Tell you what, why don't you just hit it out of here? Another thing, feathers should be worn on your head, not your ass, or didn't you go to the bang-bang movies when you were a kid?"

Pru changed her voice, lapsing into a theatrical narrative flow. "Injuns come galloping over the ridge, faces smeared with gook, wearing bird feathers up here on their noggins. Good guys down below in the valley, just sitting there on their white horses, patiently waiting to pick them off. Bang-bang. You're dead." Pru cocked a diamond-studded finger at Maggie and laughed. "You're dead," she repeated, not laughing anymore. She departed with a swish of her long beaded gown.

Maggie wished she were dead. For once in her life, even anger didn't come to her rescue. She was defeated, through and through.

Next to her, she was aware that Chance Harris was rising out of his chair, moving a bit unsteadily. He teetered forward a bit and grabbed the edge of the table to gain his balance. Instead, he knocked two half-empty beer bottles to the floor. Everything was happening around Maggie in a fog. She felt strangely disassociated from the disaster, as if she, perhaps, *had* died and was watching the events from another dimension.

"Hey, you snake-tongued poor excuse for a human being," Chance called out to the backs of Digger and Pru Bellamy. "You've no damn right to talk to her or anyone else like that," he went on. "She's a lady— doesn't matter where she wears her feathers. And a friend of mine. She's making an honest living in that costume. No way did she deserve that crack."

Pru's beautiful face changed into a different mask, ugly and pinched, as if she had suddenly aged a hard thirty years. With her eyes trained on Maggie, she said, "You're fired, doll." Turning her attention back to Chance, she said, "So how'd you like that crack?"

She remained where she was, stock-still, her husband beside her. His color had blanched, yet his expression remained like stone. When no one said anything, Pru nudged Digger and said, "Tell her. Go on. You tell her you own this place, and if I say go..."

There was a moment's indecision, then Digger said, "Sorry," to Maggie, just that, and with his arm guiding his blond wife, started away again.

Maggie's eyes had collected an ocean of unspilled tears, but behind the watershed was a pool of hatred. It was nourishing, that rage; its sizzling jolt was what she needed to keep herself going until she could get out of the sequined monstrosity she was wearing.

Everyone's eyes were on her, including Chance's.

She glared back at him.

Chance ran a hand through his hair and sighed. "Hell. Should have worn my white hat. Might have made all the difference."

"You should have kept your mouth shut!"

"That, too," Chance agreed, looking after the retreating forms of the Bellamys. The couple had stopped again to speak with another man. "Maybe I should have. But maybe not, baby. Or maybe there's some things that are just meant to happen, no matter shoulds, no matter shouldn'ts. They're just meant to happen." He grabbed for one of the full beers on the table and took a lusty swig, wiped his mouth with the back of his arm and hiked up his pants before making a dramatic, but uncertain voyage across the lounge to the steps leading into the gambling area.

Maggie's impulse was to grab him back, to sit on him if need be, and shriek her guts out at him to stop ruining her life and his along with it. But it was already too late. The human missile was on his way across the casino, and a moment later, as she, along with everyone else, watched from the railing, Chance made contact with his targets.

With a controlled sweeping motion, he turned Digger Bellamy around by the shoulder and said, "This ought to be real easy. You're not a man, you're a mouse, Bellamy." He clipped Digger on the jaw.

Digger staggered and came back with an ill-timed swing of his own. Chance was dancing around with boyish glee, ready to get into it with the other man.

But Digger was not enjoying things as much. He stiffened and gave a shout. The two security guards who had been hovering nearby, but who were obviously instructed not to intervene in Bellamy's private affairs unless summoned to do so, now stepped in to earn their paychecks.

They were big men, nimble and well-trained at their work. In a lightning movement, Chance found his arms locked behind him. His knees buckled forward as he took the brunt of a kick.

The guards held him that way, waiting for orders from Bellamy, who stood in dignified control, looking slightly down at Chance, not with anger or triumph so much as with regret, maybe even a bit of embarrassment.

"Now I know what it means to be a sore loser," Chance said.

"You'll survive."

"Yeah," Chance said. "I always do." His eyes flicked over to Maggie, whose knuckles, gripping the brass railing circling the lounge, were as white as her face had become. "Question is, will she?"

"She didn't have to bring that necklace to the pawnshop. No one forced her," Pru Bellamy said, sidling up to Digger.

"Shut up, Pru. Keep out of this now," Digger said.

Surprisingly, Pru did not argue. Instead, she seemed content to use her time to dissect Chance with her radiant blue eyes, all the more bright from the recent excitement.

"Now, I want to know something," Digger said, speaking evenly to Chance. "If you're free to walk out on your own steam, are you going to do it nice and easy and polite, or are you going to cause another ruckus?"

Chance thought about it for a moment. He looked at Digger, then at Pru, who was boring holes into him with her eyes, and said, "Well, now…" then Chance looked over to Maggie. There was nothing warm in the glance she returned. Hostility rose off her body like a mist. "Now that's what I like in a woman," Chance said, cocking his head to point out Maggie. "Sweet, docile, accommodating. Makes a man just go out of his head, you know. Can't hardly do enough to even up all that female givingness. But then, I know *you* know what I mean, Digger." Chance smiled widely at Pru.

The corners of Digger Bellamy's mouth twitched, but he was smart enough to keep silent on the matter.

"So. What's it going to be? You sobered up enough to walk out of here like a civilized human being?"

Chance nodded. "I'm sober. Nothing to sober up a man more than a blow to his ego, Digger. Not a thing to match it on this earth."

Digger nodded and the two security guards released their grip on Chance.

Chance shook the blood back into his arms, rubbing them intermittently to regain the circulation. "That's better," he said, and smiled. He took a step as if to go, then whirled and popped the security guard closest to him a good one in the jaw. The other one was on him in a flash.

Digger was yelling now, shouting orders. "Get that wild man out of my place! Now!"

And Chance, as he relaxed into being dragged from the casino, was shouting back, "I said I was sober, Bellamy, but I never said I wasn't still piss mean!"

Digger shook his head, and said under his breath, "Damn fool. I kinda like that guy."

Pru Bellamy, also gazing Chance's way, nodded. "So do I, hon. So...do...I. I mean, he's just the most genuine thing, isn't he?"

Maggie turned from the railing into a gaping sea of faces, the head waitress's among them. She hitched her head to the side, signaling Maggie to follow her to the comparative privacy of the bar's cash register.

"I know," Maggie said. "I know. It's time to turn in my feathers."

"Sorry, hon," the other woman said. "Looks like this town just isn't big enough for the two of you. What a bitch she is, anyway." She shook her head. "And who the hell was that crazy guy?"

"No one."

"Well, you sure seemed like someone to him."

"He was drunk," Maggie said, looking off to the table where Chance had sat not long ago. There were broken bottles on the floor and half-empty and full bottles on the table top. The area was a disaster.

"You'll find another job easy," the waitress said. "Good luck now, I've gotta go make my fortune on that bunch of bozos over there." She gave Maggie a parting wink and sauntered off in her sequins and black tail feathers.

Maggie had never felt so depleted. There was now absolutely nothing and no one in her life. Everything was gone. Even, she thought, walking through the lounge on her way to the employee dressing rooms, the lousy bird costume was about to be set free.

Chapter Six

She was back in her street clothes again, jeans, T-shirt and a lightweight down vest, the bird getup shed. The Azteca's list of rules stated that all employees were to use the designated employee door to exit and enter. But Maggie was no longer included in that category, and even if she had been, she still might have sauntered out through the front glass doors, as she now did. She marched out beside a man in evening wear and a woman in a full-length linx coat and enough diamonds on her fingers to blind an eye with the flash. Maggie imagined the contrast between them, she with her scarred leather bag swinging with reckless abandon, the woman with her tiny white silk purse, beaded with miniature representations of roses, clutched close to her bosom. In her worn boots, Maggie's strides were long and definite, while the woman took dainty mincing steps as they made their way in tandem down the sweep of wide marble to ground level.

After the temperature-controlled environment of the casino, Maggie welcomed the astringency of the desert night. There were still exhaust fumes from the traffic to clog up the lungs and sting the eyes, but she knew if she went out a bit from town she could breathe in the purity of the land. Just knowing it was possible made her feel better about things. All about, the night glowed. Streetlights, taillights, flashing signs—the world was an undulating rainbow, a dizzying swirl of yellow and fuchsia and green and blue. Looking up, Maggie searched the heavens for familiar stars. Only the brightest could compete against the dazzling flash of the Las Vegas skyline.

She and the resplendent couple hit the pavement together; there they parted company. While Maggie rocked back on her heels, deciding if she should blow a few bucks on a taxi to carry her back to her hotel, or if it might be better to vent some more psychic steam by walking, the couple climbed into a waiting gray limousine. The woman nestled into the plush upholstered seat and bundled her fur around her. With a dazzling smile, she briefly turned her head to where Maggie remained, indecisive, on the pavement. The woman did not see her, that much was very certain to Maggie. She was being looked through, not at, and Maggie was suddenly taken over by the giddy feeling that she was a ghost.

Well, yes, perhaps that was right, she considered, as she took off on foot along the circular drive leading from the main boulevard into the Azteca's grounds. She and the woman lived in different economic and social dimensions. From the woman's perspective, she was clearly no more than a sociological wraith.

Rather than follow the curve of the drive, she dodged between taxis and private vehicles to take a shortcut to the city street. This path led her through a parklike area directly fronting the casino.

The grounds contained a series of shallow geometric reflecting pools with bottoms exhibiting bold designs in keeping with the Azteca's Indian theme. From the street, a passing eye could follow these pools, which graduated in height, to an apex where a fountain of mammoth proportions rose off the landscape. The massiveness of this fountain made it more of an architectural monument than a mere display of waterworks, with its giant cantilevered blocks of black granite shooting off in different directions. It was a fascinating engineering feat, and Maggie stood in awe for a moment, watching as water, backlit by brilliant spotlights, spewed jet streams into the air to land, eventually, in the lower pools. Illuminated at night, it was a dazzling sight, like a giant black sun, Maggie considered. In fact, its watery rays so intrigued her that until that moment they had eclipsed the sole human form bent over the rim of the lowest pool.

It was too late to turn away. They saw each other at the same instant that Maggie started to move toward the street. At the farthest, they were no more than ten or twelve feet from each other.

Chance was in the midst of splashing his face. A moving blur at the corner of his vision caught his eye. He looked up.

For an instant all he could make out through the water washing down over his eyes and clinging to his lashes, was a blurry form of what he took to be a female. Then her face came into focus, and with it the black stare of Maggie Rand. It was a look potent enough with rage to turn a normal man to stone.

Fortunately, Chance thought, he was not a normal man, at least not if recent history was any criteria.

No, indeed. A normal, sane, well-adjusted man would have never gotten himself involved with such a mean-tempered, unpredictable woman in the first place. A normal kind of guy would not be on his knees as he was now, in front of one of the world's flashiest buildings with water dripping down his neck.

The fact of it was, as he looked into the dark, piercing eyes of Maggie Rand, he didn't know what to say. In some vague sort of way, he realized that something in the order of an apology was in keeping with the situation; but then he thought, the hell with it. He'd already said his piece, which, as it turned out, had been far too much. Nothing he could say to her would ever make any difference; better he should gurgle away to the fountain. *It* would at least gurgle back.

A thin stream of blood from a cut at the corner of his eye traced down his face. He felt its journey as a tickle and swiped at the annoyance. It hurt. His knuckles, too, were battered and slightly raw from the punches he had delivered to Bellamy's jaw. He felt foolish and unappreciated, maybe even a little bit angry, although, in fairness, he had acted on his own volition. It wasn't exactly as if she had been screaming her lungs off for a knight on a charger.

"Thanks!" Chance called, at last. He still knelt on one knee by the fountain. "I really appreciate your concern. You're all heart, woman. In the presence of what is obviously a crumbling human being, all you can do is pin me with one of your dead fish-eye looks?"

"I promise I'll cry at your funeral. Anyway, thanks, yourself. You did me one hell of a favor in there. It's what I really needed, you know. To get fired, my first night on the job."

"You're too good for a job like that anyway," he said flatteringly.

"I know, I know," she said. "Being as how brain surgery's my real specialty. Just my bad luck they were fresh out of local openings today. So, I found myself obliged to dress up like a chicken."

"Well," Chance said kindly, "I saw you more as a hawk. Anyway, it's a smart move, you getting out of the business before you were eaten. Look, baby..." he said, raising himself up, but not without a considerable amount of discomfort. He gave a moan that was genuine, but sounded theatrical, even to him. Anyway, he made no effort to hide his pain. Sympathy being out, he'd go for the satisfaction of instilling a little guilt in her.

"I'm looking," she said, with the briefest twitch of a smile. "You're dripping."

"Yes," he replied, and only that, which was enough. The situation spoke for itself. A bead of water seemed to be hanging on the tip of his nose, with another watery crystal suspended somewhat ignominiously on his chin. With all the other physical distractions, he hadn't noticed. He moved his head and the droplets continued on their gravitational course.

He also went on with what he had originally started to say, while at the same time tucking in his shirttail and stamping to settle the seams of his trousers. "You don't just come sidling up to someone like Pru Bellamy and tell her head-on she's wearing your necklace. It just doesn't work out well."

"No kidding? I don't care who she is. I say what I've got to say. Period. Anyway, I don't exactly recall asking you for help."

Chance patted his eye, exploring by touch the extent of the damage. It was tender and he flinched. "Let me tell you, lady, the way I see it, you might be a tad better off if you took a new tack in your conversational habits. Period," he mimicked.

"Maybe you'd be better off if you kept out of my business," Maggie replied, and started off down the concourse leading to the street.

"I'll go one better than that!" he called after her, "I'll keep out of your entire life!" Then added in an ironic whisper to himself, "So there. And period...baby."

Her back was toward him. There was no visible response from her, but what had he expected? he asked himself. There was just the steady gait of the long tapering legs taking her through a world in which she didn't seem to fit. With confused emotions, he continued to watch her silhouette moving against the lights of the strip, her slender body like a willow he longed to bend into him again. And again. Hell, no matter how angry she got him, the attraction was there, a cosmic fact. Whatever else she was, she was one hell of a woman. He didn't know if he meant that in a good way, or the other. She certainly caused a lot of hell to break out around her, that was for sure. Well, regardless, he thought, sighing, his attention still on her retreating form, she still had a great body. It did things to him just thinking about it.

Maggie made it back to her motel. She had walked briskly the entire way. Anyone who saw her would have thought she was a woman with a purpose. But, now that she was there, she had to ask herself, why? She stood in front of the Panda Inn's false front, continuing to wonder this, along with what she intended to do with the rest of her life. A shabby neon-lighted representation of a Chinese pagoda winked off and on. *Home, be it ever so humble.*

Deciding it might be best to keep moving for a while, Maggie began walking again. The next part of her journey took place while she was in a haze of ruminations covering the life of her grandfather. She reviewed what he had told her of his father and his father before him. The backward pass into time was an attempt to borrow some shred of wisdom or emotion from their experiences on this earth. She knew she sure as hell could use a hint or two to help her through her own existence.

Anger and despair had buoyed her along on her meandering route to nowhere in particular. Now, at last, they were earthbound weights, dragging her to a stop. She didn't know how much her mind had to do with it, but her feet had brought her to the horse farm where Darkstar was lodged.

It was three-thirty in the morning by the time she crawled over the corral fence. The moon was out and looking a trifle lopsided, just the way her life appeared these days; but away from the city lights there was shine enough to illuminate the area, and when she looked skyward now, it was into the same vast sea of stars her grandfather and his father had seen during their times on earth. There had been a story, when she was a child, about the stars in heaven being the souls of braves who had lived well and now guided their ancestors.

Darkstar inhabited a separate enclosed space, and when she saw Maggie standing in her territory she neighed a friendly welcome and trotted over.

The wired feeling from the excess of liquor—which had prompted his ill-fated heroics—had now settled in Chance like silt in a stagnant pool.

In the same bed in which he had made love to Maggie Rand only—could it be only a night before?—he now lay alone. In the past, no matter how bad things had gotten, he had been able to pick himself up, dust himself off, and march right back into the fracas that was life. Well, he didn't feel that way anymore. The inner stimulous to fight the almost impossible odds of making it in the horse racing business wasn't there for him now. He only felt tired and sore and alone.

It was this sense of the solitary, of almost not being part of existence, so disconnected did he feel from the world as he lay in bed staring at the spot where Maggie had lain, that prompted him, no, actually propelled him, to rise out of the bed, dress himself again, and set off at three-thirty in the morning.

Minutes later, in the middle of the Strip, he sat in the cab of the truck, the big engine idling roughly, as he waited for the light to change to green so he could move forward with the others. That had been his secret, if subliminal intention, to put himself back into the flow of humanity with the hope that he might be caught up in its stream.

Only it didn't seem to be working out that way.

The light turned red and everyone in line shifted, gunned their engines and rumbled forward in purposeful procession. He did not.

He did not feel part of it; he did not feel connected to any of it anymore. Because . . . he did not even want to be. And this, this sudden jolt of a realization, is what scared him. His family had been the horses, and now they were gone. There was nothing left to keep him here on the planet. No living thing to care about, nor to care about him. He was a human cipher.

A chill ran through him and he trembled. The expression that came to mind was "the hand of death." No, they were wrong, it was more of a claw actually, something not quite human, and it had set down upon his shoulder, tap-tapping, just waiting for the inevitable.

Then he remembered Darkstar.

She would not be his for long, but at least for the moment, she was a warm, alive *something* that he might hold on to.

He told himself that he was, of course, absolutely stone sober.

Then what was that out there? What the hell was that out there?

From farther back up the road, he had started looking for the form of the horse in the corral, needed to see the animal's shape with a fervent desperation. What he initially saw from the distance was disturbing enough to make him cut the lights and coast along in low gear until he was close enough to make out by the light of the moon what was going on in the corral.

His mouth went dry.

"Holy . . ." he said, "holy . . ." A wave of adrenaline washed through him, leaving him weak. His arms collapsed over the steering wheel. He shook his head, thinking of what might have happened if it had been another time. Up until a week ago, when he had sold it because he needed cash for feed, he'd kept a .45 revolver loaded with Magnum bullets in his glove compartment. The way he'd been feeling tonight, seeing a thief up on the only thing he had left to his name in the entire world, he would have blown the sucker clear up past Mars and Venus, and splattered the remnants of the son of a gun against the moon. His eyes followed the mental trajectory. Above him, the silver disk hung in the blackness like a thin, crooked smile.

And on the ground, fifty or so feet ahead of where he sat with the engine deadened and the lights killed, he watched what was perhaps the most beautiful sight he had ever witnessed in his life.

Slowly, his movements measured to reduce any possible sound, Chance crept from the truck.

A religious feeling swept over him, or what he judged might be termed such. He was filled with an exquisite joy that was also sorrow. It was a feeling that contained within it a soaring expansiveness and appreciation for—he tried to put it into some sort of verbal context—for simply being.

Bareback, in the moonlight, Maggie Rand rode atop the filly. Darkstar's coat was a silvery, liquid gleam in the night as she pranced to what had to be some silent, magical music, a symphony of sound coming from the hearts of horse and rider.

Chance tightened his grip on the railing, feeling weak from the jolt of passion that tore open his soul. He loved this woman, would love her into an eternity that until now he had never believed in.

Beneath Maggie, Darkstar moved like the soft flow of water. Relaxing into the horse's rhythm, Maggie had lost herself to time and place. With hands on the animal's mane and her thighs gripping tightly, she rode bareback with as much certainty as she had ridden the Indian ponies as a child, when her parents and grandparents had been together on the reservation. The Indian ponies were wild and jittery creatures, as unlike Darkstar as hemp was to Chinese silk.

Darkstar needed no guidance, the horse seeming to sense Maggie's change of thoughts as easily as Maggie accommodated herself to the filly's rhythm. An exquisite sense of wholeness filled Maggie. No longer did she feel fragmented and apart from herself and the world. In the night air of the desert she was home again, inside herself. The Panda Inn or the Hilton, either could be her home. Or neither. Outside there was nothing, and inside there were worlds of joy to experience, never ending and exquisite and safe.

"Come Darkstar," she whispered, leaning down close on the horse's warm neck, "run for yourself, run girl...."

Maggie felt the horse release her spirit into the night. The animal's legs were gliding, stretching out and floating over the ground as if airborne. A sense of freedom rippled through both horse and rider's bodies. The night was electric with magic.

Maggie threw back her head and laughed for the sheer joy of being alive. The heavens seemed ablaze with celebratory candles, and she knew with the deepest, the most profound sense of gratitude, that somehow her grandfather had lit her way to this spot on this night.

At a gallop, Darkstar turned and headed back in the opposite direction. She slowed slightly, on her own, as if distracted. Maggie took notice of the change in behavior, and searching for the reason, she too saw the figure at the rail.

At the sight of Chance Harris standing quietly watching them, the spell was shattered.

Maggie brought Darkstar to a walk, then a stop. She slipped easily off the filly's back, the tightness in her thighs relaxing as her boots made contact with solid earth once again. Darkstar trotted gaily over to Chance, tossing her mane and snorting, a coquette. Maggie followed behind with considerably less exuberance. She tried, without appearing interested, to make out Chance's mood. His facial expression gave her no clue. It was impossible to gauge his reaction to her stolen ride, but she doubted he'd look kindly upon it.

Chance waited silently. He found it hard work, the effort to collect whatever rational elements of his mind remained as Maggie Rand approached. Judging by recent history, and based upon present common sense, it was safe to predict another difficult exchange between them. Loving her, which was crazy, but which he had to admit he did, made everything that much harder. It was a futile love. He knew that as well as he knew he was stone broke.

Figuring that outward show was a good part of the game, he kept his eyes steady on her, careful to give nothing away of what he actually felt. The familiar swing-glide to her gait continued to fascinate him. She moved with the assurance of a wild creature perfectly in tune with its body and natural surroundings. Chance could read generations of genetic history reflected in the tilt of her head, in the rhythmic, elegant stride. The noble warriors of yesterday were not entirely extinct, living on, at least, in this one woman.

It was incomparably difficult to remain so outwardly unaffected by her presence. The moonlight accentuated the clean sweep of her high cheekbones, and her eyes glittered with inner starlight. A few more steps and she would be close enough for him to touch, near enough to love. He would throw her to the earth and cover her with himself, drown them both in the fire of his body, hammer his love into her until she was bonded to him forever.

Instead, when she reached him, he said, "Don't tell me. You've become a horse thief now." He had managed to force a tone of light annoyance into his voice.

She either ignored it, or didn't notice.

"How much for Darkstar?" Maggie asked.

There was something different to her voice, an excited, almost breathless quality that Chance had not heard before.

"How much you got?" he returned.

"Not much."

He could feel the will behind the dark eyes boring into him. "That ought to be about right," he said.

"I'm serious," Maggie said.

"The moonlight's gotten to you." He was beginning to think it had gotten him, too. The topic of conversation was unexpected and he was not prepared for the earnestness in her. He felt his rational mind slip-sliding from under him.

"I'm serious," she repeated.

She had remained on the inside of the corral. Now she leaned up against the railing and held tight to the upper bar. He could feel, as well as see, the tension in her body as she waited for his response. Just for a second, he saw her nude, as she had been the night they had made love. For a different reason, the same coiled physical expectation had existed—on that night she had wanted him, desired him. And he had satisfied her. God. He would do it again this moment, and a million times after that.

Chance paused, shifted his weight from one foot to the other and let out a bone-weary sigh as he came back to the subject at hand. This idea she had concocted in the desert moonlight was in no way a good plan, not for her, not for him, not for Darkstar. Looking at her, he said, "What in hell's name are you going to do with a horse? Lady, you can't hardly take care of your own self."

Maggie seemed not to have heard him, instead turning her head in the direction of Darkstar, who, at the far end of the fenced enclosure was playfully bobbing her head as she stomped at the ground with one hoof.

"That's a good animal. She can run. Before, when I saw her...well, I thought she might. But tonight I felt it. She can run. I know it now," Maggie said wistfully, not looking at him, but speaking inwardly.

"Come on," Chance said, "let's hit it outta here. I'll drop you off wherever the hell you're staying. Knowing you, probably on top of some goddamned cactus with the needles still on it." Except for that night, when she had hit rock bottom and had clung to him, he had never seen her soft like this. It touched him, touched him immeasurably. He had to force his voice flat to hide the tenderness he was experiencing.

There was no objection to his invitation. She climbed over the corral fence and he helped her down, not because she required it, but because he was, at least historically in sexual matters, an opportunist, and this was an opportunity to slip his hands around her waist. He held her a beat longer than was necessary, reveling in the feel of her. She had to have noticed, but said nothing, and recklessly he allowed himself the fleeting and wild thought that perhaps there might be some hope, after all.

Together, silently, they walked back to the truck he had left some distance away.

Chance did not start the engine at once. He remained slouched against the seat, engaged in an internal struggle. Two divergent impulses assaulted opposite sides of his psyche. Into one ear spoke the rational, clear chiming voice of reason; and to this he politely listened. But the voice to whom he paid most ardent heed, whispered in the breathlessly seductive tones of his heart.

No, the sensible voice said to his interior. *No, don't make this stupid move.*

Aloud, his own voice announced, "If you really want Darkstar—she's yours."

Maggie, who had been contemplatively staring straight ahead at the horse's shadowy form in the corral, snapped her head around.

"Really?" She sounded like a young girl. "You mean it? You aren't playing? Seriously, now." Her eyes were wide, waiting for Chance's confirmation.

"Yeah," Chance said, trying not to grin—he felt like a god, like a hero, like Santa Claus, like the entire allied armed force of the Normandy invasion. At the same time of this triumph, he was having to fight against the urge to touch her shoulder, her face, the curve of her neck. "Yeah, you two looked okay together. So what the hell..."

Amazed, he watched her eyes cloud.

"What the hell..." she echoed.

As quickly as the excitement had arisen, the familiar pall resettled over her, like a flimsy netting momentarily blown off by a fortunate wind. But its weight seemed formidable, and somberly, she said, "You were right. I don't have much. You know what I've got? Just the money from the necklace. And what I've made tonight. My entire fortune." In disgust at herself, she turned her head, staring out the window rather than face him in her shame.

"Yeah, well." He really was wacko, the voice inside taunted. He was out of his gourd. "I saw that in my crystal ball. Tell you what, you pay me what you've got now, keeping what you're going to need to eat on, and when she wins the Triple Crown, you can pay me off with that half."

He meant the last part, of course, as a joke. She didn't.

"I will." She put out her hand. "I will," she insisted again, and the smile was back.

It was simply for this, to view the appearance of joy in her eyes, which gladdened his own heart to its present point of almost bursting, that he had just given away his entire kingdom. Yeah. He was nuts.

Chance accepted the proffered hand, savoring the feel of her heated palm in his.

"You've got some pretty grand ideas." He wasn't just making small talk. It was an observation, a serious one, with serious consequences tagged to its truth.

"You mean ridiculous ideas?" She waited for him to go on, and when he didn't, she said, "Go on, I can take it, whatever you're going to warn me against."

With a sweeping motion, Chance reached for his hat on the dashboard. He punched it down on his head, cloaking his face in shadow. He liked being Zorro, the swashbuckler; he didn't like to be the bearer of sad tales. Even so...

"Look, babe...she's just an ordinary filly. You know? I mean this horse is not Pegasus. She's not the daughter of Seattle Slew. So, I don't exactly know what you've got in mind, but I think a little bit of reality might be in order here."

"Darkstar's what she is. She's her own self," Maggie responded vehemently. "And it's going to be enough, just being that."

"Well that's real fine and high and noble. But it still ain't realistic. If you've got some fancy ideas about running her in some big stake races, you'd better think twice. You ought to think a hundred times. Because—"

"Have you ever clocked her?"

"Sure. Of course." Chance could see her mind turning over, ten times the speed of a second hand.

"How'd she run?"

"Okay. She did okay. But she didn't set fire to the turf, either."

"On what kind of track, against what kinds of horses?" Maggie pressed.

"On a fast track against other mongrels like herself. It was just an impromptu morning workout. Nothing serious. She's still too young."

"Well, when the time comes, she'll rise to the occasion," Maggie said. "You put her up against the real competition, I don't care about what dam or sire the horse has come out of, Darkstar can, and will, take them."

"And just how the hell do you figure that?"

Maggie didn't answer him. Her eyes held something he couldn't exactly name. They were changing, swirling pools of hatred and love and loss and triumph, each emotion coming one upon the next so fast that it made him dizzy just keeping up with it all. All of that, he realized, with a renewed sense of awe, was in her; that whole crazy, passionate stew of feeling was in the woman he loved.

The show was over. Her eyes had settled flat and hard again, as she finally responded. "Because she's *got* to win," Maggie said.

Through all of it, Chance had neglected to let go of her hand, only this time it hadn't been by clever design. They had both simply remained joined during their conversation. Now, in the enveloping silence, he became aware of the feel of her again, her hand's pressure tight with resolution against his.

"Maggie..." he said, and looking down, with the hat's brim hiding the emotion in his eyes from her, he rubbed the top of her hand with his thumb. She began to withdraw from him, but before she could he reached for her and pulled her into him. "Don't fight...please," he said. "I only want to hold you—nothing else, if you don't want to. Only this. It's enough," he said, and thought of what she had said about Darkstar.

For whatever reason, be it obligation, or exhaustion, he felt her relax against him. They didn't move, either of them, both remaining absolutely still, the physical connection tentative and, to him, precious.

Maggie's eyes brimmed with tears. Her heart filled, as well. Her entire being seemed in danger of being swept off in a flood of feeling. Her mind kept wanting to shut down, but something stronger than her mind made her stay conscious of what was going on. Something had happened this night. It was something magical, something holy. It was *something*. And they were all a part of it. Chance and she and Darkstar. A triad of dreamers, she thought.

The morning was almost upon them. Off where the horizon joined earth and sky, pink light was growing out of the ground. Maggie watched Darkstar. Poised, the horse stood still, facing the new day that was coming.

"Chance," Maggie said, as she leaned against his chest, "thank you. Really thank you." She turned so that she could see his face.

"Yeah," he said and pulled the hat down farther to block out her vision of his brimming eyes.

She leaned forward and kissed him lightly, surprising herself; surprising him, no doubt. She pushed his hat away from his forehead. Her eyes held an invitation. Chance looked away.

"What do you know? Made it another day." He kept his gaze steady toward the rising sun. In the few seconds that had elapsed, a gold wash had joined the pink. There were no longer stars.

"I wouldn't mind if... I really want to be with you now, tonight..."

"Better to leave having things right, Maggie; with everything square between us. Somehow, all along, things have been wrong. Let's end things the way they are now. If nothing else, we'll have at least one nice memory to think back on."

Gently, he pushed her from him. It was, perhaps, the hardest thing he had ever done. But what he had said was true. In light of her feelings, or lack of them, for him, his emotions for her meant nothing.

He switched off his desire, and switched on the truck's ignition.

The engine was the only sound between them, rumbling as they drove back through town to Maggie's motel. A couple of times he dared to glance at her, but she sat there without any signs of pain or joy; just sat there, staring ahead and thinking her private thoughts. Well, he had a few of his own to run through, too.

The ride home was torture for Maggie. She had never experienced such confusion before. Whenever she forced her mind to think of Darkstar and their future together, something else more insistent took over and directed her mind to dwell on Chance. It was going to be the end between them. There would be the transfer of Darkstar's ownership papers from Chance to her, and that would be that. She'd be on her own, which was, of course what she had wanted all along. Only now she wasn't sure.

Somehow the idea of the three of them—Darkstar, herself, and Chance—as a team, had formed in her head. The triangular image would not be erased. What had seemed right to her, her independence, suddenly seemed every bit as wrong.

Oh, she was tired, just tired. She leaned her head against the side window and closed her eyes, losing herself in the engine's hum.

Sometime later, the silence awakened her.

They were parked in the lot of the Panda Inn. Chance was watching her.

"How long?" she asked, wiping her eyes. "How long have we been here?"

"Only a minute or two."

"Really?"

"Really."

"You're lying," she said, knowing for some inexplicable reason that she was right.

"Ten minutes," he admitted with a slight smile that was also sad and weary.

Just like him, Maggie thought, she was stalling for time. She was waiting for whatever it was to happen that was supposed to happen. Wasn't there something that was going to come and take over for her and make everything right? Where the hell was her anger now? Where the hell had her pride gone, just when she needed it most?

"I want you to come in," she said shyly. She had never offered an invitation like that before.

Chance didn't say anything for a moment, as if he were considering.

"I do," she said. "I want you. I want us to—" She was starting to cry. God, she couldn't believe it. She didn't even know whose tears these were. They were happening on their own. "I don't know!" she said, as if he had put forth an argument. "Look, I don't have any idea what's going on with me right now, but I feel like . . . I feel like I want you to come in there with me. I need you," she said. "You did this! You made me need you, dammit!"

"The horse is what you're all about, Maggie. You don't have the place to keep a man in your heart, too. I can see that now," he said, and finally looked at her. He breathed out slowly. "You've got a destination now. You've got someplace to go. I don't. And if I did, it isn't in your direction. So why come in there now and make it worse for the both of us later? The deeper you touch, the longer it takes the wounds to heal."

"Thanks for the info, doc." She pressed down on the door handle.

"I'll drop the ownership transfer papers off at the office tomorrow. Before I go," he said. Three words, three little words, such an insignificant combination of letters when one did not pay careful attention. *Before I go.* Three words, three powerful words, a monumental combination of letters turning lives inside out, if one were to truly consider each as a seed of destiny.

Maggie reached into her purse and peeled out the money she owed him. "Here," she said. "You've got more coming when we win the Triple Crown." She dropped the money on the seat between them and slid out her side to the pavement.

"Son of a bitch," she said softly, looking up at him before closing the door.

Chance tipped his fingers to his hat.

Both had tears in their eyes.

Maggie shut the door and walked off.

An electric timer suddenly shut off the lights illuminating the false front of the Panda Inn. It was, as Chance had said, another day.

Chapter Seven

Maggie swallowed, feeling dizzy with shame. This second night at work was for some reason worse than the first. The day before hadn't seemed real; she hadn't yet settled into her new role, this latest of roles. The humiliation had, therefore, been muted and bearable. It had been a visit to someone else's dream. Tonight there was no place for illusion—this was her life and it was no stopover from which she might escape, either.

From out of the tiny orchestra pit, the drums came forth with a sensuous swish-ra-tat, swish-ra-tat, while the keyboard player held to his vamp. Cocktail glasses clinked. An outburst of laughter from a man. A woman's high cackle. Swish-ra-tat.

Playing her song, they were, the music of survival.

In the wings, off the small stage, she and the others waited for the master of ceremonies to finish his warm-up patter.

Ladies and gents...Pot of Gold Casino...best odds in Las Vegas...winners last week from... proud to present...Rainbow Room...most beautiful women...dazzling moving spectrum of feminine beauty...most—

She had only done it once, the night before, but even so, for her it had already taken on a perpetual sameness. There was no real purpose for it, no joy, no integrity. In another second the gold drapes would pull back and out they would strut, a line of smiling women cloaked from toe to neck in ostrich plumes. She was in yellow. The woman in front of her wore purple, and so on down the row, human display boards for the medley of colors. They were there to carry out the theme, no more, no less. They were the Rainbow Girls of the Rainbow Room in the Pot of Gold Casino.

There was an upsurge in the drum beat. On cue, the plume procession fluttered forward in a single line to fill the stage.

I am a dazzling spectrum, not Maggie Rand. Maggie Rand is somewhere else. She is in the desert. She is on a horse called Darkstar. No, no...Maggie dreamed...moving her mind forward in time...Darkstar is at Santa Anita. She is winning the...

Applause from the audience. The tempo of the small band increased. Remember not to lose the smile, she told herself. Lose the smile, lose the job.

Oak Tree Classic. Her mind moved to California on a fall day. She could see Darkstar flying lengths ahead of the others to the finish line.

Swish. The close sound called her back. Her cloak— all of their cloaks—fell to the floor behind them. Almost, but not quite in unison they dropped; none of them were professional dancers. We only have long legs and pretty faces and empty stomachs, Maggie thought. Perhaps empty heads. No souls. Somewhere they had lost their souls behind them, too. Swish, and gone! It happened like that, life did, swish and things were suddenly over.

Chance's face rose into her mind's view. She tried to see him more clearly, but the image wavered and finally dissolved.

She and the rest of the spectrum stepped forward in their gold glitter bikinis. Right foot, left foot, dip and again...it was all so simple. One did not have to think.

The previous day she had gone in search of work. She was too late by ten minutes in one place and too inexperienced for another place to find work as a cocktail waitress. She had never thought herself the type to work in dress or jewelry shops, but she tried anyway, and discovered the pay was minimum wage and commission. With the present gnawing on her, what she needed was real cash, now.

By noon it had been safe to say it was not going to be a lucky day. She broke off from her job hunt and went to visit Darkstar, hoping the trip might boost her spirits. Instead, it only highlighted the reality of her desperate situation. This was a living breathing responsibility she had taken on. She told the owner of the farm she would be taking over the boarding expenses. For how long she didn't know.

An hour later, she happened upon The Pot of Gold Casino.

The Pot of Gold Casino was a tarnished bit of stucco on the far end of the strip. Built in the forties, it had seen multiple renovations by various owners, none of whom had the funds to lift it out of its third-class status as a gambling and entertainment establishment. Its most recent owners were, from what Maggie was told, a consortium of Los Angeles physicians who left the casino's running to a local management firm.

Maggie had responded to its newspaper advertisement, requesting applicants for cocktail waitressing. When she arrived for her interview there was a billboard in the front lobby, the sign calling for show girls. It was partly a scam, this so-called talent hunt, in that there was to be a nightly contest in which entertainment hopefuls might exhibit their bodies in bathing suits. But when Maggie appeared with her long legs and "splendid, really outstanding look," she was recruited then and there to be a Rainbow Girl.

At first she laughed. Then she considered the money, which was union scale and therefore provided a definite income with which she could feed both herself and Darkstar. She also took into account that she would not have to deal with the public. The less she had to do with two-legged critters, the better. The clincher was the hours; they were perfect. She would have her days off to work with Darkstar until she could afford a real trainer. And so, once again, she donned feathers to become that modern symbol of feminity, a chick, a bird, or most appropriately, she figured, a real turkey.

The house offered the Follies-type production gratis in a theater lounge off the gambling area, as a lure to customers to play their tables.

Another musical cue sounded. Dutifully, the line of women stepped and dipped back as the Rainbow Man—a kinetic spectacle in a gold-sequined Spandex jumpsuit—claimed the stage. His true name was Massimo and he had been a waiter on an Italian cruise ship until he'd found a rich American matron to marry. The story went that she paid for singing lessons and kept him in tight pants just long enough for him to find a job as a chorus boy in Las Vegas. No doubt, providing his pants held out, The Pot of Gold would merely be one more stop on his way to prove the American Dream still existed.

Here in the background, the blinding floodlight effect was reduced. A brilliant white spot, something special demanded by Massimo to accentuate his importance, was directed full-strength on his glittering form as he warbled an up-tempo version of "Somewhere Over the Rainbow." With Massimo as the focus, the rest of the stage was reduced, comparatively, to shadow.

Dip and turn, right foot then left, and so it went for Maggie as her mind turned over and over, the smile always in place. A few feet in front, Massimo twitched and turned ceaselessly in his elastic suit, only occasionally veering off key.

Maggie relaxed into the monotony on stage. Her eyes drifted beyond, into the smoky, purpled haze of the gambling casino. A different clientele here than at the Azteca, men in jean outfits or sports shirts or woebegone leisure suits complete with yesteryear's flared bell bottoms, a lot of polyester on women, cowboy hats and— Maggie's heart skipped a beat. A man with a fedora stood with his back to her, talking to a blond woman in a black jumpsuit. The woman laughed, and the man turned to look up at the stage. It was not Chance.

Just the same, the very thought of him being there had filled her with a numbing sadness.

"You're not smiling . . ." the girl shuffling in time to the music beside Maggie hissed between her teeth.

"What?" Maggie mumbled.

"Smile or you're dead, hon. Yesterday's cheese-cake."

"I've been worse," Maggie muttered. The girl's face was plastered into a tight mask of false joy.

"It's easy," the girl went on in her ventriloquist's whisper. "Just pretend to smile. I've done it all my life. I used to be a beauty contest winner."

"I used to be a person."

"Well, see. And didn't you smile then?"

"Never," Maggie said.

He was making a symbolic gesture, only who was to know? In a way, Chance considered philosophically, that was the whole point, wasn't it? Everything in life was a gesture. But in the end none of these valiant attempts to punctuate one's daily existence with meaning mattered any more than if you'd sat on a rock for eighty years and then croaked. Either way, you croaked. And that was that.

He stood at the side of the craps table, staring at the green felt on which he had placed a bet of a hundred dollars in chips. This was the symbolic part, this small tower of plastic. It was there now, and with a roll of dice from the man in a blue blazer and flushed red face, who was shouting "Seven the hard way, come on, come on, baby be good to me..." it might be swept away, leaving nothing but empty space. And so went life, his life, all lives.

The castle of chips was swept into away by the croupier's long stick.

Chance smiled. He felt a perverse triumph for having lost. Life was as he said it was. Predictability counted for at least something. He put out another hundred dollar stack of chips. He was a real sport, he was. And a buzzed philosopher, to boot. A cocktail waitress passed by and he stopped her, ordering his fourth drink of the still young evening. Let life pass on in a haze.

The money he was wagering had recently belonged to Maggie Rand. It, like her, would pass briefly through his life. The whole ritual he was engaged in was, in its own way, sadly meaningful. As the dice flew across the felt again, bouncing hard on the table's rim, Chance watched the play with the self-satisfied and twisted emotion of a religious zealot whose martyrdom was imminent.

He wanted to rid himself of her, wanted to purge himself of the hope and desire that had infected his melancholy since they had made love, since they had touched that one night in a way he had never thought possible. That slim promise of a future together had poisoned his resolution of detachment. If a man could die thrice in one lifetime, then he was two down already, with only the actual physical departure to await. The first of his deaths had come when the horses had been murdered, and again when perhaps the only woman he could ever love—had ever loved—passed out of his life.

The dice fell against his bet. The chips were collected.

Resolutely, Chance set down another tower of chips. It had, of course, occurred to him that he might finish with the whole affair in one wager, but that seemed too easy. There was something instructive in the slow, meditative pain he experienced as this portion of his past was reduced to nothing. He would learn from it.

A slight pressure on his shoulder roused him from his inner dialogue. Like a man suddenly come awake, he started, then immediately remembered his ordered drink and turned.

"Keep the change," he began. But he had been wrong. No cocktail waitress stood with drink in hand. "Well," Chance said, "the Empress of Trouble."

"Nope, the Queen of Peace..." Tiny folds of skin puckered at the edges of Pru Bellamy's blue eyes. She stood close. Her entire face beamed, like a piece of the sun floating crazily before him. Wallowing in psychic pain or not, he was still able to take in the blue-beaded gown draped in strategically stingy fashion over the form of Digger Bellamy's wife. She was a sight to behold, he'd give her that.

"Forgive me for the other night, oh please..." Pru said, her face now arranged into a position of contrite sincerity. "I can imagine what you think of me."

"I don't think of you at all." He would have turned from her then and avoided any further contact, except that the cocktail waitress did finally appear at that moment.

Pru took the drink from the woman and handed it to him, explaining, "Digger owns the biggest piece of this joint, too." She paused. "I'd understand if you don't want to drink it."

"Why wouldn't I? I ordered it."

"Oh," she said, with a sigh and a shrug, "maybe you'd see anything from me or my business as a moral compromise."

Chance shook his head. "Lady, I am not, nor have I ever been a noble man. I'm more thirsty than I am honorable." He demonstrated by downing half the drink.

When he looked at Pru again, she was smiling, only more tentatively than when she had first arrived. "I don't believe you—about you not being a man of honor. But I know what you mean. A body wants to get by in life, they've got to learn to face facts just the way they are," she said. "Maybe it's stretching things a bit, but there were times when I was hungry and had to decide what mattered more, holding my head up high, or just holding my head up at all."

"Yeah, well, I'll drink to your philosophy." And he did, emptying the glass.

"Listen," she said, sidling in a step closer, "I'd like to talk to you."

"What's this?" he said. "Tennis?"

"I mean somewhere private."

"Uh-uh." Chance shook his head. Her perfume made his head spin. "I'm not up to having your husband's pals bash my head in tonight. I'm tap-city in the heroics department."

"Okay," she conceded. "But, anyway, it's not what you think. It's business I want to talk about."

"So talk." He showed his disinterest by turning and placing another bet on the table. Pru's eyes went to the dwindling supply of chips in front of him. "My entire fortune," he said.

"I know about it—that thing with your farm."

"Everyone knows."

"Well I think it was rotten luck."

"Luck had not a thing to do with it."

"Yeah, so I heard. It was rotten just the same. But it looks like we could help each other out now."

"How's that?" Chance said with more amusement than interest.

"I know you're the best Thoroughbred trainer on the circuit. Everyone knows that, too. Well, the thing is,

I've got me some of the best Thoroughbreds anywhere on this planet.''

"That's the story going around."

"Yeah, sure. I know some of the other stories going around about me, too. You think I don't know what people say about me? All I am is Digger Bellamy's blond toy. Well, I've got these horses now and I'm going to show there's more to me. I want to bring in winners—my winners, not Digger's. You can do that for me.''

Chance laughed. He stepped aside, showing the latest pile of chips being collected by the house. "Honey, feast your eyes. I'm a loser.''

"No," Pru said emphatically. "No."

She said it with such simple conviction. Chance could only look at her, speechless. At the same time, he felt that he must, that he *should* deny her allegation that he was capable of winning anything ever again. He felt it an absolute moral imperative to challenge this preposterously misplaced faith. Only he couldn't quite pull it off. Something of himself stubbornly remained undeadened, and that part of him still alive vibrated tenuously to the optimism in her voice.

Pru reacted quickly. Reaching into her beaded clutch purse, she took out a folded bundle of white paper and held it out for him to examine.

Chance read the type. He flipped quickly through the pages, then went back and looked again. "This is for real?" He studied Pru, wanting to remain unconvinced.

"Absolutely. We can go upstairs right now. We can grab us a notary from the office and make it official. I'm not messing around here. Chance," she rushed on, breathlessly, "this is a deal for both of us. You win, I win. Don't let it go."

Chance looked past her into the crowded room. This was cause for deliberation. The money she was offering was more than generous; it was downright outrageous. But then Pru Bellamy was an outrageous type of woman. It made sense she'd go all out to get what she wanted; hadn't she always, from what he had heard? And he? What did he want from life?

Nothing.

That was the problem. And maybe also the beauty of it. He felt, as he looked out into the swirling profusion of strangers intent on their quests, that he was finally immune to the pleasure and the pain. He simply didn't care how things turned out.

"What the hell," he said, devoid of enthusiasm.

But, even so, the radiant sun of Pru's smile descended upon him again. "Well, hot damn," she said. "Let's go! We're gonna sign this baby!"

Chance turned back to the spread of green felt and began to gather up his remaining chips, then stopped. The moment held a laugh; silent and turned in on itself. On impulse, mocking fate, he shoved the remaining three hundred dollars' worth of plastic money to the number ten.

The dice were his to roll. Eyes lifted to him, eyes filled with hope. They clung to him as he sent the dice shooting across the table. The squares hit the back rim, then rocketed into the center and righted themselves. A united moan arose around him as several people counted their losses.

From Chance there was no response. The moment demanded a certain dignity. He waited silently, without expression, as the croupier paid off on his bet. A toss of a match, he was a poor man and broken; a sweep of his hand, and he was a man of fortune. Life was outrageous.

"See, you're on a streak already," Pru said gaily, prancing beside him as they walked through the casino on the way to notarize the employment contract.

"How's that?" Chance said.

"That bundle...out there you just won a heap of green," Pru said, incredulous that he didn't understand her point.

"Doesn't matter."

Pru looked his way uncertainly. "What does matter to you, then?"

"Nothing," Chance said.

"Don't know if I like to hear that," Pru said solemnly. "I kind of like to think winning big matters to you."

"I'll do my job," Chance said. "If you want to win, we'll win."

"That's what I want," she returned defiantly as if he had opposed rather than supported her. "Why else bother?"

"There's nothing wrong with winning."

"Then how come you make it sound that way?"

"Sorry."

"I don't get you. You used to be out there busting your britches to take first place every time."

"Yup. I thought it was all worth it."

"And now you don't."

"What do you think you're winning, Pru?"

"Not money," she said. "It's not for money. I've got all I could ever spend this very second." Walking beside him, she was absorbed in thought. After a time, she said, "For glory. For a moment of glory, that's why I do it."

Chance nodded. "And then what? That moment's gone. What do you have then?"

"What does anyone ever have?" Pru countered. "Nothing lasts anyway."

"Have you ever loved anything, or anyone?"

Pru snorted. "Oh, come on. I've been in love. When I was sixteen I thought I'd die from love. Billy Grant. Let me tell you, I've known my share of Billy Grants since then. Different names, but they all of 'em pass through the same revolving door eventually."

"Must have kicked up quite a breeze, all that spinning," Chance commented, and they both laughed.

"From what I heard, you kicked up a dust devil or two with your own action." Pru cast a hungry smile his way. "I mean if you want to point fingers."

"That I did. But I only loved once," he said. "And too damn late."

"What the hell are you talking about?"

Chance laughed. "I'm talking about winning, baby. I'm talking about love."

"Seriously," Pru said, sounding baffled and peeved.

And Chance answered, "Nothing. I wasn't talking about anything at all. Where the hell's the notary?" he shouted out, and Pru was happy again.

The bright eye of a streetlamp illumined the row of cars. Chance searched down the line, trying to place his truck among the other vehicles. Everything gleamed in artificial color; blues turned green, greens became gray, reds purpled, the atmosphere of Las Vegas distorting reality to its own vision of life.

Life! He slapped the signed contract against his thigh as he moved along. His stride was jaunty. Once more he was a man with somewhere to go. At least that much was real.

It was astonishing to be caught up in it again. He recognized the dangerous sensation of hope, tried to turn from it, but found it impossible. How seductive hope was. How exhilarating it was to be caught up in the jet stream of life. He had almost forgotten.

Only an hour before he had thought of himself as a dying ember. A flagrantly romantic notion! So dramatic, maudlin to the point of shame. Then, of course, it had seemed so appropriate, the core of his being resonating with futility. After everything, his valiant efforts had amounted to nothing more than a giant goose egg.

Life, he contemplated, was the big game of chance, a game played on a monumental scale; dreams the same as dice, shot across a vast board known as the planet earth. Easy come, easy go. He would do well to remember that in the future, no matter how bright the present now appeared, at least in a financial sense. He fought down the image of Maggie.

Spotting his truck at last, he moved to it, all the while pushing down the picture of Maggie that had materialized with the revival of hope. Images rushed at him— Maggie running, slow motion, arms outstretched wide, to him! A verdant horizon appeared in blurry focus on his mind's screen, and then in sharper relief came the horses, Thoroughbreds all, each one belonging to his farm resurrected from the ashes.

What insanity hope brought with it; different it was from the sense of despair from which he had suffered, but no less potent in its ability to upset his equilibrium.

He felt out of control again and, reeling from all of the unrealistic notions, got into his truck and slammed the door shut as if that might make him safe from the wild and futile fantasies being spun by his heart.

To be truly secure, he must see life as it was, not glossy and classy and happily ever after, but as it existed in its actual form. That was the only way to survive his ride on this spinning joke of a world.

He gunned the engine and took off in search of the back side of life. If he were going to survive, he had to be careful this time. He'd have to ground himself in the hard facts of existence.

For a half hour he cruised the boulevard, thoughts piling up one after the other, endless, like the string of automobiles on the strip. Halfheartedly, he looked for the right place in which to lose his foolish dreams. It was the name which finally attracted and prompted him to make a quick U-turn and slip into a parking space. The place—more aptly, the joint—was perfect. What could be more ironic, and therefore more curative for what ailed him, than a visit to The Pot of Gold Casino?

Merely upon entering, he found immediate relief in the casino's shoddy parody of the more glamorous casinos. It reminded him of a magic act put on by an amateur magician. What was meant to be sleight of hand and illusive, came off instead as a bumbling performance of dropped cards and rabbits appearing off cue. But that was as it should be, this was the precise anchor he had sought and he felt comfortably uncomfortable in the surroundings. The Pot of Gold contained false coins; as good a metaphor for life as any he'd heard. It was a sham world and once that was understood there were no problems.

He took a seat at the bar, where fifty feet or so beyond, a lounge act was holding the attention of blurry-eyed gamblers. A man was singing in the foreground of the small stage. He was prancing about in a tight gold jumpsuit. Chance looked past him to the chorus of scantily clad female dancers who shuffled back and forth and occasionally did a dip and revolved prettily.

It was then, during the dip-turn, that he saw her.

The room got smaller and tighter, closing in on him.

It seemed his eyes had suddenly become empowered with zoom lenses. Her face was projected before him. So vital, so close did she appear that he imagined her breath on his skin. The slash of raised cheekbones streaked with rouge and gleaming with makeup and sweat beneath the hot stage lights was poignantly familiar and at the same time strange in the surroundings. His mind flew backward, desperately trying to replace her in time. He wanted her beneath the moon, on Darkstar—even walking freely down a highway would be better. But not this; he did not want this for her!

His first instinct was to bust back the imaginary walls closing in on him. With the second wave of adrenaline, he rose and moved forward, a man possessed.

The small orchestra reached a weak, quavering crescendo just as he arrived at the side of the stage. Later, he was to ask himself what he might have done had the curtains not closed when they did. He knew what he had wanted to do, though. He had wanted to drag Maggie off that stage, kicking and screaming if that's the way it had to be done; her tearing at his hair and cursing a blue streak the whole way—that would have been all right too. Just so long as he got her out of the sleaze-bag place. Whatever the world might be, whatever its tawdry reality, she was not to be a part of its seediness. His tarnished vision of life was exclusively his, and there was no room to share it with her. He wanted her out of it, needed to believe, for whatever insane reason, that she would find a home on some shining mountaintop, that she would live in the warmth of the sun, that she would ride the clouds and sail on the wind.

He wanted these immense dreams for her with a fierceness that took his breath away and left him standing at the edge of the stage with an ache in his ribs, as if he had been brutally pummelled.

The crowd around him buzzed. No one paid particular attention to the man in the brown leather jacket, the well-traveled cowboy boots and the incongruous fedora turned at a rakish angle so that one half of his face lay in shadow, while the other exposed an eye fevered with pulverized dreams. For a long moment he stood there staring at the closed curtain.

There was simply nothing he could do. It was not his life. She was not his woman. The closed curtain, the empty orchestra pit, cosmic hints that he had better well heed. He turned and, alone, moved through the animated throng surrounding him.

Maggie tried to concentrate on the music. She wondered if it was possible to fall asleep while still dancing. And then he came out of the glare, a man, just one man among the many whose outlines Maggie could dimly discern in the darkness before her. Even so, Maggie identified him, knew this man as separate and distinct from all others. How? Through instinct? Did she detect him through some primal left-over animal sense? Or was it more conscious, this knowledge? Little clues she subliminally recalled in the way his arms swung, just so, the slight tilt of his head—a notch to the left when he was disturbed, to the right when his energy was directed from his heart—and the rhythm of his stride, easy and flowing and totally, purely masculine. Did all these diverse parts add up to one unique and whole human being who could be no other than the Chance Harris whom she had known so briefly, and yet loved so fully?

The admission of that love shook her briefly.

Until that moment, she had not put her feelings into such concrete terms as words. It would take time to adjust. But then she would have a lifetime for that; years alone in which to relive two magic-filled days of loving a man.

She would have time to remember each small thing, to reconstruct, in a hellish leisurely purgatory without the man she loved, the first glimpse of him through the window of the truck. She could internally play back his initial remark to her, relive—oh, God!—the feel of his hands on her body the night they had twisted beneath and above each other, smelling, tasting, experiencing what she now knew was the only truly valid reason there was to live in this world.

And from that, from all of that glory, she had so haughtily walked away! From that stupidity, from that arrogance, from that blindness, she would now die slowly, an endless death of hollow seconds lived without him. What she had squandered could not be regained. There had been that brief time in the beginning, when sharing their love, they each might have stepped beyond their previous lives, filled as they were with all of their concrete beliefs and disappointments and petty angers, to form what might be wholly new selves. The power of their love was that strong, that magical! But she felt all of this, knew this, only in hindsight. Life had moved on, taking its transforming gift of ecstasy with it.

Now, they lived again as who they had been before their meeting, two strangers, a man and a woman who had met on a road, just two itinerants whose personalities clashed as discordant notes. They were people playing different melodies.

Even so, she loved the music of his breath and the rhythm of his stride. She simply loved him. And it was through this purity of feeling that she knew there was no mistake. It was Chance moving forward to the stage on which she danced; if one could even call it that.

Her heart rose and fell within an empty cavity that she was dimly aware of as being her body.

With the light behind him, he was a dark shadow outlined in white glow. But a sense of caution overrode the thrill of seeing him. The tempo of his walk matched the inner pulse of what she identified as rage—tightly held, barely restrained.

To avoid collision with a waitress, he adjusted his course. Slanted swords of white light crisscrossed him, and in this position he was framed in three-quarter illumination. Still, his face remained mostly in shadow, the hat—always that crazy hat!—obscuring the emotion roiling beneath its brim.

It was all Maggie could do to continue the monotonous performance, right foot, left, dip, slide and turn, she with no hat to hide the naked emotion of her love. Inside and externally, she felt herself exposed from every angle.

Earlier that day she had dreamed of a meeting between them, so different from this as to be cruel in comparison. It was to have happened at the races—she dressed in white silk, elegant and regal, standing beside Darkstar, the horse the winner of the greatest purse in the greatest race. But instead, laughably, here she stood, glitter falling like dirty snow from her cheaply constructed bodice each time her arms came up against the material. There was no greatness in exhibiting the length of her legs and the span of her behind to a darkened arena of inebriated onlookers. There was no honor to any of this, and—exiled from love—it was honor that she held most dear. Honor, or the promise of its attainment, someday, was all she had.

She knew, ashamedly, that it was the condition of her present dishonor that Chance was seeing as he continued to plow relentlessly toward the stage. She wished to shrink, to shrivel to dust.

Against the skins of his instrument, the drummer clanged and boomed and brush-brushed wildly.

The sounds came to Maggie as rushing wind, and internally she heard the lamenting voices of an entire Indian nation speaking from her heart. *So this is what has become of you?*

The declamations rose up around her, and silently, but with equal passion, she denounced the disappointment of those ghostly forebears. "No! Wait," she pleaded to the inner voices. "Don't look at me now! Not here, not now! This is not the way it will end!"

The curtain closed then and her fervent denial died along with the music.

The others hurried offstage to take off their makeup and remove their costumes.

Only Maggie remained, staring for a long while at the curtain, feeling Chance on the other side. The barrier was not the cloth; it was flesh and blood and two lifetimes of wrong turns caused by stubborn refusal to use someone else's map. Like Chance had said, they had their own journeys to take and they were headed in different directions. It was true and there was nothing more to it.

Tomorrow he would leave and that would be that. Chance drove down the wide avenue with its extravagant palaces of pleasure blinking and flashing their invitations in manic hysteria. The street was bumper-to-bumper on both sides. Stalled in traffic at a light, he leaned against the open window and breathed in the exhaust fumes, not caring, not noticing, that his eyes stung. His thoughts were otherwise engaged. He was making rules, making plans, making sure there was no space left over in his mind to think of her.

So. He would take off around daylight with the horse trailer hitched to the truck. No horse, just the trailer, a reminder of a past that he would drag with him into the future. That was necessary, to remember some things in order that they not happen again.

And when on the road he would sing. He would let loose and blast out "California Here I Come" at the top of his lungs. He would sing and crack stupid jokes to himself, see a future in which every race was his. All of this is what he would do when he floored it straight down the highway leading from Vegas—the road taking him away from the only damned woman he had ever loved.

And with that, a vision of Maggie flooded his mind, obliterating all else. He actually felt her presence, the smell of her, the warmth of her. God! He was reeling with grief, struck with a fiery desire that made his limbs tremble.

It's over! Forget her! Over, over, over, finished...

Silently repeating the mantra of his finished love affair, he battled his need to be with her, if not forever, then for just one more time. Little by little, his equilibrium stabilized, but it was a shaky, tentative balance. The light changed and the line ahead inched forward. Weakened, he righted himself and clutched the wheel, giving the truck gas. He felt so foolish, felt much like a man who had contracted some strange jungle fever for which there was no cure, and whose return was bound to be frequent and debilitating and humiliating.

God, to think that love could wreak so much havoc.

Well hell, it was over; that was the way things were. So accept them, tough guy, because you have one last matter of business coming up.

Chance pulled the truck into the space reserved for Guest Registry. Easy, fella, stay tough, he cautioned himself as he reached into the glove compartment. The cab's interior was bathed in a shower of light from the nearby sign. The Panda Inn's pagoda facade flashed off and on, hot and cold—like some of the women he'd known and probably would know again he assured himself as he climbed out of the cab.

He was in treacherous geographical territory; thirty thousand miles over Red China with only one engine left and losing fuel. The pavement beneath him was no longer solid. Each breath he took in and let out was done with the care of a man negotiating mined land. Each heartbeat could detonate an explosion to wipe away all his hard-won resolve. Just knowing he was near her, that through some luck and possible trickery he could have access to her body just one more time, brought about a physical longing so acute as to make him light-headed. *Tough it out, fella. Tough it out.* He fought to conjure a vision of one of those women waiting somewhere for him in the future, but his talent of materializing female delacacies on whim had eroded. The only form, the sole face of his imagination, belonged to the one woman he had to forget.

In the office of the Panda Inn, the night desk clerk, a middle-aged woman with a wrestler's body, gave him a look reserved for a masked bandit. He tipped his hat back. "I'm safe," he said. "I'm just a guy who likes to wear a hat at low angle."

"I've shot men for less," the woman said in a raspy voice. "No vacancies," she informed.

"So I read on your sign. I have some papers to leave. For one of your guests." Chance presented the envelope with the transfer of ownership papers for Darkstar. "Maggie Rand."

Just saying her name made his gut tighten. How long, he wondered, did pain like this endure? He had never loved a woman. He knew only what the songs said. And that didn't look good, because most of the songs were into eternal suffering.

"She'll get 'em." Yawning, the woman put out her hand to take the envelope.

But at the moment of contact, Chance suddenly pulled the packet back. Time stopped.

"Thanks, thanks, anyway..." he said, and backed quickly away as if he expected her to make a lunge for the papers.

The clock took up again. He felt the papers burn through his fingers as he left the office. Trembling like a man who had just escaped death, he walked out the door and into the night air.

* * *

Maggie's voice called, "Who's there?"

From the other side of the door, he answered, "Me, Chance." He waited, engulfed in a vast silence, for a response. When none came, he persisted. "I've the transfer papers for Darkstar."

Slowly, as if centuries were passing, the door opened. The silence was gone, and filling the void was the thunder of his heart. Within, dread and hope intermingled crazily, and at the last second, just before seeing her, he was seized with the impulse to bolt. Of course he should not have come. But back there in the office he had felt that he would die if he did not see her just once more. An innocent look, a passing remark, the meeting between them civilized. Oh, what a mistake. He had felt and not thought and now it was too late.

The door had opened wide. She was before him, at arms reach, looking at him with the dark, glistening eyes that had so captivated the first time he had gazed into them. It would be impossible to leave while held in their depths.

At the sight of her, the papers in his hand were forgotten. She wore the same oversized Oregon State T-shirt as when they had shared his motel room, as when they had shared their night of love, he thought fleetingly, and a burst of heat erupted in his solar plexus. Her hair was loose, still damp from being recently washed, and fell in strands below her shoulders. Gone was the makeup she had worn on stage, and her natural beauty shone with a clarity that was dazzling.

Thinking of the show, impassioned by his own feelings on the subject, he forgot why he had come and spoke his mind without giving thought to hers. "I saw you up there tonight. On the stage at The Pot of Gold.

Why in hell, Maggie? That's not your world. You don't belong in a place like that!'' His voice was sharp, more brutal in tone than he had meant. He may as well have struck her.

Her face, which had been placid up until the time he spoke, suddenly crumpled. She turned from him, moving several feet into the room and Chance saw her shoulders heave slightly as she fought to regain her dignity.

"That's why you came here?'' Her voice trailed over her shoulder. "To tell me how I should make a living? How I should run my life—''

"No, no. Not to lecture.'' Chance moved in a step and, helpless to undo the damage, stopped where he was. He spoke to her back. "Sorry. It was a stupid thing to say. I had no right. Of course.''

"Well, it isn't forever,'' she said with quiet conviction. "Only to make money for Darkstar. I need to put away some cash, get ahead of myself financially.'' She glanced back at him. Their eyes met briefly, and he read torment behind the calm facade. As if the honesty was too much, she dropped her gaze. A question formed in her eyes at the sight of the envelope he held.

He had forgotten, and now with relief, seized the opportunity to uplift the conversation. "Why I've come,'' Chance said immediately. "Darkstar's ownership papers. I was going to leave them in the office, but—'' He held himself in check. More than enough honesty had been delivered for one evening. "I thought I'd better bring them in person. Too valuable to leave floating around.'' With a flourish, he handed them over to her.

Maggie held the envelope in both hands, staring down at the blank paper as if there was something important written across the surface.

"I saw you out there tonight," Maggie said, her eyes skipping briefly to his face, then returning to the safety of the papers in her hand. "I knew it was you. You were just a shadow—the lights block out half of what's going on—but I could tell it was you." She said the last with a slight laugh, the phrase ending with a sound akin to a sigh, as if she had been recalling something far in the past, something foolish, something wonderful. And again, she suddenly looked up.

There were tears in her eyes. She made no attempt to hide them, either being unaware or uncaring; Chance could not tell which.

"I think if ever I wanted to die, it was then," she rushed, the words spilling out in a torrent. "I could see, you know—I could feel everything you were thinking. Up there was this pathetic woman, a failed joke of a human being..." The bitter thought went unfinished.

A slight flush of embarrassment strained the dusky-gold perfection of her compelexion. Collecting herself took only a second. She slapped the envelope against her palm, banishing the indulgence of self-pity, and continuing in a more assertive tone, said with gusto, "I'm going to win this time. All or nothing. That, or I'll die." This last was delivered as a matter of fact, a statement without drama.

It was this lack of melodrama that propelled Chance toward her. Her conviction frightened him. "Lady, you're talking crazy." He had grabbed hold of her shoulders.

"Oh, don't worry!" she said, and in a self-parody of her melodramatic declaration, placed her arm over her forehead. "I won't gas myself."

The feel of his hands on her shoulders became the focal point of their next moment. It was an opportunity to come close, a time to mend everything that had gone before. The possibilities of the present expanded and drew out in his mind, presenting an idyllic future; yet all the while he dared not breathe, nor did he move the slightest muscle in his body. As for Maggie, she remained absolutely still.

Finally, she freed herself, moved a safe distance beyond his reach, and went on with the conversation as if they had been two characters in a film momentarily halted by the projectionist. The reel moved forward, and inwardly, Chance cursed himself again. Really, this was a rerun, nothing more, and he would do well to remember it would always end the same.

"You'll never find a bottle of pills at the side of my bed," she said in a tone that was merely conversational and lightly instructive, no different than had she been discoursing on the mechanical operation of a dishwasher. "Uh-uh. The way it works is, I'll wither away, see. That's the way we Indians do it. People think we die of disease or old age, but it isn't that at all. When our souls dry up, our bodies turn to dust." She turned from him, and then, just as unexpectedly, whirled back around, energized. "I've got to take Darkstar all the way. I've got to."

And he didn't know what to say. So he said nothing at all that would give her the false hope she sought from him, the desired affirmation that she could accomplish what he knew to be patently impossible.

He knew only that he wanted her, all of her, every part—from her outrageous, doomed dream of taking a scraggly filly like Darkstar into the big leagues, to her cantankerous, abrasive personality, to the smoldering heat of her sexuality. He wanted the woman; it was all he could think of as her impassioned words faded in the sad little room.

And he knew, from the words she had just uttered, that he could never have her. Her quest did not—could not—include him. Her's was a singular journey.

He should not have come to the room that night. He wished he had never set eyes on the woman in the first place. God, but he loved her!

"I've got to take off," he said abruptly. He saw something in the black backdrop of her eyes, a lightning flash breaking the placid reserve she had once again assumed. He took off toward the open door.

"Then we won't see each other again?"

At the door, Chance turned. "No," he said evenly and with truth. "Not again. Unless it just happens."

He tried to memorize her face, the way she stood, slightly hip-shot, the stance slightly arrogant in its composure. Everything about her was all so familiar and yet so devastatingly, excitingly new at each glance. He needed to remember the head tipped to the side, beckoning even as it warned trespassers not to stray too close. And the length of her body—the magnificent form!—its movement in bed like flowing gold, with the dark river of her tresses spreading down her shoulders like a wild waterfall. He had to remember all of this.

"Like if I'm hitching a ride on some highway?"

She said it so easily, and with a smile. He smiled, too, forgetting his inner hell for that second.

"I wonder. Would you stop for me again?" she asked.

"No."

She only nodded, and he thought he saw hurt in her face, although it might have been the reflection of his own pain. He wanted to move out, to get gone and start whatever was left of his life without her; but instead, thinking of leaving her with such ambiguity, explained, "It's torture."

"Yes," Maggie said.

It was like they were discussing a third party, not their own personal tragedy.

"Some things can't be," Chance said.

She turned her face from him, looking off to the blank surface of a wall.

"I want to stay...you know that...but—"

"Then do it, stay," she said. "Just for this one night. We can have this, at least. And in the morning, leave. No scenes. No strings."

"Those aren't my rules," he said.

"They aren't mine either," Maggie replied, her eyes full as she looked to him again. "It's just the way things are. Like you said. Like we both know. How can we erase what we are, Chance? We can't wipe away the hurt or the struggles we've known before we met. They've marked us. They're burned into us too deep for us to make it together." The weight of her knowledge drew her head down, and her lashes closed over her eyes like the luxuriant feathers of twin fans. "I feel like I'm already turning to dust, Chance. I feel like I'm slipping away minute by minute. All I have is that horse. And my big dream. And you think it's stupid. Yeah, and why shouldn't you? Well, I know the odds. But Darkstar's all I've got. I need to feel that I still exist. If even for this one night."

Before her next breath, he had closed both the door and the distance between them.

His lips were on hers and she was enfolded within his arms. "Tonight," Chance whispered, stroking the cascade of black locks smelling of soap and her natural body perfume. "We'll have tonight."

Her face lifted and, seeing the beauty of that face, he trembled, his voice a choked cry of sexual passion and sorrow, "My God, woman…my God…" he moaned.

He held heat in his arms, he danced with fire, their bodies moving hungrily in unison. Again and again, as their tongues met, he found himself slipping into the writhing flame of her soul, his body excited to the point of near madness.

Beneath the thin material of her shirt, the nipples of her full breasts seared his body. "Maggie," he whispered, consumed by the feel of her in his arms, "there's going to be a tomorrow, and—"

"Tonight. We've got now, at least we've got this," Maggie whispered, delirious with her own desire. Her fingers traveled like the kisses of butterfly wings over his eyelids, tracing his cheeks, touching the fullness of his open lips. He was hard against her yielding softness, his body an urgent demand against the inviting warmth of her skin beneath the nightshirt. His hands reached beneath the material, cupping the underside of her buttocks and driving her up against him.

He could barely fight against raw impulse. He would throw her on the floor. He would take her right then, the animal in him stronger than the man. And damn the future pain! Damn all consequence! He would have her as he wanted her!

"I need you so much," she whispered, drawing his head down to her breasts. "I can't live without this, can't live without you…"

It was just for the space of a moment, but he opened his eyes, stabbed by the hopeless words, and beyond the door he saw the red flash of neon like an electric splash of blood from an endlessly pulsating open wound. He had to remember what was real, what was false. He had to remember the pain that came from forgetting the difference.

"Maggie, Maggie listen to me!" His words had the effect of a slap. She jumped, and in her moment of surprise he stepped away, breaking the bond of their passion.

His voice was ragged with the urgency of sex. It was all he could do to form coherent thoughts. "Tomorrow morning I'm leaving. Listen to me! I'll be on the road to California by eight. I've got a job there. This is all there is . . . all there is."

She nodded. "And afterward it will hurt. There. I'm dealing with facts, not just dreams."

Her lips were full and moist, the eyes luminous and wide, a woman totally receptive to the pleasures of the body. Nothing had ever been so difficult for him. "I've got to leave now. Got to, babe." His steps were mere stumbles, leading him to the door.

"I wonder which is worse?" Maggie posed from behind him. "To live alone always, always in that vacuum, or to touch briefly—for just one night—and then burn forever in the memory of that moment?"

Opening the door, Chance stood at its portal, staring beyond the room's confines into the red light cast by the neon sign. A tall cactus armed with spikes loomed in silhouette near the office.

"To live in the memory of that moment," he finally answered.

With a push, he closed the door in front of him, the torture selected, and in doing so, shut out the world, along with his better judgment. He knew the hellish future that would await him come morning. But he loved

her, loved her now, and wanted her for this one night—
if that was all he had—far more than he dreaded the
pain that would follow in the months to come.

He turned to her and with a confused sense of joy and
shock, saw mirrored in her eyes the same sorrow and
passion and all the need of his own soul. The unity he
felt with her was staggering. It would be worth it, the
turmoil afterward. To touch Maggie, to know her
heartbeat, to feel the pulse of this extraordinary woman
against his bare chest was worth whatever pain he would
endure.

He started slowly across the room. Maggie met him
halfway. Facing him, she raised her hand and removed
his hat, the shadow of a smile, loving, tender, passing
across her lips. She tossed the fedora to the bed. Slowly,
with total concentration, she caressed the side of his
face, touched her fingers lightly to his lips. Chance shut
his eyes, the emotions rising in him almost too strong to
contain.

With a trembling hand, he took her fingers in his,
kissing each one. "Come," she said, and led him to the
bed.

Clothed still, he lay upon his back, the dark net of her
eyes holding him captive as she slowly undressed. He
had never seen a woman as beautiful—the high sweep
of her full breasts, the supple line of her shoulders edg-
ing into a straight, slender back, the curve of a small
waist and flaring buttocks, a body tense with the energy of life. The face was as phenomenal. Pagan, in its
sculpted, slightly Asiatic form, it was likewise regal. A
casual glance from the depthless black eyes might
promise the world or withdraw the universe.

Finished undressing, she stood for a moment looking down at him, then slipped atop his body and, lying

prone, kissed him. Deft fingers unfastened the buttons of his shirt, loosened his belt, felt below for his zipper, already straining.

Chance rolled over, covering her body with his own. As he maneuvered out of his clothes, his mouth roamed hungrily over her bare flesh, tasting her breasts, licking against her ear.

A slow, luxuriant sigh arose from Maggie. She stretched her body beneath him, abandoning her reserve to the pleasure he offered. His hands slipped beneath her buttocks and she arched into the length of his form pressing against her. Hard and lean, his body was as smooth as softest silk. Insistent and fiery, his movements were inspired. Driven to higher passions, she found her body responding inventively, matching him in bold ways as she discovered new ways to please and tease.

He had resisted entering, prolonging the exquisitely sweet agony of her desire until it was she who cried out for him to take her completely.

Still he resisted. His breath braised her skin, falling short and ragged and hot against her stomach. His fingers smoothed over her inner thighs and the flicker of his tongue turned her veins into a rushing, molten liquid. She was incapable of thought, unable to do more than gasp with each successive spasm of delight. Wave upon wave of sensation undulated through her. Lights burst against the midnight backdrop of her eyelids, exploding sparks into her body, liberating her with each successive burst.

"Chance...yes...yes, yes!" she called, her voice seeming to come from far away. Then, gasping, her fingers twined in his hair, she begged for him to stop. But knowing better he continued, and when she screamed, trembling, she heard his own low growl mix with her abandoned cry.

She was still high, riding the crest of the last frothing wave of ecstasy, when he raised himself. With deliberate slowness, he followed the line of her body, wet with passion, and met her mouth with his.

"Maggie..." he said, "Maggie...look at me."

Her eyes fluttered open and she saw love and desire reflected in his face. There was at that moment nothing hidden between them, nothing separate, just them, the beat of their pulses, the certain knowledge that they belonged together like this.

"It's magic," she breathed.

"No, it's real. This is real, Maggie." He buried his mouth in the concave of her neck.

She felt the tension in his body, barely in check, could feel the tide of his male desire coursing through his loins.

Then he was over her, suspended, watching her face as he brought himself slowly down and made his deliberate thrust.

Maggie was with him, matching each sure movement of his body. The pleasure they found in each other was endless. Incomparable sensations radiated throughout her body. Their union was energizing rather than exhaustive. Each time she thought she had reached her zenith, he brought her to a higher peak, extending the ecstasy until she felt herself dissolving into a pool of bliss.

His body tightened and she felt the rippling of his powerful muscles as a tremor raced through his spine. With his head suddenly thrown back, he cried out, gasping from the inner explosion. "Maggie...oh, my darling..."

She cried afterward and he held her, understanding that it was not from sorrow but from joy that these tears were shed.

"I love you," he said, stroking the damp small of her back.

"I love you," she echoed back. "I do, Chance. I do." Maggie raised herself up to a sitting position on the bed and in wonderment stared down into his face. While they had made love she had felt no embarrassment, but now she blushed, seeing him watching her expression. "What?" she asked.

"You're so goddamned beautiful. How can I ever leave when—God, Maggie." He shut his eyes.

Maggie crossed her arms, huddling into herself as a chill wind blew through her. At his words, the fullness vanished and she was a hollow vessel.

"Maybe..." she said tentatively, her voice echoing in her empty chamber, bouncing off the walls of her mind. "Maybe..."

Chance grabbed her wrist. He held her tight and said, "Not maybe...not maybe, Maggie my dearest, my darling...not maybe. But yes! Come with me, Maggie," Chance said, and rose up from the bed and grabbed her to him. His eyes compelled. His voice commanded.

"I—I want to...to be with you. For always," she said.

"Then do it. Just say yes. Only the one word and we'll have a lifetime."

Maggie was dizzy from the pressure in her head. Things were swirling around crazily, images from the distant past combining with those of the recent few days, with the remnants of their passionate union still filling her.

"Your job in California..."

"It's a fantastic job, Mag. It's better than fantastic."

He was so excited by this small bit of hope she had given him, he was shaking her. Maggie laughed, joy at his joy arising in her. "What will you do?" she asked caught up in his excitement.

"Train horses. For a sinful amount of money. But hell! Pru Bellamy's got a sinful amount of money. She's one sinful woman," he said. "I'm not stopping there, either. No way. I can start over again. With you beside me—Mag? Maggie? What is it?"

Maggie was staring at the place where he should have been, at the place from which his voice was coming from. Only she couldn't see him. A blackness had blotted him from her vision. A sickening feeling enveloped her, grew with every second and, bending over, she held her stomach and rocked back and forth.

Chance reached for her, but she drew back, scrambling away. At the edge of the bed, she found her discarded T-shirt and held it against her as she ran toward the bathroom. But Chance was quick, and intervened.

"Tell me! What is it?"

She was crying soundless tears, staring at him wildly. Then, reaching back with her arm, she brought it forward and slapped his face. Chance staggered back from the impact, stunned by the violence.

"I hate you!" she screamed. "I hate you, hate you, hate you!" And she was upon him with her fists, beating his chest, his face, before he could get control of her hands. Maggie slid to the floor, half dangling as he maintained his grip. Her face rested against his bare legs.

"Tell me now," Chance said. "Just say it reasonable like, so we can both understand. Okay?" He released his hold on her. Slowly Maggie rose up.

"I'm sorry," she said. The fury was contained and cold now. "We'd better stick to our original plan."

"Okay. Whatever you say, lady. But I think I deserve an explanation."

She considered the request. Not looking at him, she said, "I can't go with you to Pru Bellamy's."

"Because of the necklace? I swear to you, Maggie, I'll get it back."

"No you won't. I'm the only one who can do that."

"Ah, your honor."

"My honor," she said. "My life." Her face became a darkened sky against which lightning streaks of sorrow and pain and resentment flashed in quick succession. "I've spent my entire life being second best, always not quite as good, a trifle under par compared to the Pru Bellamys of this world. Do you really think I can follow you to that woman's ranch? That I can live there like some hired-hand underling? Well, I can't! I've got Darkstar now. I'm going to see that she's trained. When she wins, I win. It's me who's going to run that race, Chance. I've come too far to give in now."

"Yeah," he said. "Well, like they say, you gotta do what you gotta do." There was nothing else to say.

In a moment he was dressed. It all happened so fast. It was as if it had never happened.

The door clicked shut.

Maggie stood alone in the room. Not a thought entered her mind. Not a feeling went through her body. How could it? He had taken every part of her with him.

Chapter Eight

There was no excitement in this journey. It was a retreat. Behind the truck, the empty horse trailer lumbered along obediently, dumb to the miserable conditions surrounding its departure.

Chance, who was not oblivious to the facts of his situation, had rolled both windows down, letting in the crisp, early-morning chill to counteract his sluggishness. He had not slept after leaving Maggie. The brown leather of his bomber jacket was cold to the touch. It, like him, was scored with cracks and tears, the work of time and temperature and too much hard living. The beaver collar, turned up against the draft, was likewise frayed. It was becoming a contest as to which of them would last the longest, he or the jacket. He was not placing bets. It was that close.

A bright red Porsche sped by the truck at twice the legal limit. In its wake, a mean, keening sound knifed through the desert silence. Chance found the wail appropriate to his mood. In contrast, a few lengths down the road, he overtook a motor home towing a canary-yellow dune buggy, which ambled along without apparent concern for being anywhere in particular by any particular time. Other than these vehicles, at a spot before eight o'clock, the highway was vacant of other travelers.

The sun had recently stretched awake, and in the distance its spikey rays burst from behind the shadowed face of a mountain. The hard, sharp light of the afternoon was yet to come; now, in the earliest hours of the newborn day, the desert floor bloomed in gold and pink innocence. Above mountains and truck and highway and cacti, oblivious to the jackrabbit that made a frantic dash across the road, the sky hung as clear and blue and undisturbed as a wilderness lake.

On any other morning, Chance would have taken heart at the surrounding beauty. This day was an exception. His face was set into a grim mask of resignation as he drove down the interstate leading out of Las Vegas. No rousing rendition of "California Here I Come" escaped his lips, molded as they were into a hard, tight line. The dramatic exit he had envisioned with such unrealistic bravado the day before required more energy than he owned.

Overhead and to the right, a streak of white showed itself against the blue backdrop. Gripping the steering wheel with both hands, as if the act of keeping the truck on the road required his total dedication, Chance watched the line climb vertically to its invisible, indeterminate destination. Seconds later, the trail abruptly ended, the jet stream immediately turning into a blur of white fuzz. It took only a short while longer before it evaporated and was gone. The sky was serene once again, unmarred, as if the line had never been.

And Chance knew that was how it really was: some things came and went without a trace.

He realized then, looking up into the flat blue panorama, that it was not the haunting beauty of her face, nor the splendid, erotic body that he would miss the most. No, none of these attributes would be responsible for the full, reverberating psychic ache he was already experiencing; oddly, it was the force of Maggie Rand's restless soul, whose fate it was to ever and always reach for the elusive destination, which to him presented the most wrenching loss.

The shrill, piping voice of the woman made Maggie even more crazy than she already felt. Her hand itched to slap the spindly, birdlike form jittering around before her, refusing to listen for a single moment to what Maggie would have her understand. The woman was a small, wizened fixture on the premises, her duties restricted to cleaning out the stalls and seeing that the horses had water. The responsibility of harboring a single unroutine thought seemed more than the woman could endure.

But it was early and there was no one of authority around whom Maggie felt she could trust. There was something vaguely shiftless and too hungry in the faces of the other grooms for Maggie to have confidence that her fee would reach the proper hands. She had always lived with the fear of breaking the legal rules of those who governed the land taken from her people. The system of justice was not truly free from prejudice as she had been taught in the classes shared with her fair-haired school mates. Any of her darker-skinned friends could attest that justice worked on behalf of those who had the resources to bend the power behind the laws. It was, therefore, important in the extreme that this, and all other debts be paid.

"Yes, I know," Maggie explained to the woman for the fifth time. "The office is closed now. But I have to leave. Right now, this moment."

"You can pay in the office at nine o'clock," the woman repeated for the sixth time in her grating chirp. "That's when they get in. I don't have nothing to do with the money end of it. Money's not my responsibility."

"But I told you, I can't wait until nine o'clock." Maggie slapped the money she owed for Darkstar's keep in the woman's limp hand and closed her fist over it. "Just give this to them. Just the way I gave it to you. Like that."

"You should have planned better," the woman whined to Maggie's back.

"I should have done a whole lot of things better!" Maggie returned over her shoulder. She was running, headed for the horse barn where Darkstar was boarded.

Once with the filly, Maggie worked at a fevered rate. A bitless bridle and reins were all the equipment she had for Darkstar. The saddle had been sold to pay for feed. A new one would come later when Maggie could afford it, a saddle that was splendid and in keeping with the champion status the horse was to realize. But this was now, and Maggie sat on the filly bareback, her bedroll and the rest of her belongings anchored to her back with rope.

"What time is it?" she asked in Spanish to one of the hot walkers leading a pony into the bathing area.

"Half-past seven," he replied.

"Which way to the highway, the one to California?"

The man shook his head and called out to a comrade for the answer. Another groom joined the discussion, and one more besides. It took the lot of them three or four minutes to discuss the issue and argue over who was right based upon past fallibilities of judgment. Maggie thought she would either kill them, or die herself from nervous anticipation. When at last everyone was certain, she pushed her heels gently against Darkstar and set off on the prescribed course.

For all its desperation, the ride was still exhilarating. The very air seemed to sanction her wild journey as she lay close against Darkstar's mane, the animal's powerful, graceful legs stretching at full gallop over the hard-packed earth on the shoulder of the highway.

The implacable mountains, the plain dry land, all manner of vegetation from scraggly grasses to plump water-hoarding cacti, the frightened lizard and startled squirrel, the hawk looping overhead—each element of life scintillated with a light that seemed to emanate from the very heart of Maggie.

For this one time in her life, she was not running away from something; for this one time in her life, she was running *to* something! From the darkness of the night, to the light of this glorious day, she was leaving sorrow and racing toward joy.

It was not luck, nor was it a miracle that the truck was up ahead, Chance's truck with the trailer rolling behind it. She had known somehow and absolutely that it would be there when she was.

"Go, go girl!" she prompted Darkstar, and with a jerk of her head, the horse accelerated, its hooves sending crystals of sand scattering in the air around them like jubilant stars.

* * *

It was at first just a splash of darkness in the side mirror. Chance looked again. "Well, hell. Well, blow me away. Well *awal-riight*..." he muttered, still watching the scene unfolding behind him. And what a sight it was! A thrill such as he had never known in his life danced through every cell of his body.

Coming up fast on his side, horse and rider kept to the shoulder of the road at a pace to match the diminished speed of the truck.

"Hey! Hey, mister!"

He looked straight ahead, letting the voice bubbling through the open window enter his heart as well. "Yeah? You talking to me?"

"I'm talking to you. Noticed you've got a vacant space for a horse in the back there."

"Might have," he called back, still maintaining his profile, but nevertheless aware of her every nuance, vocal and physical. Her jet-colored hair was in a long tail, its thickness luxuriant and flung over the shoulder nearest him. She wore tight jeans and soft, high boots laced up the side like moccasins. Against the cold, she wore only a black turtleneck sweater beneath a down vest. As she cantered beside the truck, her firm straight body matched the horse's rhythm. Now, as always, the small pointed chin was held at a slight upward angle, proud, defensive and decisive, a woman daring the world to interfere with her plans; maybe even when there had been no such intention, Chance thought.

"Also noticed you got a vacant seat up front."

Like a covering of rich velvet, the black eyes fell softly upon him, her spell irrevocably claiming him. He answered noncommittally, "Might just have."

"Noticed that I'm a damned fool."

"Fine observation."

"Noticed that I love you," she shouted, bobbing along beside him. "And if you don't stop this thing, I'm not stopping either. I plan to follow you all the way to that bitch Pru Bellamy's farm, even if I've got to carry this horse on my back to do it."

Chance grinned. Even his toes smiled. The hair on his arms smiled. The mole on the back of his neck had to be grinning from one end to the other. He imagined the cracks of his bomber jacket closing themselves up, renewed. He brought the truck to a crawl, then to a stop at the side of the road.

He dared to face her fully.

Astride the horse, Maggie looked over at him through the open window. Darkstar turned her head and fixed him with an intense stare. He felt pinned to the front gate of paradise by four warm, wide, dark, luminous eyes.

"What are you waiting for, woman? Get that animal in the back. Then get your own sorry rump up here. I've got places to go."

Maggie handled the situating of Darkstar on her own. When she came back around to the passenger side, Chance leaned over and opened the door for her. Before she was all the way in, he said with utmost seriousness, "This is for good, Maggie?"

She nodded.

Chance held out his hand and she took it, climbing the rest of the way up to sit beside him.

It was one of those times when any word, any look, any touch would have been a word, a touch, a look too much. Everything they felt was contained in the space of their hearts. That was enough; everything, in fact.

* * *

Pru Bellamy's fifteen-hundred-acre horse ranch, Rancho Costa Lomas—ranch between the ocean and the mountains—was located in a green coastal valley north of San Diego.

Maggie wondered daily if such happiness as she felt was illegal. For one thing, she took joy in the small house she and Chance shared. She had never had her own place before, not something that was solid and freestanding and permanent, anyway. She lavished attention on the white frame dwelling, as if it were not just a modest shelter but a work of high architectural achievement. There were only the three rooms, living room, kitchen, and bedroom, and of course the bathroom, but she understood from reading the real estate ads that bathrooms did not count officially as a separate room.

From her place of employment, a fabric store, Maggie would purchase, at discount, yardage to sew curtains and cover throw pillows. Working at home at night, she made a bedspread and several tablecloths with a sewing machine on loan from the store, and was of late contemplating learning to upholster the furniture that came with the rented house. But her house, just the same. She was so happy, so gloriously happy. Daily, she allowed herself to submit to these extravagant, foreign emotions welling up from within her. There were times when she would be alone and would catch herself staring, looking not at anything in particular but experiencing the euphoric state of her satisfying new life. Life! Love! The words were a constant chant in her heart.

There was, however, one splash of darkness against the backdrop of her miraculous new existence with

Chance, and that stain was the intrusive presence of Pru Bellamy.

Maggie had done what she could to blot the woman's presence in their lives out of her everyday reality. Yet, every so often, she could not help but to lapse into spells of deep, if momentary, depression over the blond barracuda's controlling influence over Chance. That Pru pulled Chance's purse strings was a bitter fact, but a situation within the bounds of Maggie's endurance. However, with a female's territorial instinct, Maggie sensed a parallel interest Pru held in Chance, one having nothing to do with his professional services.

"Does Pru Bellamy know we're living here together?" she asked Chance one night. They had just finished the stew she had prepared for dinner, and Chance was gathering up his things to return to the ranch. A horse was going to foal that night, and Pru wanted him to be there for the birthing process.

"No," Chance said. The response was remote.

Maggie scraped pieces of untouched fat into a tin can. Her fingers tightened around the fork. The sight of the utensil's pointed prongs, with their co-ability to cause mayhem, sparked Maggie's imagination. A low-grade anger rose with her words. "Why's that? I don't see how you could work for her for three months without her knowing anything about me being here."

"It's never come up." Chance was checking the time.

"Well, maybe it should." She stood with a dish in her hand, looking at him coldly.

"Why?" Chance faced her, squaring off with his shoulders, legs slightly apart, ready for their first fight since she had climbed into the truck outside of Vegas. "What possible difference should it make to her what we do with our lives?"

"Not our lives—your life. There's no damned reason for you to be going back there tonight. They've got a vet. They've got plenty of other people over at the farm who can handle things."

"What are you saying?"

"You know what I'm saying. You've got to know... I'm saying that she—" Maggie's pride overrode her anger. "Nothing." She ran water into the sink.

"Hey!" He came over and put his arms around her. At contact, his hands instinctively rose to her breasts. She closed her eyes. Warmth rushed through her, countless memories of lovemaking tumbling through her mind, her body a willful conspirator with Chance's physical demands.

He spoke against her ear, his mouth brushing through the stray locks of hair that had escaped from the rubber band at the nape of her neck. The heat of his breath excited, incited her.

"You're jealous," he said with a hint of pleasure. "Why?"

He looked to see what impact his words had taken, but she wrenched her head around in the other direction to escape his amused look. Chance's smile was always slanted, as if nature had engineered his face to divide into two equal parts, angelic and devilish. Maggie had always found this look of impish sensitivity irresistible. No doubt Pru Bellamy found it likewise charming. His ego was clearly having a feast.

"How could you be, Maggie? Jealousy? When we have all this together?" She melted against him, oblivious to everything but the surge of her desire, which allowed him freedom to run his hands up her skirt, to find the elastic rim of the nylon beneath and explore the moist proof to his words.

Gently, he pressed his mouth against hers, his tongue demanding, hungry to possess her. Clinging to him, returning his ardor with her entire being, she pressed into him, and with his hands already slipping the nylon down, he lifted her into his arms and carried her to the bedroom.

He was undressed in seconds, his hard, taut form stretching over her on the bed. The arms and shoulders, tanned and smooth-muscled, rippled with the strain of his desire as he pushed aside the material of her skirt with the same sense of power and domination he might have used to banish a block of granite should it have stood in his way to have her at that moment.

So passionate was their lovemaking, it came close to mild violence; the mutual intensity of their sensual demands seeming to go beyond mere tactile pleasure, as they both reached for something past the physical.

Afterward, when Chance had hastily showered and dressed again, after they had exchanged parting words of love and he had left to attend the foaling, Maggie lay in the small dark room. Her mind elsewhere, her eyes traced the outlines of the paltry furnishings in the dim light. There was only the bed and a single, high dresser. The smell of Chance was still with her, lingering on her body, on the sheets, natural and masculine. Hanging in the air, the faded hint of cologne applied after his shower could never be as compelling.

Yes, of course he loved her, and she, him. Her jealousy of Pru Bellamy, as Chance had assured her, was unfounded.

Maggie was behind the cutting counter, the balance of a roll of fabric unfurled. Carefully, she folded the five yards of material she had just measured and cut.

"It's really beautiful," she commented to the customer, a stout, pleasant woman with apple-red cheeks and dimples that winked merrily whenever she smiled.

The Butterfly Fabric Boutique was a small countrified yardage shop, catering to the upscale clientele of the area who liked to fancy themselves as authentic rural dwellers, when the truth was they were anything but the "plain folk" they played at imitating. Most of them, Maggie had learned, were dyed-in-the-wool urban sophisticates who owned second and third homes in Los Angeles and New York, Denver perhaps, or a hideaway in Palm Beach. Even a villa in Europe was not an exception. Likewise, many of the women who frequented the shop had no knowledge of sewing, but craved the unusual and original. It was their habit and pleasure to enter with a decorator or personal seamstress, hunting for an exotic weave of silk or wool to be fashioned into a one-of-a-kind-item.

On the day Maggie stood with her dimpled customer, it was three weeks after Christmas. The California sun was a pale white ball hanging over the patch of Pacific, visible between two stores on the ocean side of the street, opposite the Butterfly. Baskets of trailing green ferns suspended before the bay window looked like fine lace and added to the cozy atmosphere. Even the bells on the door had an unusual sweetness, ringing like a cheerful voice to welcome all visitors across the Butterfly's portal.

As the bells rang now, Maggie glanced briefly away from her customer. A group of four women entered. Instantly, Maggie identified three of the women as frequent visitors to the Butterfly. They were landed-gentry types who frequented the shop mainly to find decorations for their numerous charity functions or personal social affairs, which they produced on equally lavish scales, forever in competition with the last hostess.

But it was the fourth woman who stole the pulse from Maggie's heart.

She was taller than the other three and appeared brilliantly illuminated, as if there was a hidden spotlight following wherever she moved. The effect was intentional, of course, the drama engineered, Maggie very well knew, by the flurry of pale blond hair framing the famous face of Pru Bellamy, hair that fell to the shoulders of the white riding jacket with its elegant leather-patched elbows. Her riding breeches were a light creamy beige and the gleaming high boots, clacking authoritatively over the planked floor, chestnut brown.

At the same instant as Maggie's recognition took place, Pru Bellamy's glance also fell upon her.

The smile on Pru's famous mouth froze. At the same time, her eyes narrowed like a cat's judging the distance and force it would take to pounce and destroy a mouse out of escape range of its hole.

Maggie's customer was saying something to her, and it was with relief and a still-weakened pulse, that she turned her attention back to business.

But she was not to get off so easily. The hole was indeed too far for the mouse.

After the cash transaction had been completed at the register, Maggie was overtaken by Pru Bellamy as she made haste to get to the back stockroom.

"Well, well..." Pru said, stepping quickly in Maggie's path. Her arms were folded across her chest. She appeared relaxed, in control.

Fiery heat rushed to Maggie's face. The scene at the Azteca rose sharply in her mind. *Her necklace! Her*

magnificent, cherished necklace, in the possession of
this jealous, mean, careless woman!

"I see you've given up feathers."

"Excuse me," Maggie said, and made to step around
Pru. She liked her job and needed it. It would not do to
have a scene here with Pru Bellamy and risk being
shown the door. She was not so naive as to think social
clout in these parts did not count for much. Pru and her
pals spent too much money at the Butterfly for the
owner to overlook a nasty scene; a boycott would hurt,
and Maggie's services could easily be duplicated by another person.

But Pru took hold of her arm faster than she could
get away. Prickling with electric rage, Maggie slanted a
meaningful look to the polished fingernails on the
sleeves of her navy pullover, then raised her dark eyes
to Pru. Maggie did not want a fight, but there was a
point at which she would not back down. The warning
look was enough. Apparently reassessing the climate,
Pru released her hold and stepped slightly back.

Physically she might have retreated, but that was all.
Her rancid tongue continued on its original course.
"News doesn't travel quite as fast in small towns as
one would expect, does it? Who would ever have
dreamed…?" Pru ran her eyes down Maggie, then back
up, slowly, with social insult covering every inch of the
journey. "I'm truly surprised. A man like Chance, and
you?" She shook her head with humorous disbelief.

"We're not in your casino now, Pru. I'd watch out."

"But Chance is in my employ."

"Chance is in my bed," Maggie returned with equal
coldness.

An inner darkness shadowed Pru's face. "For how
long? Do you honestly think someone like you could

hold a man like Chance Harris with nothing more than a body he can play with? If that's what you're thinking, you've got surprises ahead, doll."

"Get out of my way," Maggie said. "Get out of my sight."

Pru smiled and sauntered off to join her friends in the front of the store.

In the stockroom, Maggie leaned her head against a shelf containing boxes of sewing goods. Overwhelmed by nausea, she kept her head down and inhaled to control the rage and fear tearing at her insides.

Ten minutes went by before she was able to return to the front room. The women had left after spending over $2000 for fabric that would be used to make decorations for a charity dinner to follow a charity horse race.

Two days later Maggie leaned over the railing of Darkstar's corral, watching the animal cavort like the youngster she truly was; just a girl yet, with dreams to realize, as once Maggie herself had been long ago. For the first time since her confrontation with Pru Bellamy, a smile arose in Maggie's heart. Her fears that she had let desperation cloud her judgment as to the animal's potential were banished, the validity of her hopes confirmed, as she objectively examined the filly's lithe, perfect form.

She and Chance had searched for a place to board Darkstar, a place close enough to the house to be convenient, and cheap enough for Maggie to afford. Their search brought them to the farm of Sam Johnson, a retired trainer, only a mile from the rented cottage. If Chance had the truck, Maggie could walk the distance easily.

Maggie called Darkstar's name, urging her to come.

As if able to understand English, the filly trotted over to the railing and whinnied an enthusiastic greeting.

Maggie put her hand out flat, protection from the sharp teeth that could inadvertently snap fingers in two. Darkstar nudged her palm, tasting the salt from her skin.

For two days Maggie had been afraid to come. Quiet at work, she had gone about her duties by rote, her mind absorbed with Pru Bellamy's mocking assessment of her worth as a person and as a woman. At home she was distant. Chance, noticing, had probed to discover the cause. Of course she could not tell him. How could she! She felt small enough as it was; to voice her fears that the cruelty of Pru Bellamy's opinion of her might also be accurate, would lend credence to the allegations.

The words Pru had thrown at her in the fabric shop were like a hard, tight ball composed of every fear and hurt Maggie had ever experienced. Throughout her life, Maggie had caught that ball, the impact a blow to her gut, time and time again. Hunched and bent double over her pain, she had always quietly retreated. She had brooded her life away.

Now she would not. Lying awake beside Chance in the dark, she had listened to his easy, rhythmic breathing. She had felt the warmth of his hard body, which earlier had pressed his passionate love into her. She would not lose this man. She would not allow Pru Bellamy's words to steal her love, her very life, without, at least, a fight.

To the finish it would be, a fight to the finish line, Maggie revised, her fingers rubbing downward over the lean, smooth nose of Darkstar.

She would no longer run away and bury herself in feelings of unworthiness or fear of confrontation because of her place in the social scale.

"What do you think, girl? Are you ready to show the world your stuff?"

A response was not forthcoming from Darkstar. She had noticed a friend returning from a ride and took off with hooves flying to where two familiar forms approached.

Maggie also followed the fence around, greeting Sam Johnson with a silent smile. Sam never talked much, but then, neither did she, and that was one of the reasons, she suspected, he allowed her on the premises. They both liked horses more than they did people. She helped to unsaddle the horse and insisted on currying him down, while Sam prepared a vitamin mixture with oats.

"How much would you want for working with my horse?" she asked.

"Honey, I'm retired."

"I know, but as a favor—"

"I don't owe nobody any favors."

"I know, but—"

"You sure know a lot," he interjected.

"I don't know much about training racehorses, though. You do. You know everything."

Sam hitched his head in the direction of Darkstar, who had suddenly taken to gamboling about. "That one?"

"That one."

"Who's she out of?" he asked.

"No champion blood stock," Maggie said. "Even so, she's special. I want to race her."

"Your boyfriend...I hear he's maybe number one in the business now. You get him to help."

Maggie shook her head. "No. I can't. He's busy."

The man looked at her, shrewd gray eyes uncovering the lie.

"It's something I've got to do on my own. And I don't want him to know about it. It's kind of a surprise. Only much more."

The man still looked at her, probing more deeply now with his inquiring eyes. Then he looked to Darkstar.

"She's a weanling," Maggie said. "It's time to start working with her."

"Honey, I'm close to seventy now. I went out of this business at the top. I was number one and I worked with the number one horses, bloodlines as long as that road out there. Didn't start that way. Started with stuff like you've got here. Sometimes I won, and mostly I lost. Kept at it, though. Made my way in this business. But I might just as easy have failed. When I take my last breath I don't plan to be remembered as an old jackass who lost it in the end, running fifth-rate horses."

"You won't lose with Darkstar," Maggie said.

"What makes you know that?"

"I just know it."

"Desperation. You got something to prove? Huh, that it, girl?" He laughed, and the gray eyes slipped into her for a second, making his confirmation. There was something else in his voice when he next spoke, some added note of perhaps respect, when he said, "And just who's going to be running that race? You or the horse?"

"Both of us," she said, because it was the truth and Sam Johnson already knew it.

"I'll be watching. I'll be watching. Now you hand me that hoof pick, and see that can of oil? Give it here. Old bones aren't what they were."

Maggie returned with the items. He didn't look at her when he took them, his mind appearing absorbed by a circular lesion on the horse's hock; even so, she knew that she was already being watched.

In the next two weeks, Chance was busier than ever. Some nights he didn't come home until after ten o'clock. Maggie tried not to mind, tried hard to put her trust in him and not let her suspicions get the best of her.

Exhausted, he would fall into bed, barely having time to hold her before he fell asleep. By four in the morning, he was already walking out the door.

"I've been training Darkstar," she told him one night when he came home for dinner.

His mind was elsewhere. Finally he responded, although vaguely. "Darkstar. You've been . . . ?"

Maggie nodded. "Could you maybe come by tomorrow afternoon to see her?"

"Can't, Mag. Have to ride up to Hollywood Park to check out a new stallion Pru's making an offer for."

"The next day?"

"I've got to—" He stopped, obviously seeing the disappointment in her face. "Sure. Okay. Thursday afternoon."

But Thursday afternoon he did not come. She waited with Darkstar until it had turned dark and her teeth were chattering from the cold because the early March day had been unseasonably warm and she had not bothered with a sweater.

She was lying in bed when he slipped into the cottage at close to twelve o'clock.

"Maggie?" He stood in the bedroom door, his frame blocking the light from the other room. "I'm sorry. I'm really sorry. I tried to call you but—"

"I wasn't here. I was waiting for you."

"God," he said. "I'm so sorry. Pru had me meet with two Arabs—"

"I don't give a damn!"

"I'm doing this for us... So we'll have something good, Maggie. So you don't have to work in casinos and yardage shops and someday you can have a real horse to take the biggest stake races. It's for this I'm—"

"What are you saying, damn you? That Darkstar's not a real horse? That I'm some piece of low life because I take my body to work in places where your fancy boss lady wouldn't be caught dead? Maybe the air over there's gotten too thin for your brain. Maybe you just don't think straight anymore."

Chance had crossed the room, and in a sweeping motion, yanked her out of the bed and into his arms. "Shut up! Just quiet down, will you? I didn't mean to put you or your horse down. I'm only telling you that I have a job to do. I'm a trainer for some of the best horses on this planet. Not only is a lot of money involved, my entire financial future—not to mention my own sense of accomplishment and my public reputation—is at stake here. If it means that for a while I can't come running to you when you want me to, then that's the way it's got to be."

Maggie pushed herself from his arms. "No," she said, "I'm not going to be second place to Pru's interests. She's bought you, Chance. Your soul's gone, and God only knows she's hard after your body, too."

He didn't say anything to that.

"So," Maggie said, "it's true."

"I've never—"

"Yet."

"Whatever she feels, I have no interest in her."

"Then tell her you want nights off to be with me. And you want an afternoon now and then to help me with Darkstar."

"Okay, all right," Chance said after a long spell of silence.

Another night passed without making love. They lay beside each other, their thoughts stirring the air between them, but neither could touch the other.

At four in the morning, Chance crept silently out of bed. He was gone within the half hour.

Prucilla Bellamy's office was paneled in wormy cherry wood, antique boards taken from a dismantled eighteenth-century estate once belonging to a Virginia statesman. Framed pictures of champion horses adorned the walls. There was a fire in the hearth and flowers on the mantle, before which Pru Bellamy stood listening to Chance.

"I understand," Pru said, her brows knitted in concern. "I can understand just how you feel. Of course you're entitled to a personal life. Only for now, it's impossible to give you any extra time off. You know that, Chance. And to be honest, I'm surprised you'd even ask."

"I'm not asking, Pru. I'm telling you."

"Oh? Really." Her eyes took on a glacial quality, as did her voice when she continued. "I don't plan on being beaten," Pru said. "I'm a realistic woman. I'm flexible, and I'll do what I have to, to get what I want. I want to win the Breeder's Cup Classic at Hollywood Park. The winner's purse is $1,350,000. If you can bring Shambhala in first, I'll give you a free stud fee. But that kind of gift buys me a year of your time. I own you for that year."

The offer resounded in Chance's head like a jet engine's roar. Shambhala was a year-old colt, projected to be a champion, and sired by one of the greatest stakes horses ever known in the industry. The stud fees on a horse of Shambhala's lineage, along with what was surely to become a monumental track record, could be as much as $500,000, maybe even more before all was said and done. In the case of Northern Dancer, the outstanding Thoroughbred stallion of the century, an assignation could range up to one million dollars. Chance's mind worked like a computer: it cost a minimum of $24,000 a year to maintain Darkstar on the farm, not to mention what it would cost when Maggie raced her on the circuit—if it ever came to that—only one in a thousand horses made it to a race.

What Pru Bellamy was offering him was unbelievable. With the right mare mated to Shambhala, their progeny would have a certain chance at the big stakes winnings. After that, they could syndicate; there was literally no limit to what they could make. The money, the esteem, the freedom! All of these realities circulated through Chance's mind. A year of personal sacrifice was a small price to pay for the lifetime of heaven on earth that would follow for Maggie and him.

Behind Pru, the fire blazed red and blue and green, snapping sparks up the flue.

"Yeah," Chance said. "I see your point."

"I rather thought you would," Pru said.

"Then I'm yours for a year. And the horse *will* come in first. That's a promise."

Her diamond earrings were almost dull compared to the smile Prucilla Bellamy flashed. "This has made me so very happy, Chance. I just can't tell you, how much. You know how it is, with Digger always working, and now away on his darn world tour. Why, these horses are my entire life, my whole world. And tonight,'' Pru said, ''you and I will celebrate our new deal. We'll open a bottle of champagne, and how about lobster!'' She reached for her telephone and pressed the line to the kitchen. ''Have Manuel run down to the village and get about four live lobsters for tonight's dinner. I'm having company. No, just one other person. But my appetite's suddenly very stimulated. Very.'' She smiled at Chance as she placed the phone in the cradle. ''There,'' she said. ''Everything's handled.''

''Pru—'' Chance began.

''No, Chance. Don't start again, okay? You're not some kid. You know the score. I know the score. And so does Maggie. We all have to choose. You made a right decision. If she doesn't want you, doesn't trust you enough, then...''

''That's what this is about, isn't it? It's about Maggie.''

''Partly,'' Pru admitted. ''You can do better.''

''No, I couldn't.''

''Anyway,'' Pru said, ''I've made you an offer, fair, no matter what its motivation.''

''True. For a year you've purchased my soul. But not,'' Chance said, smiling, ''my body, Pru.''

''Agreed,'' Pru said, also with a smile, ''that's one thing I can't force. But you never know about these things. You might have a change of heart before all's over and done.''

''I've got to call Maggie,'' he said. ''She was expecting me home.''

Pru handed him the receiver. ''I'll let you handle this in privacy.''

"You're all heart," Chance said, as Pru strolled toward the door. The line was ringing as she closed the door.

Maggie answered. "Hello?"

"Maggie..." Chance began.

Chapter Nine

You could try to understand," Chance said. Agitated to the point where it was impossible to remain still, he paced the length of the small living room.

He moved with such vigor that Maggie thought his momentum would take him crashing beyond the room's boundaries. His leather jacket was draped over the back of an armchair. The light blue dress shirt he had donned, tieless and with the sleeves rolled to the elbows, early that day, now hung limp on his body.

Since he had left that morning, deep creases had appeared on his forehead. Or at least Maggie had not noticed them before. She saw him differently now, almost as a stranger. She felt she had never known him, never. The man she loved could not do this to them. Defecting. That was the word. Chance had defected.

Blue hollows circled his eyes, eyes shadowed with truths to which he would not admit, eyes that seemed to meld into the room's dim light. He looked as tired as she felt. It had been an endless night for her, waiting for him to return. She had hours in which to mull over the news he had told her over the telephone.

It was a call she would never forget.

The aroma of the roast she had prepared for their dinner had been wafting around her, even as he said he could not be home to eat it. He was going to stay at the ranch. He had been given an amazing opportunity, Chance had told her, one that would benefit them both beyond their wildest imaginings.

Well, her imagination was plenty wild. Her imagination saw the situation in full technicolor, complete with sound effects—Prucilla Bellamy panting up to Chance, offering her body, offering her money, offering her position in the world to him. And taking Chance from the Indian.

He had hung up, going off to keep his bargain with the devil.

And she? She had no one, not even the devil with whom to commiserate!

She had thrown the roast against the wall, spattering juice over the entire kitchen. It was still there. What did she care of cleanliness and orderliness, about the moon falling or the sun becoming cold?

A year, he had told her. He was to offer his total services—ha!—to Pru for a year's length of time, after which if he kept to his end of the bargain, he would have a stud right to one of the most famous racehorses perhaps in all of racing history.

It was for them he had agreed to Pru's offer. He hoped Maggie would understand.

Oh yes, she understood.

Those hours while she waited for him to return, she had time enough to comprehend the situation. At first she had exploded. Then, with a saint's forebearance, she had forgiven him his trespasses, only to rage against him the following minute. Over and over she had made decisions and again and again she had altered them as the next train of churning emotions rampaged through her mind.

Now she stood calmly by the front window, knowing the only solution to the situation was the bag packed with Chance's things placed by the door. The first light of day was beginning to seep through the Venetian blinds.

"Maggie! For God's sake! Don't do this to us!"

She reeled around. "I'm only accommodating you. Go. Go to Pru Bellamy. Work for Pru Bellamy! Be her slave, her lover—"

"She means nothing to me." Chance threw up his arms. Like lead weights, they fell again to his side. "I've told you and I've told you."

"If that's true, then tell her."

"Tell her? She knows. I don't have to tell her. She knows you're the only woman I want."

"Don't you understand what this is doing to me?"

"Yes. Yes, I think I have some idea. And I hate it. But Maggie girl, my Maggie..." He came over, placing his hand softly against her wet cheek. "This crazy thing you have about not feeling as good as other people. Well, it's—" He was at a loss. "It's just crazy. And destructive. To us. To you. It's not real."

"It's real," she said.

"No, only to you."

"Pru looked me in the eye and told me—"

"Anyone can look anyone in the eye and say anything they want. They can call me a king today, and a bum tomorrow. But who the hell cares? I know what I am."

"But I don't know who I am."

"And that's something I can't give you, that knowledge. I can't do that for you, Maggie, no matter how much I want to. You're the only one," Chance said sadly. He looked to the packed suitcase. "So." He sighed. "You're serious about that?"

"Yes," she said. "I love you too much to have you coming home at odd hours of the morning. Or maybe not coming home at all some nights. Maybe nothing would be going on. But it's too much for me, the wondering. This is all I can handle, being alone."

"Then I'm sorry," Chance said. "But I've got to do what I know is right. For me. And for us."

"For us? For us!" Maggie exploded.

"Yes! Look, I love you. Whether I'm here or at the ranch, that's not going to change. And at the end of the year, I'm still going to love you. I'll be waiting for you. Regardless."

He picked up his suitcase and waited with it for a moment by the door, allowing her the time to come to him, to say something to make him stay.

But she didn't. He grabbed up his jacket and, swinging the suitcase around, walked out of the cottage. His truck engine started up, and a moment later Maggie heard the slow crush of gravel beneath tires.

It wasn't until she had picked up the roast and cleaned the floor and cabinets of the debris from the previous night's tantrum, that she returned to the bedroom.

And there it was: the hat, forgotten. His silly, wonderful, faded, crooked and bent and dearly beloved hat, lay on the dresser. He had put it there that morning when he had crept stealthily in, thinking—hoping!— that she would be asleep.

Oh, Chance. Oh, chance, my darling, my love.

Lifting the hat, she crushed it against her face, smelling the scent of him, holding against her flesh all she had left of him.

Rising early, before her hours began at the Butterfly, Maggie worked with Darkstar herself.

Sam Johnson allowed her to use the practice track. For forty-five days, Maggie galloped Darkstar for a maximum one mile ride every morning. She walked her forward through the starting gate, then backward, to familiarize her with the fearsome equipment from which the filly would some day take off in the presence of thousands of breathless spectators.

Now only one man watched—Sam Johnson.

Silent like a wraith, he would intermittently appear in his long camel-hair coat, the early-morning, inner-coastal mist swirling around him as he stood by the fence. Always, before Maggie had dismounted Darkstar, the aging retired trainer was gone. Such was the extent of their relationship.

After forty-five days Maggie turned Darkstar out. She was to lounge in the field in the soft grass for two months. It was a time for the horse's psychological development. It was a time for meditation, animal style.

"What do you think?" Maggie said to Sam Johnson on an afternoon visit. He had been watching Darkstar when Maggie came up beside him.

"She's a good little lady," he conceded.

It was a warm May afternoon, but Johnson wore a blue padded windbreaker and a long scarf wrapped around his neck. Peculiar garb for the time of year, Maggie thought, but then remembered his age. She wondered after his health.

Sam Johnson gave a sidelong glance to Maggie. "In spite of being born on the wrong side of the paddock."

"That's *why* she's a good little lady," Maggie snapped. "Just why. She'll know how to fight hard."

Sam Johnson didn't say anything. He walked away, tending to his own horses.

She didn't see him again for two weeks. Then one afternoon, after spending time with Darkstar, she walked up the long drive leading away from the stables to Johnson's house proper. His maid let her in, and several minutes later, Maggie was shown into Sam Johnson's study.

Fully dressed in a red cardigan sweater and charcoal-gray slacks, he sat in the corner of a leather couch, looking smaller than she had remembered him. Immediately she felt her visit to be a mistake. Her presence was intrusive. Beyond the confines of these walls, he could hide his frailty behind coat and scarf and the bustling appearance of responsibility to the animals he still owned; but here she was, an invader of his refuge, and he was exposed as a lonely, slightly structured man in his waning days.

"I didn't mean to...well, I hadn't seen you in a while, and I...are you ill?" she asked.

"I'm old. But I'm still alive," he shot back. "So don't you worry. I've got some steam left, enough to—" He stopped. "How's that horse?"

"Great. I'm putting her in a stall for two weeks."

Johnson nodded. "Good, good. Put her in one of the primo ones. One of mine," he said. "You tell Rudy I said so."

They stared at each other, sharing a visual handshake.

"Thank you," Maggie said. "Thank you very much, Mr. Johnson."

"Sam, dammit. Friends—the ones who still remember me, or haven't already cashed in their tickets—call me Sam."

"Sam," Maggie said, and smiled. So did he, just a little. "Well, then...I guess I'd better be off." He didn't say goodbye and neither did she. Neither of them were much for formalities.

Two weeks later to the day, Sam appeared at the stall where Darkstar had been lodged as part of her training process. "Put her in the paddock with my horses," Sam ordered in his scratchy voice. "Might as well associate with animals of quality, get her used to the society life. Let the little lady stay there seven weeks."

This was the first absolute advice he had given her. No, it was an order. Maggie said nothing. She was afraid to, as if to acknowledge his concrete help was to break the spell that had prompted the assistance.

But on the day full training began, no guardian angel in the form of Sam Johnson appeared on the scene. She had hoped to see him there. She had looked for him to drift into view, just as he had in the past. In her wildest imaginings she had thought he might even come up with an accomplished rider for Darkstar, someone who galloped Johnson's own horses and would know how to get the best out of the filly.

Instead, she hired a young groom, inexperienced, a boy of sixteen whose Mexican family had recently been granted visas to work in the States legally. Every day Arturo galloped Darkstar a half mile, slow and easy. Afterward, Maggie would help with the filly's bathing and they would put her on a circular walker to cool her down from the exertion of the exercise.

Whereas Arturo had been a bargain-basement choice, by the time the horse was being galloped for one and a half miles a day, a period lasting for fifteen to twenty days, there was a marked improvement in his riding style.

"I love this horse," he said one day, when Maggie led them back to the bathing area after a workout. "She is going to win the big ones," he added with conviction.

So, what did he know, this kid from south of the border, this poor kid with holes in his faded jeans? What the hell did he know? She wanted that kind of statement from someone like Johnson. "You just want to keep your job, Arturo. Cut the bull."

Arturo was insulted. A curtain of gravity descended over his expression and his voice took on what Maggie recognized as the timbre of an older man, the cadence closely matching one of the professional trainers who occasionally paid the farm a visit. She realized they had something in common, she and the kid from the other side of the border. They both wanted something better for themselves. They wanted to shine, too—like those others.

"No," Arturo said. "I know this. And even Mr. Johnson, he say the same. He say, this horse going to take the big prizes. Me, too. I want to take the big prizes," he said with heated passion.

In spite of her resolve to remain unemotional, Maggie's eyes filled. "Yeah," she said, "don't we all?" Her heart went dancing on its own, leaping and twirling in an inner cascade of bright sunbeams. Sam Johnson had said that!

That he had, was confirmed three months later. Darkstar was galloping through the deep soft earth of the practice track for two miles every day. She had also mastered the starting gate, entering it as calmly as she did her own stall.

It was then that Johnson reappeared in their lives. Marching up to where Maggie watched Arturo gallop the last quarter mile, Johnson looked wan. But his voice contained a vigor Maggie hadn't heard before as he took over her life. It was clear she had no say in the matter.

"This horse's going to move to the track at Del Mar," he said. "She'll stay in my stables."

"I didn't think you kept stables there anymore, Sam."

"Well, things change, things change all the time, don't they?"

And she had to admit they did.

Balmy weather, palm trees, endless blue sky, a light breeze blowing off the Pacific—all of this was Del Mar Race Track, and more.

Here was the glamour. Here were the horses with bloodlines so rich, so rare, that the very mention of their names brought dizziness to Maggie as she walked through the stable area with Arturo and Sam Johnson. Darkstar had been vanned in earlier that day.

"You're with me now," Johnson said. "You walk proud. You're with the best. You're going to run the best. And," he said, pointedly casting a glance to both Maggie and the tiny Arturo beside her, "you two are the best this track's going to see for a long time to come. Don't forget it."

Neither Arturo nor Maggie said anything. The statement meant too much to both of them. They were the best—the wetback and the redskin. They were, their footsteps seemed to repeat, as indeed they moved proudly along beside Sam Johnson. Sam Johnson was an emperor, a wizard. He knew everyone there by first name, and everyone knew him.

He even knew Chance Harris.

Maggie saw Chance first, coming forward with his head bent low as the man beside him related some incident complete with ardent gestures. Chance glanced up briefly to where she walked with Sam and Arturo, stared for a moment, as if not comprehending, and then, as her presence registered fully, he turned pale and stopped in his tracks. The man with Chance also halted, his story cut short as he noted Chance's lack of involvement.

"Hello, Maggie," Chance said as she and the two men came up.

The weight of his stare was a bruise to her heart. "Chance . . ." Even to manage his name was an effort. Her mind had stopped; she did not know what else to say. What was there to say? They had not seen each other since the day she had set his suitcase by the front door and he had taken it, taken himself, and taken their love, away.

"How's Darkstar?" Chance inquired. He had on slacks, beige with neat creases, and over the pants an unstructured light-blue sports jacket softly blending with the cream polo shirt. He looked wonderful, prosperous, too; he looked like a man she had once almost known.

"Fine. Great. Sam Johnson's helping me . . ." Her voice trailed off. She looked to Sam for confirmation, but he and Arturo were gone. The man in Chance's company had likewise evaporated from the scene.

"I know," Chance said, nodding appreciatively. "And he thinks you've got a shot at the big stuff."

"Not a shot. Darkstar's a sure thing," Maggie corrected.

They were talking horses, but beneath the civilized talk was a different conversation. Feelings vibrated in each breath, in every casual glance, in the shrug of Maggie's shoulder and the shifting of Chance's boot in the fine, loose dirt.

"You left your hat," Maggie said.

There was a long pause. "I'll get it sometime," Chance replied finally.

"It's been six months. How did you live without it?" Maggie smiled. "I should think it would be like living without your head." Chance laughed. There was for an instant that old good feeling between them. Then the happiness died as they remembered more than the hat. "I guess you got yourself another one," Maggie said with an excess of emotion. "Did you?" she challenged.

"That one was special." The blue eyes bored into her with a meaning that was not lost between them.

"But not irreplaceable..." Maggie replied flatly. Behind Chance, Prucilla Bellamy, in tight jeans and high boots and white silk blouse, came swinging toward them. Maggie felt herself growing smaller with every step Pru took. She hated herself even more than Pru at that moment. "See you around maybe," Maggie said and retreated.

After that she did not have occasion to run into Chance alone. Prucilla became a ubiquitous presence at the track. From what Maggie understood, with Digger conveniently on his world concert tour, Pru was devoting her considerable energies to her racing enterprise. A person didn't have to be a fortune teller to know that Chance Harris figured greatly in her schemes.

The hat, Chance's hat, remained uncalled for in its place on top of the dresser. Once Maggie had inadvertently placed a small vase of flowers beside it. When she looked at it later, in passing, an image of a shrine rose to mind. Appalled, she took the flowers away. But the hat remained, untouched, as sacred, in actuality, as any icon might be to a worshiper.

At first, like a shy child in a new school, Darkstar had to grow accustomed to her strange new surroundings. Physical and psychological adjustments were made. She did not, in the beginning, take well to the large blanket thrown over her back. Nor did she immediately adjust to the charged atmosphere created by the hundreds of high-strung beasts whose Thoroughbred blood pumped with aggression and whose hooves took arrogant claim of the turf. Darkstar was no longer the singular star she had been in the small world of Sam Johnson's farm.

In the mornings Arturo backtracked Darkstar, galloping her counter-clockwise around the track, while the older, more experienced horses ran against one another in clockwise rotation. "She wants to go with the others," Arturo bragged. "Already she wants to compete," he told Maggie and Sam.

And Sam gave the okay to let her gallop around the outside of the track. They were light workouts at one and half miles a day, nothing clocked. It was too soon.

"Nice stride," Sam commented, Maggie watching at the rail beside him. "Action's together."

The workouts continued at one run every six days or so. Then Sam brought the time down to five day intervals, telling Arturo to ask for more speed.

The horse responded, moving with freed, dynamic joy over the black softness of the track.

Darkstar had a full workout in early August. She was running six furlongs and clocked in at 1:12 flat from the gate.

Sam, Arturo, and Maggie were ecstatic. Darkstar pranced pridefully past the other horses, her step more regal, her head higher than before, as if even she knew that she was, indeed, a very special lady.

The success of that practice run was not lost on someone else. Pru Bellamy had been watching at the sidelines that morning. Chance was with her, and when Maggie walked past them, he said, "Looking real good, Maggie." His blue eyes twinkled with gladness.

Infected by the warmth, Maggie found herself smiling, even in Pru's presence. "Good enough to win the big one?"

"Never can tell," Chance said.

And that stung. She had wanted to hear a resounding "Yes!" She wanted his total vote of confidence. And she especially wanted it in the presence of Pru.

After that, she put even more effort, more love, more energy, more time—as if it were possible!—into Darkstar's training. Darkstar would win, Darkstar would take it all someday: she and Darkstar, and Arturo, too.

The Situation, as Maggie thought of it, occurred as did all major moments in life: unexpectedly and with enormous consequence. Had Maggie planned it, dreamed it up in her mind, it could never have been arranged as perfectly.

It happened one morning in mid-August. Several horses were cantering slowly around the track after their initial timed workouts. Their riders would be taking them in for bathing. All was usual, nothing extraordinary. Maggie had given no real notice to the other small bands of owners and trainers and just plain race-track groupies observing the track scene.

And then something started to take place on the track that held everyone's attention.

The gleaming brown colt, Pru Bellamy's pride, was keeping pace with Darkstar, who on her own suddenly increased her speed. Arturo, surprised, was almost thrown as Darkstar stepped up the pace even more as the colt moved past them. Three horses fell behind, their paces dwindling to no more than halfhearted straggles as the black and the brown horses flew ahead. It was like the roll of thunder, hooves against the turf, great lungs drawn in, expanding out. It was a full-on race.

Arturo leaned into Darkstar, low and floating in rhythm to the animal's strong, determined gait as she outpaced the colt.

"Go, go Shambhala!" screamed a familiar female voice.

"Darkstar!" Maggie shouted.

"Shambhala! Take it over!"

Maggie glanced to her human competitor, and saw that Pru Bellamy's neck muscles were taut, her fists rigid. Pru was not there alone. Three of her friends were with her, all garbed expensively, impeccably. The four women stared at Maggie for a fleeting moment, as if stunned that any contest at all could exist between the likes of her and the likes of them. But a contest it was, a race extraordinaire.

And one that Maggie's black filly took by an easy three lengths.

Of course it was all unofficial. Of course.

Maggie's blood pulsed through her body with the force of dammed water being let into a dry reservoir. Such victory, such triumph! Ah, the feeling, the bliss of winning!

"Weren't you the lucky one today?" Prucilla Bellamy said, coming up alongside Maggie as she led Darkstar back to the stable area. Arturo walked next to Maggie.

"Lucky?" he said, taking exception to the statement. "This horse was breezing. I could hardly hang on."

"Well, you'd better learn, sweet cakes, 'cause when we run a real race out there you'll be eating dust."

"That was no freak luck," Maggie said calmly. "My horse is a champion."

"She's a mutt."

"She's what she is. Which so happens is faster and stronger than anything you're going to see on that track next season."

Pru stepped in front of Maggie. Her face was very close, her words spattering against Maggie like shrapnel. "You have some nerve. You don't belong in this league. You're out of your element. That horse is out of its element. You're both jokes around here."

"It wasn't such a joke today. We won. And we're going to beat you again. And again. Every time."

"Show me, just show me..." Pru laughed and walked off.

A week later, Pru was there with Chance at her side. It was this, more than anything else, that made Maggie do the unexpected. She was tired of having everything taken away from her by this woman. It was time to fight back, to reclaim a bit of her life, bit by bit. She did not have the patience to wait until next year.

She was very clever, knowing just her presence was enough bait to spring the trap, as she sauntered by Pru and Chance at the railing. They were there that morning with several other people, men and women who looked affluent, who looked in possession of some secret, magical ingredient that made the world their playground and everyone else in it mere props for their pleasure.

So she walked by and, sure enough, just as she knew it would happen, Pru could not resist the temptation to perform before her cohorts, and said, "Well, I see you and Darkhorse are still hanging in where you don't belong."

"Darkstar," Maggie corrected sweetly, having stopped.

Chance's eyes were on her. She could feel his suspicion. He knew she was not sweet. He knew she was up to something. Maggie did not dare look at him directly, for fear she would burst into laughter.

But, of course, in another way, this was all very serious. Very serious.

"Darkhorse, Darkstar, the same difference," Pru said. "You may as well call it Longshot."

"My horse took yours. Or have you forgotten?" Maggie said, now not quite so sweetly.

"My rider was holding back."

"Sure," Maggie scoffed. Her laugh, added a beat later, was in the form of a wink to Pru's friends. Maggie started off.

"Next year will tell," Pru called with bored confidence.

Maggie turned. Walking backward, she said, "Next year, now, what difference does it make to a real winner? My horse is ready. She was ready the day she was born. You can stand by that railing for the rest of your life and talk big in front of your friends. The truth is out there!"

Everyone looked to where the horses were galloping.

"Right on," Pru said. "But we can't run a race now. It's illegal, sweetie."

"We ran a race the other day," Maggie said.

"That was unofficial. It just happened. Animals out of control."

"It could happen again."

"Maggie!" Chance said.

She ignored him. So did Pru. The two women were squared off now. Maggie moved forward toward Pru and her group. A second more and it would happen: the glove would be thrown down officially.

"Fine," Pru said, not looking absolutely confident. "This time put your money where your mouth is."

The glove was down. "Terrific," Maggie said. "I've got a hundred dollars saying Darkstar will take Shambhala."

"Be serious! That's not a bet! Make it interesting. Something that matters. Maybe another necklace? Let's play for that."

It was the meanest, most low-down taunt Maggie could imagine. To Maggie, owning the necklace was the same as if Pru possessed a piece of her soul. She burned from the image of the beautiful jewelry belonging to her people on the neck of Prucilla Bellamy.

"I don't have another necklace."

"Oh, too bad," Prucilla cooed. "I would so have liked a pair." A cold light took residence in Pru's eyes.

She said, "Tell you what. Why not really make it interesting? Let's play for the necklace. Try to win it back."

"I only have a hundred dollars," Maggie said.

"And the horse. Put the horse up."

There was silence all around. Faintly, in the distance, Maggie could hear—could sense—the labored breath of the horses as they ran the track.

Chance did not intervene. It would have been futile. It would also have been an insult. Thank God he granted her this moment of dignity to act independently. Maggie's eyes passed quickly over his face. On it was a look such as she had never seen: fury and pity, love and anger. He was afraid for her, sorry for her, aware that she was at this very moment a woman who had gone quite mad.

"Okay," Maggie said. "Darkstar for the necklace."

Pru nodded and smiled. "Winner take all. Tomorrow?"

"We'll be here," Maggie said.

Chapter Ten

Of course the contest was illegal. If the track stewards had the slightest inkling of what was to take place on the turf with horses not officially old enough to race, there would be blood to pay, if not worse. But to the small group assembled there that morning, no threat was severe enough to deter them from holding their unsanctioned event.

Maggie swore Arturo to secrecy. As far as anyone was to know, what would happen would be due to a spontaneous outflowing of equine energy. If Sam were to find out it was anything other than that, Maggie knew he'd wash his hands of her.

"You are loco," Arturo grumbled as they led Darkstar from the stable area to the track. Light had only just seeped through the night, yet other horses were already in the middle of morning workouts and others were even being led back to their stalls. Passing Maggie and Arturo, hot walkers, grooms, and riders nodded and exchanged greetings.

"I'm not nuts," Maggie returned. "I'm just tired of being put down."

"You can lose her!" Arturo exclaimed passionately. "She'll win."

"Shambhala is a good horse, maybe something more than good. A great horse," Arturo said, again sounding wiser than his years. "He has bloodlines, the best blood. Darkstar has heart, but I don't know." Arturo shook his head. "Shambhala can be greater even than Darkstar."

Maggie whirled around, snapping the reins out of Arturo's hand. "Don't you ever, ever say that again!" Arturo jumped back, as if to save himself from a whipping with the leather straps she twitched with lethal intent. "You think of Darkstar as the winner, the best, and nothing else!"

"But—"

"There are no buts!" Maggie said in a fury. "When you go to win, you think only one thing...that you'll win. You allow nothing and no one to influence that thought. You got that, Arturo?"

He nodded, looking even less convinced of her sanity now than before. "I think nothing but to win," he reiterated obediently.

Maggie gave over the reins and again they moved on.

They were all there. The small band of Pru's socialite friends were spread out like birds along a fence, already watching Shambhala canter around the track. The horse was majestic, sleek and brown, every line and muscle of the animal built for speed.

Chance was there, too, hatless, but dressed in his old bomber jacket, the garb of the old days, those times when he would have been at her side and not Pru's. As the memories invaded, Maggie experienced a sharp, bittersweet stab of pain. She saw Chance look as she approached with Darkstar. By the tension in his face, by the way in which he held himself, she felt he might come to her.

But he didn't. To do so would have been unthinkable, tantamount to committing professional suicide. Still following her with his eyes, he held himself in check, foregoing the flamboyant recklessness that had characterized the personality of the Chance Harris she had loved. *That* man, charming in his spontaneity, had been at times too brusque in his honest approach to life and had paid the price society exacted for being an individual.

That man, Maggie thought, as she parted from Darkstar and Arturo, scarcely existed anymore, other than in her memories.

But the old bomber jacket! Consciously or unconsciously, she knew he had worn it for her. It was a reminder of the past, of his roots, and of her own. And as Maggie came up to the fence, she needed more than ever to be in touch with her origin. She needed the pride of her people to pilot her through this treacherous course she had undertaken. In her heart, she knew Arturo was right. She was crazy.

There could be no opening to the ceremony at hand. Anyone might have noticed the planned intent and reported it to the stewards. The race commenced, therefore, in much the same way as it had innocently begun the previous time.

Shambhala and Darkstar were only two in a straggling series of eight other horses. The riders of both horses kept their distance, then, as Maggie watched, her hands balled into fists, Darkstar galloped closer to Shambhala.

For a time they kept pace, and then, as if both horses sensed the moment, they picked up speed on their own without visible urging from the jockeys.

Arturo leaned forward slightly. And the race was on.

Hurtling around the track, the two animals—one a gleaming brown, the other a radiant jet streak—vied for the lead. Other horses scattered, some spooking, becoming fractious as the horses passed.

Shambhala was in the lead by two lengths. Maggie could see Arturo leaning lower into Darkstar's neck, becoming part of her. She felt the tension in the rider's legs, gripping the horse, lending his will to the animal's.

But it was still Shambhala in the forefront.

Maggie's stomach had become weightless. She felt herself floating, disembodied, as if she were no longer connected to this world. Her life was nothing anymore. All that was, was happening before her on the track. All that would ever be was happening before her on the turf. She felt herself being born and dying over and over again, with every rise and fall of Darkstar's hooves.

There was an eighth of a mile left to run.

Shambhala was in the lead by five lengths. Darkstar was slowing. *God!* Maggie shrieked silently. Win, win! You will lose yourself, Darkstar! You will lose me!

Her eyes moved to the side, to where Pru Bellamy stood, her hands coolly at her sides, a smile on her placid face. In her hands she held the necklace, the silver dripping carelessly through her fingers.

Chance stood off from the others, his body rigid as he followed the race being won by Shambhala.

The moment was at hand, the distance shortening to the finish line. Maggie could hardly breathe. The air was thin. She felt she was on a high, cold mountain and all was suddenly still. In her ears she heard a ringing, then the thunderous intake and expelling of breath from a giant bellows as if she had entered the place where all winds were born. She was in the wind, she was the wind, and the wind was suddenly Darkstar, the animal's powerful lungs working to drive the body of muscle and flesh and bone...and will!...forward.

Maggie felt the change; felt it as surely as if a switch had been activated. Darkstar was electrified, energy streaming through her movements.

The distance closed. Four lengths, then three, only two...the finish line ahead by only feet, only feet...and Darkstar bulleted past Shambhala. To win.

Maggie did not move.

No one else moved.

Every cell in her body was charged with a sense of thankfulness, of fullness. Her heart was at peace. Her mind was clear. She had done what her ancestors would have done. She had believed in herself and in nature. Nature had supported her. Life, because she had not denied its power, had lifted her and carried her dreams to their fulfillment. It was this knowledge that her grandfather had imparted when she was a child. Then she had only half believed. Now she knew. It was so, it was so.

Prucilla Bellamy stood her ground, the loser not coming forward with a hardy handshake of goodwill. So Maggie walked into the midst of the silent enemy camp. She was aware of Chance, who stood on the fringes. Maggie would have liked to meet his eyes, but not now, not now. This moment of victory was for her grandfather, for her people, for a young Mexican and an old man, and for a horse devalued by those who bought important names instead of ability. This was a race run in the name of dignity.

Standing before Pru, Maggie extended her hand. Slowly, she opened her palm. "The necklace is mine."

Pru waited a beat, as if she might have been thinking of a way to renege at the last moment. But of course she could not, and with seeming disinterest she dropped the necklace—not into Maggie's hand, but on the ground.

Laughing then, Pru backed off. The others looked on silently. The necklace gleamed in the grass, there for Maggie to retrieve on her knees if she wanted it.

Only in the next second, it was gone. Chance bent, scooped it into his palm and stood before Maggie offering the silver to her. "Congratulations!" he said loudly. "You have a hell of a horse there."

"Thank you," Maggie said. "Oh, thank you," she said in a softer voice, prickles of love and gratitude radiating through her.

"And you are one hell of a woman, Maggie Rand."

Their eyes locked, and they flew together into a secret world whose boundaries were crossed into only by those who truly loved and truly lived. It was the same thing, Maggie thought, smiling, to live was to love, and to love was to live.

That night Arturo got drunk and told Maggie that Darkstar was the greatest horse in the universe, but that it didn't make any difference because, regardless, Maggie was crazy. He had thought he was going to die out there on the track. Sam Johnson pulled up in his truck while Arturo was still in her living room. He cussed them both out, then had a drink along with Arturo. "If you ever do anything like that again, I'll personally see you never run this horse or any other horse on any track in the country again."

"She's crazy," Arturo said, and belched.

Maggie's third visitor came late that night.

She had been waiting. The sound of the truck's wheels was music this time, the engine a loving purr.

He did not have to knock. Maggie was at the open door waiting as he came up. The black cotton T-shirt dress she wore was comfortable and clung to her body. Over it, the silver necklace gleamed like a thousand smiles.

"I thought this was as good a time as any to come around for my hat," Chance said. He was wearing his bomber jacket.

"It's in the bedroom," Maggie said. "Where you left it."

Chance passed her by, owning the house again, owning her, just as surely. She followed him into the bedroom.

They undressed silently. Maggie spread her body over the length of his, feeling the hard, wonderful limbs again, shivering from the heat arising in her groin as his hands reached around and cupped her breasts.

"Welcome back, Maggie Rand," Chance said, looking into her eyes. "I'd say you found a big chunk of yourself today."

She had removed all but the necklace. Her fingers touched it, and the metal felt warm where it had been pressed against his chest. The strands of her long hair formed dark cascading tributaries over her shoulders.

"I'd say you did, too," Maggie said.

Chance touched the necklace. "Yeah," he said, laughing. "I tell you, it felt damned good to be bad again."

"You haven't lost your touch, Harris..."

"No, I haven't." Chance let his fingers slip down to the valley between her high, full breasts. Cupping one, he brought his mouth upon the nipple. Maggie sighed as with his free hand he guided her to take him.

They could move only slightly before the fire they shared grew too intense. So they would rest, and in the stillness of each other's body they would experience another kind of pleasure, concentrated and intimate, exquisite.

She did what she remembered he liked, and now, after the months of separation, she had grown, it seemed, more inventive—or perhaps more hungry for him—and found countless new ways to bring him to peak after peak of tension just short of release.

Maggie looked up once, just before arching into him, a heartbeat before her eyes closed in the trembling mystery of their union and saw, through the window, the heavens watching. The moon was frozen in the sky, the stars unmoving. It was a night of love, a night to last forever.

"So, you were with her," Pru said.

Chance had found her in her office. She had not shown up at the stables that day. No one had seen her. Finally, he had gone to her, needing to discuss the sale of one of the stallions to a farm in Kentucky. The butler told him she was not seeing anyone, but Chance pressed past the man, regardless. The ensuing conversation never touched the subject of the stallion.

"It's my business where I go. But, yes, I was with Maggie."

"At least you don't lie, even if you do cheat."

Chance raised his right brow, challenging the statement.

"You weren't here for me last night! I came over to your cabin because I wanted to talk to you about—"

"Oh, cut the baloney, Pru. You have never needed to talk to me about anything at night. Every time you've come over, it's smelling of perfume and booze, and you're half naked in a costume that would do better on a runway with black lights and drums than padding around a horse farm at eleven at night."

"That's quite enough!"

"Right! More than enough. Having to say any of these things to you is degrading for both of us. That little scene you pulled yesterday, dropping the necklace in the dirt, that was more than enough, too."

Prucilla came to the front of the desk. Fire was in her eyes, and her skin had gone pale against the navy-blue jumpsuit she wore. He waited for the rage to come hurtling out, for the vitriolic dismissal. He was prepared.

But he was wrong.

"Maybe you're right," Pru said, her entire demeanor relaxing into what was not quite defeat, but perhaps a stance of reasonableness. "When I want something I tend to get carried away. A little flaw. I'll have to watch it."

Chance was almost too stunned to reply. He said, "I'd appreciate it. My personal life is—"

"Your personal life," Pru finished in a singsong tone. "No need to rub my nose in it. I quite understand."

Chance had forgotten the business about the stallion and was almost to the door when Pru's voice rang out again. "But, you are one-hundred percent mine as far as work goes. Aren't you, Chance?"

Chance turned back. "Yeah. We signed on it."

"And if you had to beat Maggie Rand's horse on the track, you'd go all out to do it. Wouldn't you, Chance?"

He was quiet. Then he said, "We signed on it."

"Just so you remember," Pru said. "Good, very good."

Chapter Eleven

It was all for real now, the whole wonderful world, the exhilarating world of horse racing, with its accompanying glittery social scene. And Maggie, like some majestic, newly formed star, dazzling to behold, had burst into the rarefied atmosphere populated by the beautiful people of leisure, the monied people for whom the real stakes were not dollars but ego strokes, and the desperadoes whose psychic systems were oiled by the incomparable highs of gambling.

It was an all-or-nothing world, and Maggie had, for once in her life, all of everything.

Darkstar had won her maiden race. Darkstar had gone on to race other two-year-olds in her league, winning many of the meets and placing in the others.

Had she the bloodlines to match her triumphs, the attention would not have been shown to the extent it was. But as it was, Darkstar was fast becoming a folk hero. Darkstar the renegade filly was becoming a legend in an industry that might publicly dine on odds and ratios, but whose members, in private, devoured myths and snacked greedily upon superstitions.

Sam told Maggie to play it up. "It's good press. Good press is good publicity. Good publicity brings bettors, investors. Flaunt yourself."

He ordered her to dress for center stage. He made her strut her stuff through the air-conditioned club houses and private turf clubs reeking of one hundred fifty dollars-an-ounce perfume, through the back stretches of the tracks smelling of hay and horses and red hot *chili con carne* simmering over Sterno pots, and into the private homes of the racing Czars who held lavish postrace parties.

And like Darkstar, Maggie had her own inimitable style. She was what she was, what she had always been, but had not recognized, and now she paraded her individuality with the pride of a conquering empress. She had quit her job when it became clear she could live off Darkstar's earnings, and she blossomed fully. Eschewing pearls for her Indian necklace, she dressed in custom designed leather outfits, high-style and provocatively sensual. To the media she was clearly a stunner with her dark, sultry coloring, the clean, glistening sweep of her high cheekbones and the pointed determination of her jaw. The wide black eyes were frank, appraising, and often startling with their gleam of contempt for any softness or sham met in the course of social congress. People stepped aside from the challenge in her stride. Slender and tall, she moved with the animal grace of a tigress inspecting her territory. Her words were still measured, but confident, the tone of her voice ranging from the assured purr of a mighty jungle cat, to the biting snap of a bull whip levied against an unjust act.

And in all of this, Chance also reveled.

"You're lucky I'm not the jealous type," he said one night after a celebratory gathering at a socialite's Pasadena estate. They were driving back to the cottage they once again shared together. "That oiled down Brazilian with the Steinway smile was ready to take a bite out of you. Lucky I happened by when I did."

Maggie cast him a sidelong glance, the fringe of her black lashes creating a fan of shadows beneath her eyes. "Happened by?"

"Yeah, well, I might have been there. In the vicinity."

"He was only talking horses," Maggie said innocently.

"He was talking horse *shit*, was what he was doing."

"And you were hovering on the other side of a potted palm. Admit it! You're jealous," Maggie accused flatly, loving the whole situation.

"I'm in love with you," Chance said.

"Still, you shouldn't hover. It's undignified."

"You're right. Next time I'll be more direct. I'll reduce the guy's smile by three octaves."

"You always do things with flair."

And style Chance did have. In abundance. If there was one absolutely fatal charm Maggie possessed in terms of the opposite sex, it was that she cared nothing at all for anyone but Chance. Elusive and unavailable, she was all the more pursued for her disinterest.

It seemed that the perfection of their life would go on forever. Only it didn't. Exactly when things began to change, it was hard to say. But later, when Maggie thought back upon those days, if there was to have been an actual time when the ride on the golden sunbeam had come to an end, it was on that morning early in March when a disturbed Arturo mentioned the stranger.

"I didn't like him," Arturo said. He was outside hosing down Darkstar after her bath. In spite of the sunlight, Arturo's generally robust coloring was gray. Maggie had never seen him so agitated. Taking the small metal bar, she raked water from the filly's coat while Arturo railed on about the unwelcome visitor.

"I told him she was not for sale. But he would not go. He look here, there, at everything. His eyes, always they are on Darkstar. He goes to the tack room. Big eyes everywhere. And he ask questions, questions! All kinds! None of his business. No, I did not like him."

Maggie was thoughtful. She trusted Arturo's perceptions. After all, he worked with animals. That alone said much for anyone's sensitivity. "He had a pass though."

"He had a pass. But he did not belong here. I know it. I feel it." Arturo hit his heart with his fist.

"Keep your eye on our girl," Maggie said. "We'll hire someone to sleep by the stable."

"I will. I'll stay here," Arturo said possessively.

And he did. The man did not return again, or could not return again, due to Arturo's constant and compulsive vigilance.

So the days went by one after the next, with nothing tangibly different from former times. Yet there was a change to the mood, a slight tension to the air which did not dissipate, regardless of Darkstar's continued winning streak.

Then it happened that the pendulum swung in this area of her life, too. Darkstar's record began to lag. Out of four races, she lost three to horses in Pru Bellamy's stable.

"Congratulations," Maggie said to Chance at a dinner she had prepared for the two of them in the cottage. "Maybe I should save myself the trouble, and make a recording of that." She raised her goblet, but she sounded down.

Chance peered across the top of his wineglass. "I'm doing my job, Mag. Winning *was* a legitimate part of the deal."

"It just doesn't seem right. Darkstar racing against your mounts."

"You mean Darkstar losing against my horses. That's the problem here, isn't it?"

Maggie glared at him. "I hate that word. You know how I hate it."

"Losing?" Chance smiled his crooked smile and shrugged. "It happens sometimes. You had a streak of good luck. But losing is still part of the master plan of life. Especially life on the track. Can't have a winner without a loser."

"Fine, then I want to be the winner." She drank her wine down and poured another full glass.

Shadows continued to grow, sweeping more deeply into the once sunlit territory of Maggie's life with each succeeding race. Darkstar took one first place, then lost the next two. There were nights when Maggie could barely sleep from obsessing over the losses. And her recently won personal confidence was also in decline. Undermined professionally, those newly claimed parts of herself faded with each succeeding disappointment.

She picked on Chance, seeking an outlet for her free-floating angst, yet he ignored her efforts to create a serious breech in their relationship. His acceptance of her ill-directed fury riled her even more. The simple truth was, there was nothing for which she could actually fault him or anyone else, for that matter. Around Prucilla Bellamy, he was professional and aloof. Pru, herself, seemed to have adopted a whole different tack when relating to Chance. She was polite, but distant, and several times she had even said good morning to Maggie, herself.

But again the pendulum swung, and swung broadly.

It was the end of November. In southern California, Christmas decorations were already in the department stores. It made no difference that the temperature was more appropriate to late June, colored lights were strung in twinkling, intricate webs across boulevards and nested, blinking, in palm trees.

But at Hollywood Park this seasonal activity was barely noticed. Quickened pulses were due to far different reasons that the coming yule season. The Hollywood Starlet, a race for two-year-old fillies, with a purse of half a million dollars was to be run. A second race, in which the fillies were to race with the colts, was to be held two weeks later. The purse of one million dollars clearly exceeded any visions of sugar-plum fairies.

Darkstar qualified. Maggie was ecstatic, rushing home to Chance with the news.

"I've heard," he said. He was seated in the big chair in the living room, his legs stretched out long before him. In his hand he held a drink. At the base of the chair was a half empty liquor bottle.

The sullen picture he made diluted Maggie's enthusiasm.

"It's half a million, Chance. Doesn't that get just the tiniest rise out of you?"

"Pru's got two fillies running."

"So?" Maggie challenged.

"So they're damn fast horses. So I don't want to be around if you lose." At that, Chance roused himself from his half-reclining position and stalked into the bedroom.

Maggie followed him. "What's that supposed to mean? That you don't think Darkstar has a chance?"

"Of course she has a chance. Every horse out there has a chance, or they wouldn't be in the race. But this is the big league, Mag. The biggest league. It's not going to be quite the same out there."

"Don't worry about it."

"Darkstar's running against my horses, Maggie. I've got a reponsibility to bring a horse in first place. And there's a good likelihood, a damn good likelihood that I'll do it for the Bellamy stables. Are you going to be able to accept that?"

Maggie's eyes lowered. Of course she couldn't accept it. She couldn't even bear to think of the double defeat it would be. "No," she answered, raising her face to his. "Truthfully, no. I don't think I could. That's why I'm going to win."

What Chance had predicted proved out. It was a tough lineup; a band of the toughest competitors Darkstar had ever gone against. Maggie didn't know, she really didn't know if there was a chance to pull it off. Arturo, on the other hand, had no such doubts. "First place," he said. "First place, first place," he repeated over and again to Darkstar as he saddled her before the race. "Do you believe that, or has your record stuck?" Maggie asked, partly annoyed by his self-possession, partly gratified by his loyalty. "First place," Arturo continued, ignoring her. And she smiled, remembering her advice to him. *Think only one thought: to win.*

Maggie watched the show from the Turf Club. She was seated at a table with Sam Johnson, who was trying to appear calm and wasn't succeeding. The odds were not in Darkstar's favor. She left the gate at eleven-to-one, and she left slowly. Out of the thousands watching, there was only silence, as if the sound had been cut while the ten horses on the far side of the track seemed to float surrealistically above the earth. The favorite, Malaga Malaga, a Bellamy horse, took the lead and held it against a two-year-old owned by a male movie star. Pru Bellamy sat at her own table surrounded by her pals, all of them dressed to the nines. Chance, diplomatically, had remained below near the rail.

The race was three-quarters over, with Darkstar straggling fourth from the end, when with a definite change in gait, she moved forward, the long, black graceful neck extending itself to lead the powerful legs in the direction of the finish line. A murmur arose from the stands as the filly passed two horses, then swept by two more contenders.

Maggie rose up, her fists clenched. Sam no longer pretended; beads of sweat made a necklace on his forehead. He, too, stood.

Some people were beginning to scream out the numbers of their bets, the names of the horses. Maggie had no voice. Not even her heart could comment. Fear had stunned it.

There were two horses in the lead. The finish line loomed ahead, too close, coming up too soon.

Darkstar's gait changed once again, altering to longer strides, strides so powerful it seemed she was pulling the

earth from under her, gathering the world as if it were
no more than flimsy silk over which she skated.

And then there were only the two of them: Darkstar
and Malaga Malaga.

The stands had gone frantic. Maggie, too, and Sam—
they were screaming, sounds arising from their guts,
primal energies spilling into the ethers, arrows made of
hopes and dreams shivering through the air.

And Darkstar became a black streak, tendons straining, hide glistening beneath the sunlight. The other
horse strained forward. Both jockeys were high in their
saddles, almost separated from their mounts.

The rider's encouraging whip-prod to the flank of
Malaga Malaga pushed the filly forward by a nose.

And at that, Darkstar flew ahead on her own, legs
synchronized with the soul of the wind; and with the
invisible wings of the eagle she soared ever forward...

...first over the finish line!

First! It was Maggie's moment of glory. She grabbed
Sam and hugged him, intermittently crying and laughing, until the crush of well-wishers made her intimate
celebration impossible and the ritual of glad-handing
strangers was imposed upon her. Amid the confusion,
she caught a glimpse, through the shoulders of tall men
and stout women packed around her, of Chance entering the room. His eyes scanned the crowd and Maggie
raised an arm high above the surrounding pandemonium to direct him to her position.

Her greeting went unseen, however. At that precise
moment he was intercepted by Prucilla Bellamy. Chance
made to move forward, but Prucilla grabbed hold of his
arm. Maggie saw Chance's face darken, and as he
wrenched himself free of Pru's restraint, he said something that made Pru stand still. For once, stunned to the

point of muteness, she merely watched as he waved to Maggie.

A rush of love filled Maggie as he plowed through her fans to lift her into his arms, kissing her fully, deeply, possessively—completing her. It was, in all ways, her moment of glory.

"Do you think I'm a bad winner?" she asked languidly, stretching her body over Chance's as they lay in bed three days later.

"I think you're a lousy winner," he grumbled and nibbled on her neck while running his hands along her buttocks, squeezing slightly as he ground his pelvis against hers. "But you're a good lover. Exceptions can be made."

"I'm going to win the next one, too," Maggie cooed. She shivered with desire as her hand found him ready again.

"You think you can make it against the boys? That's a rough, tough league, baby."

"You mean Shambhala's a rough, tough guy, don't you?"

The passion in Chance cooled. Separating himself from her, he sat higher on the bed and said seriously, "Shambhala's going to take that race, Mag."

"We'll see about that!" She was laughing, but he wasn't.

"I mean it."

"Yeah," she said, coming down off her high, "I can see you do. Only you don't have a crystal ball."

"Mag, Shambhala's in prime condition. Shambhala's got the time, the bloodlines, the rider. He's got the race."

Maggie pulled herself off the bed and, grabbing her robe, threw it on, pulling the sash tight enough to cut off her circulation. "I'm going over to the track," she said. "I'm going over to see the future winner. Darkstar."

Arturo was frantic when she arrived.

"He was here again!" he said.

"Who?"

"That hombre with his big nose and the big eyes. I would like to put out his lights," Arturo said, having added the lingo and inflection of late-night television reruns to his expanding English repertoire.

"What did he want, Arturo?"

"Nothing. That is what is wrong. I know he wants something." They both looked to Darkstar.

Maggie made the call to Sam Johnson immediately. "Sam, I want to van Darkstar over to the farm right away. I'd just feel safer if she's away from here. It's just a feeling," she explained. "A bad feeling."

That evening Sam sent a driver with a trailer for Darkstar. Arturo rode shotgun in the pickup, determined not to let the filly out of his sight.

The accident occurred on the freeway near San Juan Capistrano.

Chapter Twelve

Maggie's breathing had almost slowed to a stop. Chance stood behind her in the office, holding firmly to her shoulders as she waited, suspended in a state of fear, for the vet to make his pronouncement.

"A quarter crack to the front leg," he said finally. He handed the X-ray prints to Maggie.

Maggie stared without comprehension at the fuzzy images in her hand. The veterinarian pointed his finger, identifying the break in the bone.

"What's the chances of it healing?" Chance asked.

The doctor frowned. "She'll be able to do some easy running." A light came up in Maggie's eyes. The vet paused, having taken note of the unfounded hope. "But nothing strenuous," he added. "I'm afraid racing's over for this one."

"No," Maggie said, and then again, "No!", the second denial coming as a kind of wail.

The doctor's face blanched. He was a professional in a world of professionals. For the majority of his clients, the horses he treated were not pets, but financial properties to be bought, sold, traded, and on occasion, retired. He was used to displays of disappointment, but the outburst from Maggie clearly stunned him.

Chance's hold tightened around her. "Maggie." That was all; there was nothing to say that could make any difference. "Come on, babe. Let's go home."

"No, not yet," Maggie said dully. She pushed out of his arms. "I want to go to her first." Eyes brimming, red forming at the edges, she started for the door, then stopped. Turning back to the veterinarian, she said, "You don't know Darkstar."

"No. But I do know about bones that can't be put back together."

"There's more to an animal than bones and flesh."

Chance and the veterinarian exchanged glances. Maggie bristled. "I don't need your condescension. I'm not a child. I don't believe in Santa Claus and fairies. I'm not off my rocker."

"I'm sorry," the doctor said with obvious sincerity. "She was a beautiful animal."

"*Is* a beautiful animal. She's not dead. And she's not finished on the track, either."

"Maggie...?" Chance opened the door, and Maggie swept defiantly past him.

Over her shoulder, she called, "But I do believe in spirit!"

Her life had been put on hold. The flurry of activities that had characterized her previous days and months came to a halt. Maggie visited Darkstar daily, sometimes spending hours at a time doing no more than talking to her. Arturo found extra work with Sam Johnson, but his mood, too, had changed. It was as if neither of them could believe, nor accept, that the magnificently proud animal in their care would never fly over the turf again. Maggie put copies of the X rays up on her kitchen wall. Each morning with coffee, she would sit at the table, staring hard at the prints. Each evening, she would focus her mental energies on the black-and-white photos.

Except for the plastic support Darkstar wore, all was the same on the outside. The damage being unseen, it made it all the more difficult for Maggie to accept the finality of Darkstar's career as prophesied by the veterinarian.

But for Chance, the world continued to whirl at its former dizzying pace. The Hollywood Futurity was coming up.

"You don't have to act like someone's died. Not on my account!" Maggie snapped one night at dinner. "I know you're excited. I know you're high. So you don't have to martyr yourself for my sake."

"Fine," Chance said. "Shambhala looks better than he ever has before.

"He'll win then, won't he?" Maggie said bitterly. She shoved her chair back and stood up to clear the table.

Chance caught her hand, held it for a beat and then dropped it, her resistance a strain on them both. "Mag...I know what this must be like for you. It's rotten. I wish the accident didn't happen. It's the worst possible luck. I don't see how the hell something like that—" He broke off abruptly.

Maggie turned around slowly, the towel in her hand forgotten as she tried to read his expression. "Something like...? What are you thinking, Chance?"

Chance was staring into the distance, his eyes unfocused, a man watching something in another dimension.

"Tell me," Maggie pleaded.

His vision returned to the world Maggie occupied, then in a single flowing movement, he left his chair, grabbed his jacket and hat, swept up the keys to the truck and started out the kitchen.

"Chance!" Maggie cried. She followed quickly after him, caught in the jet stream of his mysterious burst of energy. "Dammit! What's happening?"

"Later!" he called as he bolted through the front door. Then, spinning back around, he demanded, "Where's Arturo?"

"At the stable, probably. At Sam's."

A moment later, she watched in bewilderment as he roared off in the truck.

Arturo was with Darkstar, just as Maggie said. When Chance found him, he was brushing the horse and talking to it as if to a fellow human.

"Hey, hombre," Chance said, standing spread-legged in the stall's doorway. Surprised, Arturo looked up from his work. His congenial expression wavered in the presence of the tall man, whose eyes glowed dangerously as he went on to say, "We're gonna talk, pal."

Ten minutes later Chance had the answers to match his suspicions, and with the knowledge, his face had darkened to a black fury. He felt sickened to the point of dizziness. A vile, poisonous anger gripped his gut, tearing away his humanity. He knew at that moment what it was like to want to kill someone. He knew why there was such a thing as justifiable homicide.

* * *

Prucilla's houseman answered the door. No longer in his uniform of servility, he had on slacks and a sweater. Keys dangled from his palm and Chance realized he was about to leave.

Dispensing with formalities, Chance pushed him aside and strode into the entrance hall. "Where is she?" His voice was a whip crack.

"She's in her suite, Mr. Harris, but—"

"Which way?" Chance didn't wait for a response. He set off on his own, taking the most likely route down the hall.

Prucilla jumped as the double doors to her vast peach and white and sea-green suite slammed open.

Chance stood in the doorway, fire coming from his eyes. "So," Chance said, "it was you who hired him. A nice little deal, huh, Pru? How much did it take? A couple of thousand? Well, you aren't through paying yet, baby. You haven't even begun."

Prucilla's face had drained of its pink and white alabaster color. She wore a blue taffeta gown. Her hair was loose, framing her face. She wore no makeup, but the scent of expensive French perfume permeated the air.

"Ruthless, that's what you are." He moved slowly to her. "Heartless. Without soul or conscience. You're despicable," Chance said. He had arrived in front of her.

Still, Prucilla said nothing. She stood like a statue on a winter's day, eyes hollow and icy.

"You can't prove anything," she said. Her voice was cold-edged, like a sharp wind.

"Oh—" Chance laughed, the sound of his own voice equally forbidding "—there you're wrong. So wrong, baby. I've got enough people who've seen him. I've seen him—your hired man. He's the same sick, demented bastard someone else hired to burn down my barn and kill every horse. All but one, just one little survivor made it: Darkstar. And then he came back—thanks to you, baby—to finish her off, too. A job well done. I remembered tonight. It all came clear. It was fuzzy before, but the picture suddenly made sense. It was his face I saw just before my barn burned. What a pair you two are, what a pair. Two professional destroyers." They were mere inches apart.

Pru's face was twitching, from fear or fury, he didn't know or care. Overcome with a murderous impulse, he reached out suddenly and, grabbing a fist of long pale hair, yanked her face up to meet his eyes.

"If you lay a hand on me, I'll—"

"You'll what?" Chance pushed her to the side, letting her go out of disgust. "You'll do nothing. Nothing, baby. By tomorrow I'll have that dude's name. Connections, honey. You're not the only one with them. I know people, too, maybe not like your fancy friends, but they've got tongues that wag just the same. I don't exactly relish turning over rocks to get to the slime. I don't have your stomach for it. But in this case, you've given me a good enough reason to go hunting through the muck for his name."

"He won't say a thing," Pru said confidently.

"Oh, he'll talk. Because if he doesn't, he's not going to have a tongue left. He's a businessman. And you? I can have you kicked off every track in this country. You'll be hated. And, I can have your cold ass hauled up before a court of law."

Pru was trembling. Her entire body had suddenly been transformed into an earthquake of agitation. Propelled by the anxiety, she fled to the other side of the room, held onto the bedpost for a moment, and then collapsed like a limp doll onto the mattress.

"No," she said in a voice reduced to a mere vapor, "please. What do you want? It's yours; name it. Whatever you want."

"Write a full confession out. Here. Now. And you're going to pay for the best vet in this country to take care of Darkstar. And you are never, never to insult Maggie Rand again. You are never to interfere in her life ever again. You are to hold up your end of the bargain as far as Shambhala is concerned. I get a free stud right if I do my job."

Prucilla nodded weakly. "Thank you."

"No graciousness intended. I'm keeping your tail out of the slammer because I want to win that race. I want a horse out of Shambhala."

Fifteen minutes later, Chance folded the confession and slipped it into his jacket pocket. "Thank God you didn't have the gall to say you were sorry. That I couldn't have taken."

"I'm not sorry," Prucilla said.

"You will be," Chance returned. "Count on it. What goes around comes around."

It happened as Chance had predicted. Shambhala, living up to his heritage, rising to the promise of his powerful musculature, sailed across the finish line five lengths ahead of the next closest competitor for the one million dollar purse. The Hollywood Park Futurity was his. The day also belonged to Chance.

As lavish homage was paid to Chance, Maggie stood off to the side. She wore a smartly tailored red suit with black-and-gold epaulettes. Her hair was coiled into a neat chignon and on either ear were the ruby-and-diamond earrings Chance had given her for Christmas. She might have been the dutiful wife of a political candidate, a mere necessary backdrop, no more than a luxurious accoutrement to complete a prescribed image. Only Maggie did not wear a canned smile, and although the winter sun shone brightly, the impression she gave—had anyone cared to notice—was of a woman standing in a pool of deep shadow.

In comparison, Prucilla Bellamy's smile eclipsed those of all others. Like a single, perfect diamond surrounded by tones of smaller and lesser quality, she radiated the confidence of the ultimate victor to those who came to celebrate her achievement. Her eyes flashed as she bantered brightly with the television newsmen, their microphones thrust in salute, minicams borne on shoulders like gifts.

And in the background, Maggie watched, not patiently, but overcome with a wan feeling of—if not final acceptance—insufficient energy to rouse resentment, to rally anger, or even to spark jealousy. And she realized that true defeat brought not the dark, racking sorrow characteristic of the old times, but a kind of disassociation of all feeling. She might have been dead.

In contrast, Pru giggled and simpered and wiggled and clowned for the media. She smiled adoringly up at Chance, and while the cameras recorded the moment for the world to view, Pru slipped her arms around him.

A flick of the eyes, and Pru was staring directly at Maggie. Maggie nodded back. Her lips formed into a small, tight smile of acknowledgment. Turning, she sauntered off, unnoticed, the scene left to those who were winners in life.

*   *   *

He introduced himself to Maggie as Carey Mc-Donald and said that he was a friend of the veterinarian who had originally seen Darkstar. His interest in the filly was scientific. He had a few ideas on how to work with fractures and breaks. There was a chance for complete rehabilitation. Maggie, who had finally given in to what Chance referred to as "the reality of the situation," was not initially impressed. But from Sam Johnson, Maggie learned McDonald was the top animal doctor in the racing business.

"So how much would I have to pop for, to have you work your voodoo on Darkstar?" Maggie asked, after the doctor and the horse had met.

"Nothing. It's a research project," he said.

Chance, who was along for the examination, was unconvinced. "Look, I've been around horses all my life. There's nothing short of a miracle that can put this horse back onto the track. Forget it. Let's take off, Mag."

"Wait just one minute," Maggie said, with a shriveling glance his way. Turning to McDonald, she said, "This is my horse, not his. I say it's worth a try."

"You're just heading for more disappointment," Chance objected.

"Well, at least I'm heading somewhere. That's a whole lot better than where I am now, which is nowhere but in your way." She extended her hand to the doctor. "You've got yourself a term project."

As McDonald slipped his hand into Maggie's, Chance, behind her, winked and gave the doctor the thumbs-up sign. The doctor smiled. Their collusive ruse had worked.

* * *

"Why don't you leave her?" Maggie asked, lying beside Chance in bed. "Your year's up. Devil-woman no longer has claim to your soul."

"I get ten percent of each purse I win, babe. That's one reason."

"And the other?"

"What else would I do? Just hire on for someone else, and I'm already with the best, far's money goes."

"Start your own farm again."

Chance, who had been holding her, withdrew by a subtle shift in position. Maggie felt it, and propped herself up on one elbow to better study what lay behind his expression. "You're afraid!" she accused. "You, Chance Harris, Renegade Harris, are afraid?"

"Mag..." He sighed deeply, not denying the accusation.

"Look," she said, "I'm trying again, aren't I? I'm picking up the pieces—in more ways than one!" she added, laughing. Then, more seriously, she said, "I've got a surprise. Well, I was going to wait and tell you over candles and wine and all that, but..." Chance waited, his eyebrow cocked in amused expectation. "Darkstar's going to enter the Santa Anita Derby on April 1. Did you hear?" she asked, when he didn't respond at once.

"It's for certain?"

"Yes! Yes!" With a happy bounce, Maggie drew herself into a cross-legged position and went on to explain the details. "She's going to make it, Chance. McDonald said she can run again."

"Mag, it's a hard race."

"Two hundred fifty thousand," Maggie went on, ignoring his statement. "So it's not a million, but there's always later. Who knows? Maybe even the Breeder's Cup. The Triple Crown! Chance, you haven't watched her lately. She's more alive than ever before. It's like...like she's matured or something. It's almost as if she can sense that she's been given a second chance in life and this time she's not going to let anything blow it for her.''

"That's great, Mag. Baby, that's...it's wonderful."

Maggie noted, but outwardly ignored the lack of enthusiasm in his voice. "I'll tell you what's going to be more wonderful. When she wins that race on April 1."

Her eyes were shining with such bright hope that Chance had to look away. Shambhala was scheduled to run that race. And Shambhala would win. There was no doubt in his mind.

"You can't be serious?" Prucilla said, seated behind her desk. She pushed the offensive piece of paper farther from her.

Chance shook his head. "That's my letter of resignation right there, black and white."

"Just like my confession?" Pru said with a sneer. Chance said nothing. "Look," Pru said at last, leaning into the soft leather of her chair, "what happened between us happened. I say let it be water under the bridge. We've got a business thing going here. I'm paying you more than any other trainer in this country is pulling in. Your life's your own. It's a good deal. so what's your beef, Harris?"

"No beef. I want to strike out for myself again."

Prucilla's eyes widened. "Give me a break," she said, laughing. "You've got that kind of money?"

"Almost," he said. "Enough to start off."

"Enough's never enough. Not in this business," Prucilla countered. "If you haven't heard, this is called the sport of kings. For good reason."

"Well, this time it'll have to be enough. Because," he said, nodding to the resignation lying on Pru's desk, "as of the last day of the month, I've signed off."

"Stay one more month," Pru wheedled.

"No, the last day of March. That's it."

But it was not entirely it, as he had planned. The following day he was to have told Maggie at a surprise candlelight dinner, complete with champagne and lobster, that he had emancipated himself from Pru's gilt grip.

The dinner was canceled. As it happened, Chance had little appetite that evening. In the morning, Pru had sought him out in the stable area.

"Okay," she said, sidling up to him in her regulation sprayed-on denims, boots and a blouse whose gauze fabric accentuated peaked nipples. "I did some research. Now I've got the picture. Darkstar's running in the Santa Anita Derby. You don't want to run against her. That's it, right?"

"You've got it, Sherlock."

"Look, hon, you know your woman better than I do, but I'll tell you something just the same. From what I can see about Maggie Rand, if she knew you were going to back out of a race because you thought you'd beat her, she'd spit nails. She might not ever forgive you, Chance."

"That's none of your concern."

"You run that race for me, with your name up there in the racing form as trainer, and I'll give you half the purse."

"Forget it, Pru. It's over."

"The whole purse."

Chance stared at her.

"I mean it."

"God, you must really hate her," he said.

"Yes," Pru replied candidly. "She took away something I wanted. I don't like losing."

"Well, at least you're more honest than you used to be."

"So what's it going to be?" Pru drilled.

He looked away, hating himself for even considering the offer. She was offering him the world with one hand and taking away the world from Maggie with the other. "That kind of deal—"

"Could buy you a whole lot of prime horse flesh."

She was so, so right. "Stinks. I can't turn it down."

Prucilla nodded with satisfaction. "I didn't think so. And you know the terms. Go for it, doll. All the way and no fudging. If I find out that race's been thrown, I'll see you never set foot on another track. One way or the other."

Chance started away. His back was to Prucilla when she suddenly called out. "You know, Harris, we could form a different kind of a deal. All of this could be yours, every last horse."

Chance's mouth turned into its crooked smile. "Woman, I've got this real streak of independence, see, and an offer like that goes way against my grain. Fact is, I've always picked my own fillies. My taste runs counter to what you've got to offer."

It did not disturb Maggie that Shambhala was running against Darkstar. If anything, it seemed to rev up Maggie's internal motor. She was in bliss; ignorant bliss, thought Chance, as he watched the morning workouts at Santa Anita a week before the derby. He'd spoken to McDonald personally and the vet confirmed what Maggie had told him: Darkstar could, in fact, run a race. There were, however, no absolute guarantees. This is also what he had tried to impress upon Maggie.

"Intellectually, she might have heard it," McDonald told Chance, "but on an emotional level I don't think she took in my caveat. If it's an easy race, there's a good chance. Beyond that, we're looking at God's will."

"Or Maggie's," Chance said ruefully.

If Prucilla was adamant that the race be run clean, Maggie was even more so, and Chance realized that what the blond ex-chorine had said was, in fact, true. Maggie would never have forgiven him had he bowed out for fear of hurting her chances. It was important for her to prove herself. It was not Darkstar who had been given a second lease on life, but Maggie.

He walked in on her before the race. Absorbed with Darkstar, she didn't hear him. Her face was pressed against the side of the filly's long nose. Darkstar, as Maggie always claimed, did seem to be listening. "This is for us, girl. You go out there and run like you've never run before. None of them can beat you. To lose is to die. Win for me, Darkstar. Win..."

And Chance moved away, unnoticed. At that moment, *he* wanted to die, rather than live out the rest of the afternoon to its all-but-certain conclusion.

There was the pageantry—the horn piercing the air with the electric promise of fortunes to be made—never, of course, to be lost; the top-hatted stewards' ride in the open coach drawn by the proud, prancing horses; pungent smells of hot dogs and beer and hundreds of various colognes and perfumes and cigarette fumes spiraling into the acidic blue sky of Los Angeles; the snap-flutter of thousands of racing forms and newspapers being turned between nervous fingers, and always the scratch, scratch of pens marking out the sure bets.

On the electronic tote board Shambhala was the favorite at two-to-one odds. Darkstar was the long shot at thirty-to-one, her injury duly reported on the form qualifying her for the race. This did not dismay Maggie; it made her all the more determined.

Maggie had dressed for her victory. Chance had left the house earlier, and when he saw her enter the Turf club, his mind stopped momentarily at the sight of her beauty. She wore a vibrant blue leather suit. At the neckline was the silver necklace bequeathed to her by her grandfather. Her hair was long and straight down her back. In her simplicity she was the most regal, most stunningly beautiful woman in the room—if not the entire world, thought Chance, as her eyes met his.

They took their professional places, at separate tables in the room. Like a piece of cement, Prucilla remained seated by his side, immovable, implacable, and totally confident.

But so was Maggie. Chance could see it in her quick smile, as she spoke to Sam Johnson, beside her.

It began. They came out of the starting gate, all nine horses flying bullets. The announcer's voice followed the action, his British accent cutting through the room's tension. Shambhala was in the lead to begin with and kept his pace strong and steady, never allowing another horse to get within a full length of his powerful flanks.

In the center of the pounding storm was the smaller Darkstar, a glistening black dot neither distinguishing herself nor falling into disgrace.

Chance glanced to Maggie. Her gaze was totally fixed upon the horse, her concentration so intent that one would think it was she running.

Shambhala was two lengths in the lead. Darkstar had fallen behind another horse. Chance's stomach turned. He closed his eyes, unable to watch the rest. He could feel her, could feel Maggie's heart breaking, straining along with the animal's. *God! He could not bear the pain; her pain was his; her pain was theirs!*

The atmosphere changed, at first subtly, but enough that Chance, sensitive to the fluctuations of energy in this most familiar of territories, knew that a horse was making a surprise move on the track. Opening his eyes, he dared to watch the debacle. With amazement he saw the fleeting form of Darkstar passing a second, then a third horse to take fourth place. He glanced quickly to Maggie. She sat like a stone, her eyes trained ahead as if in a trance.

Maggie, my love ... Maggie ... win for her Darkstar! For God's sake, fly little horse!

Darkstar lifted into still another speed, the legs stretching above the ground, an animal sailing on the wind. She was in second place. Chance rose out of his seat as the horses approached the finish line. Everyone in the Turf Club had jumped up, eyes devouring the monitors as closeups of Shambhala and Darkstar, the dark horse, were beamed onto the screens. The announcer's voice had risen to a high, frantic pitch. The only person who remained seated, immobile as a granite mountain, was Maggie Rand. Her full attention was on the immense drama unfolding before an audience of writhing, shouting, cursing, praying bettors.

Darkstar took the lead. Maggie stood. Her fists were clenched at her sides. Her body moved forward, straining with the animal's movements hundreds of yards below.

Chance's heart flooded with warmth, with a sense of joy encompassing the entire cosmos. He had never experienced such love before, such gratitude for all that was good in life.

And then it was Shambhala in the lead, Darkstar suddenly veering off to the side, the barest stumble, perhaps—Chance couldn't be sure. It was so slight, the change in pace, but the other horse—his magnificent brown colt—took off and was a clear length in the lead with no more than ten lengths to the finish line when the filly burst forward.

"Darkstar!" Maggie screamed. "Darkstar!" And Chance turned, hearing something in her voice that did not belong to triumph, but to horror, the most abject sadness ringing above the pandemonium filling the room.

The little black filly had fallen. Chance watched, not believing, as the horse struggled to its feet, took two steps and collapsed on its side, the body heaving, the head thrashing, as if even now—with only the few lengths to go—it struggled with the sheer, mighty will of its heart to take the race.

And it was Shambhala across the finish line.

Maggie had run to the window overlooking the track, and at the last moment, her nails raked the glass, clawing at the surface, as if to burst through and save the animal below. Now, as Chance ran through the crowd to reach her, Maggie bolted another way. He caught one glimpse of her face, crazed with violent grief.

She was on her knees when he reached her, covered in the dirt of the track, the blue dress of her intended triumph smeared with horse sweat and stained with

Darkstar's blood. She held the animal's head in her lap, talking to her, willing her now just to live, the race forgotten. Darkstar's eyes closed. Maggie turned horrified, questioning eyes to the veterinarian laboring over the leg, where the bone had splintered through the flesh as the horse had pushed itself to win the race.

The vet denied her worst fear. Darkstar still lived. "She won't race again," he said. "Not ever. Do you want me to—"

"No," Chance said. "Save her. It doesn't matter if she wins races. It never did," he said. Only Maggie wasn't listening.

Chapter Thirteen

Maggie shoved another carton onto the back floor of the Jeep. A shining strand of black hair swung like a silken rope across her cheek. Absently, she swept it back behind her ear, and with thumb and forefinger nudged it into the copper clasp at the nape of her neck.

Her mind settled on the remaining boxes by the steps of the cottage. She saw them as tiny, oddly shaped coffins, each holding an aborted dream. Across the yard, golden light tumbled upon them through the branches of the large oak at the house's side. A few dry leaves jittered to the ground, breaking the stillness. Soon the rain gutter would be clogged with leafy overflow. Someone—but who? she wondered—would have to sweep them away. A feeling of responsibility, of possession, of even protectiveness, enveloped her. This feeling she swept away; the leaves she could do nothing about.

Maggie's eyes moved farther up the steps, following ghostly memories of Chance into the cottage where they had laughed and fought and loved and finally parted two days after Darkstar's last race. How many endless nights and empty days would pass before the dull ache of losing him would end? How long would it be before her craving for the exquisite sweetness of life would dwindle and leave her anesthetized by apathy? Oh, God, would the constant roof chatter of her mind never cease!

Her mind tormented, going on like a hysterical gossip. Yes, the fracture to Darkstar's leg was irreparable. And yes, this mid-September, three years after she had stuck her thumb out on a burning hot desert road and found her entire being swept up into a whirlwind of passion and desperate dreams and explosive wins and shattering losses, her life was also beyond salvage. Yes, all of it was miserably, absolutely true.

Lately, she had taken to reviewing the facts as they were, not as she would like them to be. It was a painful enterprise, but necessary. Continued practice was building up emotional muscles grown flabby over the past years with Chance. Perhaps her dreams had withered and died, but her body, and Darkstar's, still lived on; two demanding machines that required maintenance. No matter how sorry she felt for herself, practicality dictated that she accept the fundamentals of existence. Just like everyone else, she had to live somewhere and eat something and give in to sleep. Just like everyone else.

Sighing, Maggie eyed the boxes on the steps again and wondered if it would not have been just as well to sell the household treasures she had collected and start completely over. But no, she wasn't quite that tough yet; maybe in time, God willing, but not now.

A large fly landed boldly on her arm and annoyance broke the sentimental course of her thoughts. She slapped at it, missed and, freed momentarily of nostalgia, set off again for the cottage.

For one or two days, fall had shown its profile, then coyly departed, allowing the ripeness of summer to linger a time longer. The heavy fruityness clung to the air, weighting Maggie's mood as she continued to trek back and forth from the cottage to the new Jeep, purchased for the exodus to Arizona.

Nevertheless, to those who knew how to listen, an occasional wind bore messages from the high country. Maggie, trudging along with an armload of clothes, sensed the changes as naturally as others tuned in to the evening news.

She knew that delicate frosts had arrived, leaving lacy imprints on the emerald fur of moss. Caressed by winter's hand, the green velvet would have withered to a pale ghostly blanket. The air that came out of the high country was flavored with excitement. Brilliantly garbed for the arrival of the new season, the leaves of aspens and birch chattered insecurely about the new guests. They were calmed by the sonorous chorus of pines who spoke in the voices of ancient, invisible wizards. And in those secret places where man's footsteps did not fall, Maggie imagined the green giants speaking of circular seasons, of time never ending. They spoke of the cone and the seedling and of the gray bough rotted at the base of their towering forms, and of the tiny brown pod growing in the spongy log stomach of a fallen relative. They said that this was the way things were and would always be. They said not to worry.

Maggie climbed into the Jeep and rearranged several boxes to make room for those yet to come. Her jeans were hot on her legs, and the red cotton tank top clung moistly to her torso. Fatigue bore down on her. Outside the Jeep, she leaned against its sturdy square back and closed her eyes. A kind of peace came into the dark space behind her lids, and behind the breathing of her heart she heard her grandfather's voice.

Overlapping the sounds of trees and wind, Maggie heard his voice laughing, calling to her in her mind. For that instant she was a child again, safe in his strong brown arms smelling of the desert earth and of sunlight itself. He, like the trees and the wind, had told her not to worry for she was a part of it all. "Of Life!" he had answered when she had not understood.

Darkstar, tied to the fender of the Jeep, snorted. Maggie awoke from the past. The filly was tossing her mane, wanting to take off with a butterfly circling her head.

Maggie laughed, and with it came new energy. "Patience," she told Darkstar. Maggie smoothed the tousled mane, then started off from the Jeep to complete her packing. "You'll get to go, too." In Arizona, she and Darkstar could chase butterflies, or just plain houseflies, forever. *What neither of them could do was to race again.*

Clothes, each item bearing its own memorable history, were placed in neat piles atop the boxes in the Jeep's back. She had also decided to bring the scrap books, hating the idea of herself as a sentimentalist, but needing even more the tangible proof of the most magnificent three years of her life.

It was two in the afternoon when Maggie climbed into the Jeep, ready to go. She sat there for a moment, watching the play of leaf and sunlight against the white of the cottage. Her eyes closed and she held in the image as she turned the key in the ignition. What she saw would need to be remembered an entire lifetime. It was her home; really her only home, no matter what came to pass in the future.

A small scruffy dog running alongside and barking at the tires, was their only witness as the Jeep, towing Darkstar in the van, pulled away from the cottage.

Five hours later, the lights of Las Vegas twinkled in the distance. For only a few more minutes, the mountains would hold the purple twilight; then, Maggie remembered, the spirits of darkness would rule over the desert and she would not be able to find the site, as her grandfather would have known how. He had told her that as a boy he had made friends and aligned himself with the nature of the night spirits; and for ever after, even beneath the very blackest of skies, he was always assured of guidance.

Maggie pulled the Jeep over to the side of the road. She was almost certain of the general location, but in three years the desert floor was bound to have changed and from the car, at least, there was no sign of the mound. Leaving the Jeep, she walked into the gritty terrain, searching for a small rise of earth in the vast surrounding flatness.

In minutes, the inky darkness moved in with the swiftness of a rushing tide. Fuzzy shapes were drowned, landmarks obliterated, and the mound, if it still existed, became the property of the night spirits. Sensibly, and with regret, Maggie abandoned her search.

She had already made it halfway back to the road and was thinking of where to spend the night, when she stumbled on what turned out to be an old piece of lumber. Her hand broke the fall, but a nail cut into her palm and within a second the warm wetness of blood spilled from the puncture. She stood, holding pressure against the wound, feeling the throb of her pulse dancing with the pain.

It was then, while facing the lights of Las Vegas, that she saw silhouetted against the glow, the barest rise of earth, no more than a bump, and on its flattened summit, a crown of spindly stalks.

How anything so delicate could survive the treachery of the desert Maggie could not guess, but as she bent to gather the pods of the Ancestor Plant, she did so with the proper respect, opening her heart to the spirits of nature as best she was able, and just as her grandfather had instructed.

The house was a modern ranch-style adobe. Its location was a forty-five minute haul from Phoenix, which Maggie rarely visited unless to see a dentist or to purchase some special item for Darkstar's maintenance that couldn't be gotten any other way but through a personal trip. With her previous winnings, she had a barn and corral built for Darkstar. Slowly, in the silence and the sunlight of the desert, the healing process had begun for both of them.

From Chance she had heard nothing, but then how could she? As far as he was concerned, she might as well have disappeared off the face of the earth. No one but Sam Johnson, who was in the hospital, knew what had become of her, and that was the way she wanted it to remain.

But she thought of Chance. In the beginning, she thought of him with every breath, and there were nights when her soul was on fire to have his body possess hers again, one more time, for an eternal time. Then, as the months progressed, the intensity of longing waned. She would think of him less frequently. Yet, just when she thought she was free of the torment, the yearning, the fire in her heart and loins would flare with strength beyond anything she had yet endured. It was as if clouds built of passion had assembled silently in her soul, becoming a monstrous force that, when unleashed, humbled her. This love of hers seemed the power of life itself; and she knew that if her grandfather were there with her, he would say that she must go with life, join with love, if she was ever to save herself. He had said that love was the only freedom. But since she could not, she would lie awake wondering if, on those occasions when she was caught in the apex of the storm, Chance was also, somewhere, tormented, as well. She did not know. She only knew she loved him still; and would forever.

Her one trip to Los Angeles was for Sam Johnson, and emotionally, the trip cost her a great deal. For one thing, Sam was not going to make it. One lung had collapsed and the other was riddled with disease. Their conversation had been painful and brief. Sam had held her hand, and in the barest of whispers, in a death rattle of a voice, he had asked her about her life in Arizona and of Darkstar. He told her that Chance had come to see him, and that he had started his own farm. It was doing well, too. He told her that she was a fool. Life did not last long, Sam said. It was his final statement to her. The next day, when she returned to see him, he was no longer there. He had gone peacefully in his sleep.

Life might not last long, as Sam had said, but to Maggie it was beginning to seem endless. The days drifted into months, the routine never varying, for there was no occasion for change.

When the boy suddenly appeared in Maggie's life, she was not certain if she was glad or bothered by the added presence of a human being. He was ten and the grandchild of a couple living a mile or so down the road. His parents had divorced and somehow or other, he had fallen through the cracks of their lives. Every day he went to school on a bus crowded with jiggling, screaming children, but after school there was no one within ten miles with whom to play.

Jake pedaled into her life one spring afternoon. Long shadows stretched out behind the bicycle frame, with the boy's own spindly body magnified angularly against the sandy blacktop. In the flesh, he was small and colorful, with red hair and bright blue eyes that looked wise and lonely. But that moment when Maggie first saw him, the blue globes shimmered with delight. He was watching Darkstar.

With reluctance, Maggie invited him into her own solitary life.

Jake was entranced with Darkstar. The horse might have been a beautiful woman and he a smitten suitor. There was no detail about Darkstar too minute or mundane for Jake not to want to know about. And Maggie, in spite of her resolve to guard her heart, found the hinges slowly opening to the young boy's enthusiasms.

"She was brave and magnificent," Maggie finished, after relating the story of Darkstar's last race.

"But now she isn't?' Jake asked, looking sorrowfully at Darkstar.

"She lost the big race," Maggie said.

"But she's still the same," Jake objected. "You said her heart made her run. And her heart is still there, isn't it? Isn't it? Isn't it?" Jake prodded in a shrill voice that in no way matched the quiet wisdom behind his azure stare.

Maggie barely fought down the inexplicable urge to strike him. "Don't be so stupid! It's not her heart that counts when you run a race. It's her legs. And her legs are ruined! And if your legs are ruined, and if that's the only thing you've got going for you in the world, then what good are you to anyone, or even to yourself!"

After that, Jake didn't return for a few days, and Maggie found herself missing him. She stood by the corral, waiting, looking down the road for his familiar form, which did not appear. She felt miserable. The words she had spoken so harshly resounded in her head until she thought she might scream from the jackhammer of their repetition.

When Jake came back a week later, she made a point of being more kind. She baked cookies and had lemonade waiting for his daily visits. Together they would feed Darkstar a treat of a carrot or pieces of apple. While walking Darkstar, Maggie would relate to Jake the same stories her grandfather had told her as a girl.

"You should be a mom," Jake said one afternoon. Cookie crumbs trailed from the corners of his mouth. "Don't you want a kid?"

"If I did, I have to get a husband first. That's the way it works, at least to do it the right way."

"Why don't you get a husband then?"

Maggie laughed. "Because you only get one when someone loves you. Come on, let's give Darkstar her treat."

Jake's expression was contemplative as they walked to the corral. "I love you," he said.

Maggie looked down at him. "Thanks, Jake. I love you, too. But you're a little boy. You can't be in the husband business yet."

"Some grownup man could love you."

"No," Maggie said sharply. "I don't want it." A look of hurt fell over the small freckled face, and Maggie bent quickly and held him. "Jake, Jake...I'm sorry. It's just that I don't have anything to offer. Me and Darkstar...we ran our last races."

"But you love Darkstar anyway," he said, and Maggie found herself drowning in the blue of his eyes, until she realized the tears were a pool of her own making.

Maggie excused herself. She said she would get them some more lemonade. She walked quickly into the house and shut the door. Then she leaned against the kitchen counter and held tight to its tiled edge so that her knuckles went white. But the pain she wanted to squeeze away would not leave. The pain would not be soothed by lemonade. The pain was in her heart.

A moment later, she brought out the two glasses of lemonade in tall plastic glasses. Her eyes sought Jake first, and then suddenly, horribly, it dawned on her that neither Jake nor Darkstar were there.

The gate to the corral swung ajar.

"Jake! Jake!" Maggie screamed. Only silence answered. The bicycle, which had been propped up against the rail, was no longer there.

The earth slipped beneath her as she started to run one way, then, aimlessly, chose the other direction. The only living creature on earth she had to call her own had somehow been removed from her life. In all directions,

for as far as she could see, there was no sign of movement, no sight of a smallish black horse.

"Darkstar!" Maggie screamed, the wail lasting forever in the desolate landscape.

And in the empty silence, came an answering call
from around the back of the house.

In the cool shade on the north side of the adobe,
Darkstar was happily munching on the Ancestor flowers
Maggie had planted there from the seed pods gathered
in Las Vegas.

"You bad, bad girl," Maggie sobbed, and threw
herself up against Darkstar's gleaming black neck.
Darkstar nuzzled her, the large head jerking up and
down with the pleasure of freedom and from having
happened upon the unexpected dessert whose remains
spilled from her mouth. Wet with saliva, the seeds of the
Ancestor Plant clung to Maggie's open palm. "Now
see . . . you've eaten grandfather's plant, and—"

Maggie stopped. She stared down at the pale, flat
seeds in her hand and as the idea took form—the current of life flowed once more through her veins.

One man was from England, another from France,
and the third, dressed in flowing white garb, was a genuine sheikh whose kingdom sat upon more oil than
sand. All three men listened with rapt interest as Chance
explained the final details of the syndication that had
taken four days of hard negotiations to conclude.

So engrossed were they, that it was only the sheikh,
always on the alert for deals or assassins, who noticed
the Jeep with the horse van, moving up the long gravel
drive toward them.

Chance glanced up from the documents he held.

"Who comes here?" the Arab demanded. "You have said for certain we would be alone."

Chance paid him no attention. His mind was fully on the woman, whose face he could now clearly see.

"We will conclude this transaction?" the gentleman from France called peevishly, as Chance moved away from their circle and toward the vehicle which had stopped.

"Later..." Chance said. "Later, sometime."

"I believe we are speaking about three million dollars!" enjoined the Englishman.

"Right, something in that ball park," Chance said over his shoulder.

Maggie opened the door to the Jeep.

Silently, with starved eyes, Chance explored her face. The eyes were as full of dark mystery as he had remembered, but now there was something more added. The resentment and sadness and distrust that had lodged behind the thick curtain of black lashes had been replaced by a tenderness, a gentle wisdom. She had come back to him whole.

"Chance," she said—only his name—and he closed his eyes briefly, the moment a dream he had imagined a thousand times on lonely nights. When he opened his eyes, her hand was outstretched to him. Slowly, he reached to take it, thinking to help her down. But, instead, she placed her palm over his and he felt the fall of items small and flat tumble against his skin.

Lying, warm with life, in the cradle of his hand, were several seeds.

Maggie smiled, her eyes luminous. She nodded to the gifts he held. "My grandfather tried to teach me so many things. Ah, but I was so stubborn." She sighed, remembering. Then she glanced at Chance with a curious light of mischief. "Those seeds...well, they're very peculiar. Belonged to my grandfather. Seems they grow no matter where you plant them. They grow with water or without. In the sun or in the shade. And every time, the plant that comes up has more beautiful flowers. Strange, a plant like that." She shook her head. "I think," Maggie said, "it's what my grandfather said. When you plant them, you must touch them with your whole heart and mind."

Maggie's eyes had filled. She looked away, her gaze sweeping over the green expanse of property, with its whitewashed stables and whitewashed slatted fences. She listened to the neighing of horses and to the calls of stable hands to each other. In the breeze she caught the scent of a new season coming. "Spring," she said. "It's spring on the way."

Chance nodded. He closed his palm over the seeds, squeezing them tightly into his flesh, wanting to bury the part of them that was her into his skin so that she could never leave him again.

"You've got some nice land here," Maggie said tentatively. "Looks like a lot of it. You've done okay, cowboy." Then with assurance she said, "These would grow here, Chance."

"Can we plant them right?"

"I know how now. Absolutely," Maggie said.

"Show me," Chance said. He took a step forward, and Maggie slid from the Jeep, melting into his arms.

The colt was born to Darkstar on December 23. Shambhala was unfortunately unable to attend the festivities surrounding the birth of his son, having moved to Kentucky where he was now under new ownership. Prucilla Bellamy fought a good fight in court, trying to maintain her rights to the horse, but Digger Bellamy wasn't well disposed to seeing Pru's point of view. Digger had, it turned out, found a newer, truer love in Japan, while on tour. His current wife very much enjoyed the stock market and thought it would be nice to have extra cash—lots and lots of it, in fact—on hand for her hobby; thus, Pru's own hobby dwindled in the final settlement to what Digger liked to call "a single nag, just like herself."

The new colt was black, a shining jet black, and was named Garuda after a legendary bird who hatches fully grown and soars into the sky, stretching its vast wings beyond any limits.

On the day Garuda won the Hollywood Futurity, making racing headlines, Chance brought Maggie a single flower. It was the first bloom of the season of the Ancestor Plant they had planted together. Its petals were a vibrant orange, larger and more brilliant than those of subsequent years.

The press asked Maggie about Garuda's showing. "With the spirit of Darkstar and the bloodlines of Shambhala, heaven and earth are combined." She looked to Chance, who took that moment to tip back his hat. Maggie's breath stopped for an instant, seeing him again for the very first time—the heat rising up off the desert floor, wavey lines pulsating from the truck's hood, the engine singing for an audience of mountains and lizards, the crooked grin he wore as he ran his eyes along the length of her body, eyes shining with all the light of the universe.

"How," Maggie said, looking at Chance, "how can anything beat that combination?"

Silhouette Brings You:

Silhouette Christmas Stories

Four delightful, romantic stories celebrating the holiday season, written by four of your favorite Silhouette authors.

Nora Roberts—*Home for Christmas*
Debbie Macomber—*Let It Snow*
Tracy Sinclair—*Under the Mistletoe*
Maura Seger—*Starbright*

Each of these great authors has combined the wonder of falling in love with the magic of Christmas to bring you four unforgettable stories to touch your heart.

Indulge yourself during the holiday season ... or give this book to a special friend for a heartwarming Christmas gift.

Available November 1986

XMAS-1

Silhouette Desire

**Available
October 1986**

California Copper

The second in an exciting new
Desire Trilogy by Joan Hohl.

If you fell in love with Thackery—the
laconic charmer of *Texas Gold*—you're
sure to feel the same about his twin
brother, Zackery.

In *California Copper*, Zackery meets the
beautiful Aubrey Mason on the windswept
Pacific coast. Tormented by memories,
Aubrey has only to trust...to embrace
Zack's flame...and he can ignite the fire in
her heart.

The trilogy continues when you
meet Kit Aimsley, the twins' half
sister, in *Nevada Silver*. Look for
Nevada Silver—coming soon from
Silhouette Books.

FOUR UNIQUE SERIES
FOR EVERY WOMAN YOU ARE . . .

Silhouette Romance

Heartwarming romances that will make you
laugh and cry as they bring you all the wonder
and magic of falling in love.

Silhouette Special Edition

Expanded romances written with emotion and
heightened romantic tension to ensure
powerful stories. A rare blend of passion and
dramatic realism.

Silhouette Desire

Believable, sensuous, compelling—and
above all, romantic—these stories deliver
the promise of love, the guarantee
of satisfaction.

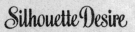

Silhouette Intimate Moments

Love stories that entice; longer, more
sensuous romances filled with adventure,
suspense, glamour and melodrama.

Silhouette Romances
not available in retail outlets in Canada